# A GLASS OF MILK

## JO EDDY

**A Glass of Milk**

Cover design by Anamaria Stefan (Instagram: @ancustefan)

# CONTENTS

# ONE

"I might get my hair cut short."

"Don't you dare."

"It's so hot though."

"It won't last. Haven't you heard—we live in England."

"It'll be a lot less effort to wash and dry if it were cropped."

"Yeah, and it'll ruin our sex life."

"Seriously? Is that all you can think about? Anyway, might improve mine; not having my hair yanked out of my scalp every time. It hurts. Wish you'd stop doing it." He laughed. "It's not funny, Tim."

"You love it really. All that moaning and groaning—"

"In pain."

He snorted. "Yeah, right." He reached for her hair. She slapped his hand away. "Gosh, you are in a funny mood. PMT?"

"Why do you always think it's that? Maybe you're just annoying."

He backed away; hands splayed. His lips clamped together, but eyes smiling.

Gemma walked over to the mirror. It was all a joke to him. Whatever she said. A joke. She had a good mind to head for the hairdresser's first thing tomorrow. But then she would have to face his displeasure... the sulk of the century... and no sex until he got over it. No, a haircut wasn't worth the aggravation. Gem zero. Tim... must be in the millions by now. Sod him.

"How do I look?"

"Fine."

"Thanks for the confidence boost," she grumbled.

The full-length mirror reflected Tim standing at the foot of the bed, fiddling with a leather belt. Had he even noticed her new outfit? Doubtful. Gemma pulled at the shoulder seams to straighten the collar of the teal blouse, then thrust her hands into the pockets of the stone-coloured trousers. She flapped the loose-fitting fabric, "Loving boyfriends would say 'you look great whatever you're wearing'."

"You read too many romantic novels. You look OK. Prefer you in a dress."

"Have you ever seen me in a dress?" The mirror image threaded the belt through the loops on his jeans. Eased the strap through the buckle and pulled tight before securing the prong. She sighed, *Take your time, man...* "Have you?"

"Hang on." He tucked the tip into a belt loop. "No. But I can imagine it. Those nice long legs on permanent display..." The half-naked reflection strode up behind and placed its hands on her thighs. Tugging her to his groin, he whispered in her ear, "...No obstruction to carnal activities." He nibbled her lobe. "Definitely prefer you in a dress."

"I don't wear dresses." Her nose twitched, irritated by his strong perfume.

"You wear a skirt to work sometimes."

"That's different. It's part of a suit." Her thumb knuckle rubbed her nose. The tickle subsided to be replaced by another on her neck. His lips brushed against the skin below her ear. Her head tilted to give full access.

He stopped, "It wouldn't hurt to wear a dress occasionally. For me."

"How about not wearing aftershave FOR ME?"

He winked at her via the mirror, "The shorter the better."

Her head straightened. Being viewed as a sex object didn't sit comfortably. Approval for her outfit was one thing; suggesting she—a twenty-nine-year-old accountant—should flounce around showing her knickers to the world was another. "I wear shorts in summer."

"Short shorts?"

"One pair is pretty indecent. I went a bit far with the jean hacking."

"Ripped denim. Tanned legs. I can go for that, but not for a meal out."

Not that she'd ever have the courage to wear the cut-offs in public. They were definitely 'last resort' in the clothing stakes. A groping hand squeezed her right breast in an attempt to turn her around. It failed. The mouth renewed its devouring of her ear. Teeth plucked at her unadorned lobe. Two wayward hands tried to slip down her trouser front. Hard to ignore but all she wanted right now was an answer. Some sort of approval that would mean she hadn't contravened her green credentials for no good reason.

She grabbed his hands, "So, what about this outfit? Surely, it's good enough for a restaurant?"

"No. Got to be a dress. What more can I say? Do you want me to lie?"

"Unbelievable! Don't know why I stick with you."

She stepped to the left to escape his groping. Spun to plonk herself on the edge of the bed. The perfect perch to grapple with the straps of her sandals. This was her first brand-new outfit in a long time. Top, trousers, bra, knickers, shoes, bag: the whole hog. Guilt appeased someway by making sure they were all made of eco-friendly materials, but remorse lingered over not sticking to her rule of only buying pre-loved. And why had she broken that pledge? Because Tim's buddies had teased her mercilessly the last time they met up. A big mistake to reveal all her clothes were second-hand to the designer-clad crowd. Not an evening she was keen to repeat. But given Tim's comments, why had she bothered with the shopping trip? There was no appreciation for her efforts and his friends would probably tease her all the same.

She leant forward, dropping the flat sandals to the plush carpet. Her ringless fingers swooped the brunette hair away from her face and tucked the misbehaving locks behind her ear. Wrapping drifted down to rest on her toes. She kicked the plastic away and glanced up at Tim shaking out his latest purchase: a plain navy t-shirt. Not that he didn't have enough shirts already. Her eyes wandered down to today's favoured jeans. That was something, at least.

"What?" asked Tim.

She nodded to his legs, "Not new."

His eyes widened to scrutinise his trousers, "Can you tell?"

"No, they're fine."

"But how did you tell they're old?"

"Hardly old."

"Fair point, but how did you tell? Is there some dirt?" He twisted to check the back.

"I watched you iron them twenty minutes ago... after getting them out of the drier." Whether they would remain in favour after a third wash was debatable. The amount of clothes he got through was so frustrating. If they were worn out and beyond repair, it would be understandable. But no, they were discarded—or rather abandoned in the depths of his expansive walk-in wardrobe—as soon as that brand-new look faltered. "And no packaging for them. Amazing. Am I finally getting through to you?"

"No. Just too busy to order a new pair."

She sighed, "How on earth did I end up with you?"

After smoothing the t-shirt over his slim frame, the mirror won Tim's attention, "Look at me. I'm quite the catch. Good job, good prospects... seriously good-looking." He broke into a beaming smile which, after a long pause, he turned and re-directed towards her. "You lucky so and so."

It was true. At the age of thirty-two, Tim was a successful barrister and tipped to go far. There was the possibility of becoming an MP sometime in the future, which filled her with dread; they didn't exactly see eye to eye when it came to politics. And he epitomised the dark handsome love interest of many a novel. Raven-black hair. Sparkling blue eyes. A strong jawline. Clean-shaven when working. A roguish stubble when not.

He bent over to kiss her. She responded but then cut the kiss short by ducking away to do up the buckle on the second sandal. "And why do you stick with me?"

"Good job, good prospects... seriously good-looking. We were made for each other, Gemmie. And I love the fact you don't leech off me. Been caught by that before. You should've seen the credit card debts my last squeeze ran up. Eye-watering."

"So, good-looking and cheap to run?"

"Basically." He guffawed as he sat beside her to pull on his socks.

"Sometimes I don't know whether you're joking or not. You're a real pig if you're not."

"And you don't want kids."

She stiffened, then turned to stare at him, "Who said I don't want kids?"

"Thought your career was important to you."

"You can have both, you know."

"Yeah, but why would you want snotty-nosed brats sticking their messy fingers all over my lovely house?"

She glanced around the pristine bedroom, decorated in shades of grey and silver. You'd think they were in a luxury hotel suite. This was the handiwork of the 'ex' as was the rest of the five-bedroom house—except for the kitchen which was down to Tim. It was all very show-homey designer stuff. Not her style at all, but as it was not eco-friendly to strip it all out and start again, she would have to live with it. Even if she did accept Tim's offer of a total re-vamp, they would never be able to agree on a style. The kitchen debacle had proved that. Yes, 'living with it' was the preferable option. The alternative would be a much-loathed confrontation. And to argue with a man who had no qualms over using his legal training in a personal setting, she was on a hiding to nothing. Only two outcomes were possible: lose the argument or just give up to keep the peace. Winning didn't come into it—a pointless exercise to even try.

"I wouldn't mind."

"Are you sure about that?"

"Yes. Joys of parenthood."

His bottom lip curled to the left, "Not my idea of fun." He picked the label off the sole of a black desert boot, before shoving his foot in. "So, why on earth do you think you want them?"

"Err..."

He smirked. "You can't think of a reason, can you?"

"Give me a minute. I can think of plenty. Just organising my thoughts."

"Playing for time, me thinks." His elbow nudge sent her slipping off the edge of the bed. Her foot whacked into the carpet. Close. She stood to face him. Confronted by a smug grin from ear to ear, she racked her brains. This was one argument she had to win. A family was a long-held dream. But why? It was surprisingly hard to think of a good reason.

"Nurture them... watch them grow... play with them... err..."

"You can do that with my sister's kids. Though she might think it's a bit creepy."

"That's not the same. I want my own children. When am I going to meet your family?"

He laughed, "Excellent deflection, Gem."

"It's not a deflection. It's a genuine question. We've been together six months now. You've met my parents. When am I going to meet yours?"

"I'll sort something out." Jaw jutting, his wide eyes bored into her.

"Good."

Tim still stared, tight lips suppressing a grin. His head tilted, eyebrows shooting up.

"What?"

"So, why kids? Why not just be an auntie?"

"It's... biological instinct." She smiled. As good a reason as any.

"I would've thought, given your views on climate change, you wouldn't want any." Her smile dissipated as he continued, "A whole new human must have a high carbon footprint. And, according to you, we'll all be dead in a few years anyway, so doesn't seem much point."

"I'm hoping things will change. Politicians will see sense. People will alter their lifestyles. If we stop having children, it's like we're giving up. You've got to have some incentive for a better future. Some hope."

"Other people can have the kids. I'm happy like this... just the two of us." He reached out and, taking hold of her hand, attempted to tug her towards him.

She stood her ground, "Maybe we should go our separate ways. We clearly want different things."

"Don't be silly. You're just in a funny mood. Tomorrow you'll be back to Gemma, career woman, and you'll have forgotten all about the stinky babies."

Tim flashed her a smile. The super-white teeth glinted in a ray of sunshine. Her desire to continue the argument nullified, she turned away. Out the window, the immaculate garden cried out for a sandpit, climbing frame... and a vegetable patch. There was a perfect spot for veggies at the bottom of the lawn, but Tim had vetoed her suggestion as 'out of the question'. He spent thousands on the landscaping last summer, including the services of a famous designer, to achieve the minimalist look. He wasn't about to let her stick a spade in the perfect carpet of green any time soon. Well, ever. She had surreptitiously sowed a few beetroot and carrot seeds amongst the meticulous borders of Japanese Forest Grass about a week ago. Whether they would survive the eagle-eyed gardener (Tim insisted on retaining despite her offer to take over) was doubtful. A bit of sweet-talking was required before the seedlings appeared, otherwise they were doomed. She had a good rapport with the elderly gentleman, though they'd only met on the few occasions the weather forced him to come at the weekend. But, despite her plying him with mugs of tea and chocolate biscuits, she was unsure he would take instructions from her, especially if they were in direct conflict with Tim's own directions. It was Tim's house after all.

In many ways, she felt like a guest. A rather put-upon guest. Despite having her own career, she did most of the cleaning and all the cooking; though Tim often opted to eat out or order a takeaway rather than accept her vegan offerings. But it wasn't as though he was lounging about doing nothing as she wielded the vacuum cleaner; the barrister was a very busy man and divided his time between his firm's Guildford and London offices. Rarely home before 10pm on weekdays and often working at home at the weekends, you could hardly expect him to pick up a duster in the little free time he had.

A pigeon landed on the lawn and proceeded to peck away at the lush grass, searching for a tasty worm. Whether the wriggling mud-eaters could survive the gardener's monthly soak in weedkiller was debatable. She watched the bird as it scratched away, willing it every success in its destruction of perfection.

A sigh escaped her lips. Her dream was slowly slipping away. Her parents put the first nail in the coffin four years ago by retiring and relocating to Wales. With them went her free board and lodgings. The subsequent rental and then mortgage costs put a serious dent in her savings plan. Moving in with Tim five months ago hadn't solved the problem because, somehow, she ended up buying him a whole new kitchen in lieu of her contribution to household costs. That wiped out all her savings. At this rate, retirement age would be reached before she could afford that yearned-for smallholding.

And if she stuck with Tim, that dream would disappear totally. He was never going to leave his luxurious lifestyle to live off-grid in the middle of nowhere. But leaving him would take her back to square one. What if she didn't meet someone new for years? What if the menopause struck early? That longed-for family might never happen. At twenty-nine years old, was dumping him a risk worth taking? It wasn't as though she didn't love the man. Despite all her doubts, the differences of opinion, the arguments, he was good company and all her friends agreed with his claim to be 'a catch'. 'Opposites attract' they pointed out whenever she expressed her doubts. And he did have a point about the carbon footprint...

Another tug on her hand. She relented this time and let him pull her onto his lap, "We'll be late."

"They're my best friends. They're used to it."

# TWO

Tim had arranged this night out, so Gemma wasn't surprised that none of her own friends had been invited. Not least her best pal, who he avoided like the plague—literally. Following in her father's footsteps, Louise was a drainage engineer and Tim seemed to be under the impression she was a hot bed of E. coli and god knows what. It was kind of funny a farmer's son could be so worried about a bit of poo—not that Louise didn't scrub herself down at the end of every working day. Anyway, her pal hadn't been invited so Gemma couldn't take delight in watching Tim squirm as he tried to avoid shaking hands and kissing cheeks. Louise, of course, knew his game and loved the challenge of forcing herself upon him in a great big bear hug, followed up with quadruple cheek kissing. Yes, it was a shame her BFF wasn't coming. Instead, the evening would be spent listening to a bunch of high achievers discuss the latest news in the world of corporate law.

Tim had chosen a posh steakhouse for the meal. She despaired at how inconsiderate he was at times. Well, most of the time, if she were being honest. Apart from herself, there was only one other present who wasn't in the legal profession—Olivia. The blonde was new to the crowd: the latest girlfriend of Harry. There was a pretty woman somewhere under all the make-up; her face was perfectly proportioned with a lovely bone structure. Why she needed to hide behind a thick mask of foundation, Gemma couldn't fathom. And what on earth had the girl done to her eyebrows? They looked like they had been stuck on as an afterthought. Why on earth did women do that? Surely, your genes designed the perfect eyebrows for your face. Yes, even she indulged in a little bit of plucking to keep them tidy, but why change them for something so fake?

Tim was busy listing out the gadgets in his new car which resulted in a bit of 'mine's better than yours' banter between the four men. The two female solicitors were discussing a case: a contract dispute between manufacturer and retailer. Gemma listened for a while, but her interest waned. Surely there were more interesting things to talk about on a night out other than work?

Bored of the pre-dinner conversation, she caught Olivia's eye across the table, "What do you do, Olivia?"

"I'm a make-up artist. Would you like me to give you some tips sometime?"

"No, I'm OK. I prefer the natural look."

"There's natural and there's no make-up. I believe you fall into the latter category. You should try a bit of light eye make-up. And some lip gloss."

Ouch.

Tim interrupted, "My Gemmie is a bit of an eco-warrior. Doesn't wear make-up. Wouldn't wear clothes if it wasn't illegal."

The group all chuckled.

"Tim, call yourself a barrister. It's not technically illegal to bare all in the UK," Harry pointed out. "Feel free to strip off, Gem."

Laughter roared around the table.

She forced a smile. "It's a bit chilly. I think I'll pass."

The men all exaggerated their sighs of disappointment.

"So, why are you so opposed to make-up?" Olivia pressed.

"Oh, so many reasons. Animal testing. Excessive unrecyclable packaging. Pollution. It just seems so unnecessary. After all, men don't—well, most of them—so why should women?"

"A lot of men should," joked Olivia before facing her boyfriend, "Not you, of course, Harry."

"There's nothing wrong with being as nature intended. Most men get that. I just think it's a shame, us girls don't."

"Most men are just lazy about their appearance, though a lot of the younger ones are now taking more care with their looks," argued the make-up artist.

"You're making me depressed. More plastic. More waste. More carbon emissions. We need to buy less, not more, if we're going to save the planet."

Tim's elbow nudged her in the side. She turned to confront the frowning face. He mouthed, "That's enough." Gemma glowered back. She was just getting started.

"What do you do?" Olivia reversed the direction of the original question.

"I'm an accountant."

"Oh, right."

Gemma could tell from her voice Olivia was unimpressed and, to confirm her indifference, there was no follow-up question about her employment. Mind you, she wasn't that interested in probing Olivia further either. Based on the conversation so far, there was zero chance of them becoming friends. It was a pity Louise wasn't here. Her boisterous enthusiasm would have livened things up. Her pal wouldn't be letting the lawyers talk shop and she would wind up Tim big time, teasing him mercilessly. Which was another reason why he hadn't invited her.

Sipping her wine, Gemma listened as the rest of the group moved on to discussing under what Acts she would be arrested if she went naked in various locations.

"Public indecency."

"There's nothing indecent about my Gemmie. She could go naked anywhere and there'd be no complaints."

A small smile crossed her lips at the rare compliment from Tim.

The conversation paused as the main course was delivered to the table. Tim had a massive steak on his plate. Blood oozed as he cut into the almost rare meat. He stuck his fork into a chunk and, noticing she was watching, offered it to her, "Want to try some?"

Gemma shuddered, "No, thanks."

She stared at her own plate. An unappetising pile of roasted cauliflower covered in vegan cheese, with some random purple and orange flowers scattered across the top to pretty it up; an attempt to justify the inflated price for a simple meal anyone could cook at home. She hated vegan cheese, but there'd been nothing else on the menu for her. Picking off a tiny sample with her fork, she dotted the stringy yellow sludge on her tongue. Tasteless rubber. She scraped as much as possible off the cauliflower and just ate the vegetable, washed down with a second large glass of red wine.

Her choices for pudding weren't much better, so Gemma declined and instead re-filled her glass. As the rest of the group tucked into various extravagant desserts, she glugged down the wine. Tim topped up her glass again. Her head swam in the babble of nonsense coming from the other diners. Across the table, Olivia talked in Tim's voice. Ravi's reply was drowned out by raucous laughter. She blinked her eyes wide. Tried to focus on Harry's mouth. No, the caught snippets of words made no sense. Her eyes dropped to her goblet. She swirled the liquid around and around until it came close to sloshing over the edge. Gulped down the contents and plonked the glass on the table, knocking a small vase of flowers in the process. Only Tim's quick reactions prevented disaster. She'd drunk a lot, and with not much food in her stomach to soak it up, standing was going to be a challenge once the time came. Harry reached across the table to pour her another glass. An inane smile thanked him; speaking required too much effort.

The plates were cleared away and several bottles of champagne appeared on the table. The blurry friends were fiddling with their mobiles. Maybe they were waiting for her to fall over? All remaining control was focussed on staying upright, though her body seemed determined to do a face-plant into the table. She swayed backwards and forwards as mind fought body. The rocking lulling her eyes to sleep.

The arrival of a waiter allowed 'mind' to gain a temporary victory. The lad popped open the first bottle and poured out a glass for Tim to try. Her fella nodded his approval and the waiter left. Tim picked up the bottle and started to pour her a glass.

"Not fooor me, Tim. I've had toooo mulch," she slurred.

"Just one glass. A small one. I insist."

"Go for it, Gem!" Harry shouted.

She gazed in his direction. The lawyer was pointing his phone at her. A lazy scan around the table revealed they all were.

"I'm nooot going to poooke."

Everyone laughed.

Tim handed her the glass, "Drink up."

There was only one way she was going to get this down: one big gulp. Gemma lifted the glass and poured the whole contents into her mouth. Something hard stopped her from swallowing. Instead, she coughed and spluttered. Across the table, Olivia flinched backwards. Tim whacked her on the back. The object dropped from her mouth into her hand. The huge ruby stared at her, the surrounding diamonds twinkling, wet with champagne. She looked at Tim. There were two of him. They were both on one knee by the side of her chair. Tim One stole the ring from her and grasped her left hand. Tim Two totally missed.

"Gemma, will you marry me?"

She blinked away the double vision, shaking her head.

"YES. YES. YES..." the friends chanted.

"YES. YES. YES..." the whole restaurant joined in.

Hot and dizzy, flustered by the attention, it was hard to think straight.

"YES. YES. YES..."

Her eyelids drooped. A desperate need to lie down and sleep. Anything to make them shut up.

She balled her fists and shouted, "YES!"

# THREE

Eyes struggled under the weight of their personal shutters. Burdensome lashes refused to unstick. A tiny slit was forced open, but swiftly reclosed. The sun streamed through a crack in the curtains, hitting Gemma right in the face. It burned into her forehead, compounding the throbbing headache. Her mouth dry and furry, she cupped her hand to check her breath. Bad. She had no recollection of brushing her teeth last night. No recollection of going to bed... or even coming home from the restaurant. Thankfully, Tim was absent. Wrinkled sheets and an indentation in the pillow were the only signs of an earlier presence.

Keeping her eyes shut, she slithered out of the bed onto the floor. Crawled to the ensuite. Her shoulder bumped into the door frame and she fell flat on her face. Her head was last to leave the ground as she pushed up into a crawling position. A glimpse of something pink under the bed caught her eye, but she was too hungover to investigate. She staggered to her feet and plonked herself down on the loo. Quickly stood again and lifted the lid.

After relieving herself, she brushed her teeth and drank copious amounts of water. A new adornment on her finger glinted in the mirror. She whacked the tumbler down, missing the target. It slipped into the basin and rattled around the porcelain.

"Yeow!" Her face scrunched as sluggish reflexes failed to stop the dancing cup. After a final pirouette, it came to rest. Awoken by the clatter, her brain turned its attention to the ring, "What the hell happened?"

There was a vague recollection of multiple Tims staring up at her as 'yes' chants filled the restaurant. It seemed surreal. Unreal. If it weren't for the jewellery, she'd think it a dream. But no, the engagement ring was boldly adorning her finger, where no ring had gone before. But surely, she wouldn't have been so stupid to have said 'yes'? She had too many doubts over the relationship to even consider marriage and that was before Tim's revelation yesterday that he didn't want children. A worried face stared back from the mirror. The brow wrinkled. Maybe, just maybe, it was some sort of bad joke. She wouldn't put it past Tim, especially with Harry in cahoots. It could be she never actually answered, and they just put the ring on her finger as a prank. What she needed was proof... and before Tim returned.

As she came out of the bathroom, she dithered, but the comfortable bed proved too hard to resist. The pink thing would have to wait to be retrieved from its hiding place. It was probably something to do with her predecessor as she never vacuumed under the bed further than the edges. As she climbed in, she grabbed her phone off the bedside table and pulled the summer duvet up to her midriff. After stuffing Tim's pillow behind her back, she started to search through her social media accounts.

There it was—the evidence—several copies from different angles. As she feared, she'd only blooming well gone and got engaged. After the enthusiastic 'yes', she had keeled over. Planted her face in Tim's groin. Then slumped to the floor. Out for the count. Her fella's efforts to revive her were not that impressive: a glass of champagne chucked in her face, then some ice from the bucket shoved down her shirt. She couldn't remember either. The final scene was Tim carrying her out of the restaurant over his shoulder. There were already lots of comments.

Her best friend, Louise, had written, «*He had to get her drunk first!*»

Someone else added, «*Does it count if you're wasted?*»

"Does it?"

What the hell was she going to do? The thought of marrying the man had never entered her head. The thought of marrying anyone hadn't even been contemplated. She didn't need a piece of paper to show her commitment to the right man. Was Tim the right man? Did she want to spend the rest of her life with him? She flicked the screen to find the note-making app. She gave it the title 'Tim???' and a subheading 'Positives'. Her finger patted her top lip, before returning to the phone. Deleted 'Positives' and replaced it with 'Negatives'.

- Selfish
- Sulks
- Doesn't care about the environment
- Climate change denier
- Meat eater
- Capitalist
- Has to win at everything

Her ultimate dream was to buy a smallholding somewhere remote and live off-grid and self-sufficient. He was never going to agree to that. She condensed the point to...

- Urbanite
- Doesn't like hiking or camping
- Doesn't want a family

She thought for a moment, then typed in 'Positives'.

- Good sex

She deleted the 'good' and replaced it with 'great'.

- Good conversation
- Makes me laugh
- Handsome

Deciding it was a bit shallow, she deleted 'handsome'. She also prided herself on being financially independent, so it didn't enter her head to consider his career and wealth.

Gemma studied the list. All the positives weren't exclusive to Tim. There must be other men out there with those attributes and none of the negatives... or less of them. Without warning, the slam of the front door reverberated through the house and hit her sore head like a bullet. She just finished tapping 'slams doors' before Tim charged in, hot and sweaty from a run, and threw himself on the bed.

"How you feeling?" he asked.

She placed the phone face down on the duvet.

"Grotty. Head hurts."

He tapped his finger on the back of her phone, "Seen it then?"

"Yes." She grimaced.

"I was thinking, maybe we should do a re-shoot. With you sober. We could go somewhere picturesque like Paris. Next weekend. What d'ya think?"

She twiddled the jewel on her finger. Pulled the ring to the knuckle. Just that one action would wipe the great big grin off his face, but he looked so happy lying there propped up on one arm. And to break the engagement without proper consideration was unfair to him. She couldn't do it. She let go of the ring. Anyway, her head hurt far too much to cause a scene. The best she could do right now was avoid a repeat performance, "No, let's leave it as it is."

"Yeah. It was rather funny. Have you seen the comments on Instagram?"

"Hmmm."

"I was so relieved you didn't swallow it. Do you like it? It's antique or should I say reused? Just how you like things. That's why it's got some weird engraving inside."

She tugged the ring off and read the inscription out loud, "Mabel & Sid. 14.05.1960." Tiny love hearts were engraved before and after the words.

"I can take it to the jewellers in my lunch hour and get the writing removed if you want, but I thought you might like to keep its history intact."

She feigned a smile, "It's fine how it is."

He leapt off the bed, "Come and join me in the shower."

"In a minute."

He walked into the ensuite. Leaving the door open, he undressed and dropped his sweaty clothes in the laundry bin. He still had an all-over tan from their Easter holiday in Florida; apart from his bum which looked like a pair of white pants until he spun to expose himself to her. He jiggled his proud erection while grinning; an attempt to entice her. He disappeared behind the door. The water came on and, shortly after, he started singing.

She stared at the ring. The ruby was big and showy. Not her style at all. But he'd been thoughtful about getting something old. Maybe he was changing? Finally growing up? She glanced at her phone. The list had been replaced by the lock screen, but there was no need to rush into a decision. They didn't have to set a date for ages, so she had plenty of time.

She crawled out of bed and headed for the shower.

# FOUR

Gemma tipped the contents of the kitchen bin into the sink and proceeded with her weekly task of sorting out all the paper, plastics, and tins that Tim refused to put in the recycling bin. At least, being head chef meant food waste was minimal, and what little remained she'd already deposited in the caddy provided by the council. Still, the odd rogue item, courtesy of her fella, lurked amongst the pile of rubbish. She plucked out an apple core and a couple of blackened banana skins and dropped them into the caddy.

She growled in her throat, eyes throwing death rays at the culprit. He remained engrossed in a laptop screen on the far side of the expansive island.

Two beer cans were retrieved and placed on the black granite counter to rinse out later. A couple of yoghurt pots beckoned. Tim did love his yoghurt. In went her hand. Grabbed the first pot. Yuck. Slimy. Notes of vanilla scented the air as she plonked the container on the worktop. She snatched up the dishcloth and wiped the dairy from her fingers. A contamination too far. Grimacing, she plunged in for the second tub.

"There's a whole pot of yoghurt in here."

"Out of date," he replied without raising his head.

"Only by a day. You have to sniff it. If it smells OK, it's fine to eat."

"Go ahead then." He looked up and laughed, "I'll visit you in hospital."

"Ha ha," she retorted, pulling off the plastic lid to sniff the contents. The overpowering aroma of strawberries made it difficult to tell if there was anything 'off' about it. The pot still felt cold though. "Have you only just chucked this?"

"Hmm."

"There's a mouse in it."

"Hmm."

"So, you'll only eat vegan food from now on?"

"Hmm."

"Do you know what you've just agreed to?"

"Hmm."

She sighed. After replacing the lid, she wiped the pot clean, then placed it on the counter to the side of the sink, ready to put back in the fridge once she had finished sorting the rubbish. Picking at a cotton thread caught on her engagement ring, she glanced at Tim, "You're not supposed to be working on a Sunday."

"Not working."

"Not more clothes? Haven't you got enough to last a lifetime?"

"Not clothes."

"What are you doing then?"

"Choosing where to go for our honeymoon."

"Oh... don't I have a say?"

He stared at her, brain ticking over, but no hint of guilt upon his face. "I thought I'd surprise you, but seeing as you're so fussy... I was thinking Dubai."

She scrunched her nose, "Couldn't we go somewhere a bit cooler, and closer, and greener... in all senses of the word. I'd rather not fly anywhere."

"I want somewhere hot and sunny. Limited choice at that time of year. Unless you want to go further? Like Australia, maybe?"

He had totally ignored her comment on not flying, but that wasn't of immediate concern.

"What time of year?"

"Christmas."

"Next year though?"

"No, this."

"We're getting married this Christmas?"

"Yes. Boxing day."

She scowled. "Six months! Thanks for letting me know. Do I at least get a say in the venue?"

"Sorry, all sorted. Amberley Castle."

"Very posh.... You know, I would've been OK with just a registry office wedding followed by a meal in a pub?"

"Yeah, precisely why I didn't ask you. I need a nice venue to impress clients."

"You're inviting clients?"

"Just a few important ones."

She shook her head. She couldn't be bothered to argue. He would get his way in the end whatever she said. And if she protested too much, he might go into one of his sulks, and he would still end up getting his way because she would inevitably back down. Anyway, she still hadn't worked out what she was going to do. Settle or move on? Now he'd dropped his time bomb, she couldn't afford to procrastinate. If there were to be a breakup, the longer she left it, the worse it would be.

"Do you, Gemma Williams, take Timothy Starling to be your lawful wedded husband?"

"No."

God. That would be awful. Mind you, she'd probably say 'yes' just to avoid an ugly scene. Then she'd have to divorce him... No. From now on, she'd spend all her lonesome evenings pondering the matter. Set herself a target. End of the month? End of July? It didn't help, Tim was so keen. And super-efficient. He'd probably already sent out the invites. Chosen the food. Done the seating plan—Louise as far from himself as possible. All she'd have to do was turn up. And if she dumped him? Well, he wouldn't like it. There'd be shouting. Tears? Swearing? Begging? Whatever, it would be awful... and her fault. She hated letting people down, to the extent she would often do things just to keep someone happy. But marriage was too important to go ahead with, just because Tim wanted it. She was going to have to be strong. Make her decision and stick with it.

Tim had gone back to researching hotels on the computer screen, so her attention returned to the stinking pile of rubbish in the sink. She salvaged an unopened bag of rice and, after examining the 'best before' date, rinsed off the plastic packaging under the tap, "This is fine too. No 'use by' date." She placed the rice next to the yoghurt. Then a ketchup bottle next to the tins. Sighing, she pulled out a foil takeaway carton with an envelope glued to its side with curry.

"Having fun?"

"Not really. If you put this stuff in the recycling in the first place, I wouldn't have to do this."

"No one's forcing you."

She huffed. "You could at least leave things on the side for me to sort out. I wouldn't have to pick through all this putrid waste then."

"Putrid? Thought you said it's all still edible?"

She threw him her best glare.

He was smiling, enjoying the exchange. He seemed to find it thoroughly amusing to piss her off. She looked at the yoghurt... snatched it up and threw hard. He caught the pot one-handed. Amazingly, the lid remained secure. But not for long. Tim's eyes focussed on her, a slight smirk upon his lips, as he slowly tore off the lid and discarded it on the worktop.

"Don't you dare."

"You did it to me."

He leapt off his stool and raced around the island.

"I'm sorry. I'm sorry," she laughed, running sideways to keep the island between them. If she could just get to the door...

"You will be."

She ran from the room. He grabbed her from behind. Both laughing, he pushed her against the wall. His left arm held her tight, stopping her escape. His right plopped the cool creamy yoghurt onto her head. The thick goo slimed its way down the side of her face.

"Hmm, my favourite. Strawberry Gem."

Her eyes closed as Tim did a great slurping lick across her cheek. She struggled, "Get off, you're tickling me." She squirmed and giggled as he worked his way down her neck. "Stop it," she blurted out amongst the laughs.

"Yep. You were right. Still good to eat." He held a dessert-covered finger in front of her face, "Try some."

"No way!"

She tried to duck away, but he held her tight. His fruity lips fell upon hers. With trepidation, she responded. As long as she didn't swallow, she reckoned her vegan credentials would remain intact. Well, that was the excuse she was going to use, because right now she quite frankly didn't care. She wanted him. Animal products and all.

# FIVE

Spread-eagled across the bed at right angles to her lover, her head rested on his undulating stomach. Her feet pointed towards the open window allowing the occasional wave of cool morning air to brush over her naked form. Naked except for that blasted ring. Attempts to pull the gold band off her heat-swollen finger had proved impossible. Now the ruby eye just taunted her: "If you could remove me, you'd be lovely and cool." Instead, she simmered. If only the breeze would pick up. If it rained (some hope), she'd be outside in a shot. Sod the neighbours—dancing naked in nature's shower was a dream she couldn't shake.

An arm embraced her. She pushed the warm flesh away. It was too hot for cuddles. Too hot for sex. Too hot to do anything... and definitely too hot to go visiting the future in-laws.

She puffed a blast of air up her nose, "It's sooo hot. Can we postpone? Go another day?" The gentle breathing continued. "Tim? Are you awake?"

His body shifted from under her as he turned on his side. After rubbing his eyes, he looked down at her, "What?"

"Do we have to go to your parents today?"

"Thought you were desperate to meet them."

"I am. Just not today."

"Why?" He laid his hand on her shoulder. She shrugged it off.

"It's too hot. I feel like a boiled lobster."

"You don't look like one." He laughed, "More like a poached prawn." He leant over.

"Thanks," Gemma retorted, before exchanging a brief kiss. "So, can we postpone?"

"No. It's all arranged. Dad's taking time off work especially. You don't want to piss him off by changing things. Say after me, 'I must be extra sweet to my future father-in-law'."

Her brow lifted and mouth slackened. Really?

Tim repeated, "I must be..."

"I must be extra sweet to my future father-in-law." As if she wasn't going to be on her best behaviour when meeting his parents for the first time.

"Talk about tractors and cows. Do NOT talk about accountants and lawyers."

"Oh, good grief. This doesn't bode well. Does he know I'm an accountant?"

"Yes. Told him ages ago."

"And he's OK with it?"

Tim chuckled, "Well, he swore quite a bit."

"Great.... Why does he hate us accountants so?"

"Think they're always moaning about his records. He still does them in tatty handwritten cashbooks. Can't be persuaded otherwise."

"Maybe I could have a chat with him. Show him some software."

"You gotta death wish or something?"

"No. Just trying to be helpful. Does he really hate us that much?"

"Don't worry. He hates lawyers more."

"Does that include you?"

"A lot of the time." He flopped back on the pillow, laughing.

She didn't quite know how to respond, but Tim obviously thought it hilarious. "And you're sure we can't postpone?"

"No. We'll go after lunch. Aim to get there by three."

"What's the time now?"

"Err..."

Her head bent backwards to watch him search amongst the legal books and case files piled up on the bedside table. Tim's idea of a relaxing read. "Has it fallen on the floor?" He leant over the side of the bed, giving her the hazardous delight of having his bum pushed against her head, "Don't fart."

He let one rip.

She sat up, "You disgusting pig!" and shoved the sniggering beast. He slipped out of the bed, crashed into the table, and the folders from the top of the pile slipped off. She crawled to the edge. Tim was scrambling over the floor, gathering up paperwork. He laid the folders in a row. Scrutinised each loose sheet before placing it into the correct file.

"Cheers, Gem."

"You deserved it."

He shoved the folders back on the table. A more precarious mountain than before. His hand dived behind the pile. He waved the watch at her. "Found it," he snapped before checking the time, "Eleven twenty-three."

Gemma dragged the grey sheet up from the bottom of the bed and lay down; her head upon the pillow and the silk pulled to her neck. A retreat from sociability. The mischievous gesture had backfired. Expectations of a playful fight. Hot sex. Replaced by Tim's grumpiness over the muddled papers.

"While you're down there, can you retrieve whatever it is under the bed? Something pink."

Tim crouched low. "Disgusting under here," he grumbled.

He stood up. Waved the pink G-string in the air. A ball of dusty fluff floated towards the bed. Tim grabbed it before it landed.

"Not mine."

"Must belong to the ex. Don't you ever clean under the bed?"

Since when had that been her job? "You can clean under your own bloody bed."

"Touchy," Tim commented, striding across the room. He dropped the skimpy article into the fabric laundry hamper.

"I don't want them. Put them in the bin."

"Thought you would, given your love of second-hand clothes."

"Even my enthusiasm wanes when they've been up someone else's bum crack."

"Hypocrite. I think you should keep them. Ripped shorts, G-string... sexy. Maybe Dubai isn't such a great idea—you'll be locked up for good." Yet again, his demeanour had changed. Back to the cheeky lover. He crawled under the bed sheet and sidled up, kissing along her shoulder, up her neck. He paused at the frowning face, "Smile, please!"

That sparkling beam got her every time...

# Six

"Are they from a charity shop?"

"Yes, but the shirt's never been worn. It still had the original price tag on it."

"Still been in someone's grubby house."

"I have washed them." She glanced at Tim. He was sneering so, tongue-in-cheek, she countered with a proposition he would never agree to, "You should come with me sometime. They have designer stuff. Real cheap."

"I'd rather have new. And I'm not exactly broke."

"That's not the point. It's—"

"I know. I know. Don't go on. But you do realise, don't you, that you need some people like me to buy new, so stuff can end up in the charity shop in the first place. We can't all be wearing a never-ending cycle of second-hand stuff."

"There's probably enough clothes in existence right now to do just that."

"Probably? I think you're just making things up," he retorted, striding out of the bedroom.

Another argument lost. In the first few months of their relationship, it had been a challenge. She'd enjoyed the banter and hoped talking about such things would eventually make him see sense and come round to her way of thinking. But she had become frustrated by her inability to out-argue the barrister and, as time wore on, it became increasingly obvious he was not going to change. And it wasn't just when they were arguing about the environment or climate change; any decision they needed to make, always ended up going his way. That was if he even consulted her in the first place. Quite often he didn't bother and just went ahead; like he had done with the wedding and honeymoon.

He was good at that—getting his own way. His first tactic was his gorgeous smile and gift of the gab. If that didn't work, he would just sulk until she caved. She hadn't noticed this side of his character until after she moved in. Which, given she'd only known him three weeks at the time, was hardly surprising. Mind you, it wasn't until after she had sold her flat, thereby committing herself to the relationship, that she got an inkling of this flaw in his otherwise perfect persona. They had been choosing a new kitchen to complete the renovation of his house. He, of course, wanted the most expensive from a high-end shop. Black and shiny. Yuck. She proposed something crafted from recycled wood.

"We don't live in a bloody cottage!" he had shouted.

"I'm not saying it has to be rustic. Modern with a sustainable twist."

"I'm not having mucky old germ-ridden wood in my house."

"Wood has antibacterial properties."

He glowered, then stormed out the room. He blanked her for the rest of the day. Ignored her attempts at conversation. Shrugged off acts of affection. All over a blooming kitchen. She hated his choice but had given in, to get back in his good books.

Since making that list in her phone a couple of weeks ago, this aspect of his character had grated on her nerves. It was becoming soul-destroying.

Everything was about him and what he wanted. He never put her first. It was so one-sided. It made her miserable to think she was becoming a doormat... was already a doormat. Where had it all gone wrong? She'd been a strong independent career woman before she met Tim. From an early age, she had resolved never to be financially dependent on a man and nothing had changed in that regard as far as she was concerned. But recently, Tim had even been hinting that she wouldn't need to work once they were married. God knows how he was expecting her to fill her time if a family was out of the question and the garden off-limits.

She was now certain she didn't want to spend the rest of her life with Tim. The sacrifices she would have to make were just too much. She wanted those kids. She wanted that smallholding. The fact she was even debating leaving, proved she was not 'in love'. If she were, she would surely be willing to put up with anything to stay with him. But she wasn't. She had to leave. It would be better for both parties in the long run. She just had to tell him. So far, she'd failed miserably on that last point. The time never seemed right. And when it was, she just couldn't do it. Couldn't find the words. Couldn't stomach inflicting bad news. It wasn't as though she hated living with him; she just didn't want it to be forever. They were too different. It didn't help that he was so set on the idea of marrying her.

And when she did eventually pluck up the courage to tell him, she would need to stick to her guns and not let him sweet talk her around.

She would have to find somewhere new to live. It would take a sizeable deposit; Guildford wasn't cheap. "Shit." What a stupid idiot, agreeing to pay for the new kitchen instead of a contribution to household costs. Twenty-six grand instead of a couple of thousand for the five and a half months she had lived there. She doubted he would pay her back, especially if he were upset about being dumped. Some accountant she turned out to be.

Now to find the right moment to tell him it was over. *Get through today. Tell him tomorrow. No more putting off. Hang on. Not much point meeting his parents if I'm going to call it off.*

"TIM," she called out.

No reply forthcoming, she ventured onto the landing. The house was quiet. Usually, he had music playing over the downstairs sound system.

"TIM."

Still no answer, she took three steps down the stairs and leant over the glass banister. The oversized oak front door was open and swinging on its hinges in a gentle breeze. A car engine started. An impatient horn beeped three times. She ran down the rest of the stairs. Grabbed her phone and bag off the hall table. A quick tug allowed the door to slam shut as she rushed to the car.

Whilst she was still settling in her seat, Tim started to reverse out of the driveway.

"Hold on a minute. I need to talk to you."

"Tell me while I'm driving. We're already running late."

That seemed like a bad idea. She didn't want to cause a crash.

"Can I drive?"

"Seriously? You want to drive it after all that fuss you made about me buying a petrol car?"

"Well, you got it anyway. We're using it. Someone's got to drive. Does it matter who?"

He puffed his cheeks and rolled his eyes, "No. I don't think you should be allowed to drive my car seeing as you were so opposed to it." He turned to her and, with a glint in his eye, whispered "Hypocrite."

She squirmed, "Yeah... fair enough."

"Stick to your toy."

After clicking the seatbelt in place, she put her phone in the bag. She had lost yet another argument. The man was far too charming. He had a way with words and an answer to everything. No wonder he was such a good barrister. He also had a way of diffusing any disagreement with a beaming smile. She presumed he reserved that tactic just for her. As the car sped off down the road, she allowed herself a half-smile at the thought of him grinning at a frowning judge.

"What do you want to talk about?"

"It can wait."

# SEVEN

"This is my bedroom. Was my bedroom," Tim corrected himself.

"Like the wallpaper."

"Bit of a goth in my teens."

Gemma giggled. It was hard to imagine the barrister in black eye make-up. He had the hair colour for it, mind. "I need photos."

"You can take a running jump."

"Aw." She smiled at her lover. This was the jokey banter she would miss if she left him. The other type—the annihilation of any opinion held—she could do without. But the messing about, the teasing, the inevitable way it always concluded; that would be missed.

"I've destroyed all the evidence."

"Surely, someone in your family must still have some?"

"I was thorough."

"You forgot about the wallpaper."

He perused the skull-embossed blackness that adorned one wall. The other three were painted dark purple and festooned with tatty gig posters. Small clean squares delineated by odd bits of

Blu-Tack were, presumably, the site of long-gone photos.

"I'm not on the wallpaper."

"True."

He grinned at her. "You could be though."

She should've seen that coming. So predictable that he would work the situation to get to where he really wanted to be. Inside her knickers. But to get from a discussion on wallpaper to the subject of sex, you've got to hand it to him, the barrister was a top-class manipulator. Not that she was objecting. The primal lust had taken over. Leaving him no longer seemed like such a good idea. Still, she should at least put up a show of resistance, if only to delay his ultimate victory. She smiled back, her eyes blatantly scanning the room in a mock search for witnesses, "Tim! Not in your parents' house."

"My bedroom."

"Still, they might come in."

"They won't. They're getting tea ready."

"A quick one then?"

"Whatever."

She rolled her eyes. "You're so romantic."

He walked her back against the wall and got to work on her trouser button. "Now, if you wore a dress, this would be so much easier."

"I could say the same to you." She tugged his jeans down below his bum just as his dad walked in. The man swore and walked straight back out. Gemma yanked Tim's jeans back up and stopped his efforts to undo her zip.

"He's gone. We can still—"

"No, not in the mood now." She sighed. "Great. He now thinks I'm degenerate as well as a bloody accountant."

The latter two words being the farmer's exact under-breath muttering as he shook hands with her on arrival at the farm. Tim's mother had been much more welcoming and had shown her around downstairs before handing over to her son for the upstairs tour. Mrs Starling had seemed somewhat flabbergasted by the size of the ruby on her engagement ring but, given the simple functional surroundings in which she lived, Gemma wasn't surprised.

"Ignore him." Tim strode out of the bedroom. He called out, "Dad, what did you want?"

"NOT TO SEE MY SON'S LILY-WHITE BUTT!"

There were further mumbles of conversation Gemma couldn't make out before Tim returned, "He wanted to know if you would like a tour of the milking sheds. I said you wouldn't."

"Wish you'd asked me."

"Why? You'd hate it."

He was right on that point. As a committed vegan, a tour of a dairy farm was way out of her comfort zone. It would have involved keeping her mouth shut: not asking about the baby calves and their mothers, distraught upon separation; not complaining about the forced pregnancies or the fate of the unwanted calves; not arguing about the carbon emissions or the inefficient and unsustainable use of land. She would have to concentrate on the one good thing going for the Starlings' operation: it was organic, so at least the poor cows got to go outside and eat real grass.

"True, but it would've been a chance to get in his good books. Now I'm doomed. Can you at least tell him, this thing here was your fault?"

"What and you're a perfect little angel?"

"Something like that."

"And I'm the evil bastard who seduced you?"

"If you would."

"No chance."

"Tim, please. I'm so embarrassed. Please say it was your fault."

"No, I'll only get a load of grief."

"But what about me? I'm trying to make a good first impression."

He laughed, "Failing miserably."

From downstairs, a woman's voice shouted out, "TEA'S READY."

Gemma ignored the call, having other things on her mind right now, "So, will you do it."

"No."

"Why not?"

"You'll get way less grief than me, so better for him to think his sweet little boy was led astray." With that, Tim left her standing alone in the bedroom. She sighed, her shoulders slumping, then followed him downstairs.

# EIGHT

It was quite a spread. Sandwiches, cupcakes, jam tarts and a massive gooey chocolate cake, all laid out on a simple red and white tablecloth. It must have taken an age to bake all those goodies, pipe all that icing, and fill all those roughly cut slices of homemade bread. Tim's fussing mother placed a flower-decorated tea plate in front of Gemma, "Help yourself, dear."

Presumably, Tim had told them she was a vegan so she could just tuck in. She picked up a sandwich; salad and tomato escaping from the sides. Closer inspection revealed a hint of brown meat—beef. She placed the sandwich on her plate and, like a dutiful girlfriend, passed it to Tim, taking his plate in return. She eyed the rest of the feast. Shot a glance at Tim.

"Eat up." He sucked in his lips.

Her hands clenched under the table. He hadn't told them. Bastard. She smiled. Nodded. How could he? She was already in his dad's bad books. If she didn't eat... She scrutinised the offerings. The cakes and tart pastry would have butter in them. Eggs in the cakes. Perhaps she could just lick the jam off the tart. Height of bad manners, mind. Not that declining to eat would be viewed any better. Should she just come clean and admit her dietary requirements? Or just feign an unsettled stomach and hope they didn't assume a grandchild was on the way?

At that point, the absent Mr Starling Snr entered the kitchen via the back door. Surprisingly, he came to her rescue and removed the plate. The relief was short-lived though; a drink replaced it, accompanied by unwelcome detail, "Fresh out the udders."

She stared at the glass. Should she? Could she? What made it even worse was the milk was warm and frothy—straight from the cow. And he'd milked it specially; just for her. It must be fifteen years since she last touched dairy, but it was clear her hosts were oblivious to this fact. Why hadn't Tim mentioned it to them? She glanced across to him. He was smirking. Trying not to laugh.

She stuck out her index finger and pushed the glass a miniscule distance away. "Sorry, I'm vegan."

"Surely organic's OK?"

Tim was sniggering now, hand over mouth.

"Not really. Water would be better."

The no-longer potential father-in-law snatched the glass away and gulped the creamy liquid down. He stomped over to the sink, rinsed out the glass once, and re-filled it with water. She knew what was coming next. This was going to be awkward. Any support from Tim was not going to happen. She knew that now. Waste of space.

The angry farmer plonked the glass down in front of her. A milky residue swirled within the liquid. A smear of white froth remained a centimetre or so from the top. She breathed deep. There was no alternative. She had to do it. Her hand reached out and grabbed the glass...

No. She was better than that. Yes, it was tempting... so tempting. But she didn't want to be seen as the vindictive bitch. That was not her. She had dignity.

As she stood, her hand still clasped around the glass, she hesitated. In her mind's eye, the water slowly dripped down his shocked face. The smug smirk turned to dismay. A panic over his hair. The carefully coiffured quiff, he spent hours perfecting every morning, would flop in a damp swamp... so tempting.

But, no, she wouldn't take that route. That was not her. She strode past the elder man, knocking his arm. But she didn't apologise. Her eyes remained focused on her destination. Three pairs of eyes were burning into the back of her head, but she wasn't going to turn and face them. Stick to the plan.

Upon reaching the sink, she turned on the tap. As she waited for the hot water to come through, she squirted a splodge of lime-green washing-up liquid into the glass. Deciding against the manky dishcloth, she opted for the slightly cleaner brush. Scrubbed gently but purposely. An exuberance of froth flowed. She rinsed diligently—several times—before filling with fresh water; not so much she couldn't drink it in one go, and not so little the effect would be lost.

She gulped the water down in six mouthfuls. Perfect. She placed the glass in the sink. Turned and headed to the backdoor. She did not return the stares. She did not say goodbye. She walked straight out, closing the door firmly behind her.

# NINE

Gemma paused outside the door. She'd done it. Ended it. A somewhat more drastic end to the relationship than she had imagined, but it avoided that tricky conversation; the one where there was a good chance he would persuade her to stick with him. Slightly disappointing he wasn't chasing after her, but at least that avoided a painful confrontation.

She took a deep breath. The back garden. Somewhere not shown on her tour of the house. A narrow concrete path led away from the door to the right and disappeared around the corner of the building. She shrugged. Not much choice unless she wanted to go traipsing over fields.

Around the corner, an obstacle blocked her way. The rusted five-bar gate was secured by padlock and chain. Damn. Her heeled sandals weren't the most suitable footwear for climbing, but she wasn't about to turn back and lose face.

Pausing at the top of the gate, she brushed a speck of dirt from her crisp white summer top. Bought especially for the occasion from a charity shop, the sleeveless blouse sported a new pattern of orange streaks. Her lemon-yellow jeans were also now embellished to match.

Her right leg swung over the top bar. She twisted her body, before following with her left. She glanced at the ground. Yuck. Shuffled along the rail to the fence post, then stepped down onto a patch of dry grass. She turned away from the gate and faced her next challenge. Clearly the route the cows took to the milking sheds, a patchwork of cowpats formed an unruly tapestry before her. The gaps between filled with a stinking slush of brown.

"GEM. GEM."

The voice spurred her on. There was no going back. She had to get out of there and fast. She hop-scotched a few steps, dodging the pats. Wet splashes fell upon her feet. Moisture seeped between her toes. Best not think about it.

"GEM. It was just a bit of fun. Don't go."

Where was the apology? Where was the 'please'? Distracted by these thoughts, she lost her balance. Her foot plunged into the warmth of a recently composed deposit.

"Urghh."

A guffaw bellowed behind her.

"Good one, Gem. You better come back now. We'll hose you down."

"You're supposed to be supportive. Stick up for me. Not poke fun."

She grimaced at her feet. The damage was done. There was no point pussyfooting anymore. She ran. Slid. Jumped. Slipped. Hopped. Squelched. The end of the nightmare in sight, she tripped and fell.

That familiar laugh again. More raucous and out of control this time.

"Classic! I'm putting that on YouTube, Gem. We'll be millionaires!"

*Doesn't he get it? It's over. How can he not realise?*

Standing up, Gemma stared at her hands. Gross. What to wipe them on? She glanced about, then to her trousers. Pretty much all brown from the knees down, a bit more wouldn't matter. She rubbed her thighs. Where next?

She splashed through the excrement until she reached the front corner of the farmhouse. Jumping from the mucky trail, she spied Tim's car. His new car. His very expensive gleaming new coupe. Keys? Damn. He had them.

Now out of sight, maybe she could allow herself a treat. One tiny little bit of revenge. Didn't she deserve it after all? She stepped back to the stinking path and scooped up the biggest, freshest pat she could find. Skipped to the car and deposited the shit on the sparkling bonnet. Then smeared the revolting mess over the windscreen and across the doors, paying particular attention to the driver's handle. Serves him right.

She stepped back and admired her handiwork. Her cheeks dimpled in a smirk. *Excellent job, Gemma Williams*. She dusted her mucky hands. Chuckled at the fail. Then strode out of the yard and onto the open road.

# TEN

It was a good ten minutes before Gemma saw a flaw in her plan. This was her first visit to Tim's parents' farm, so she had no idea where she was or where she was heading. Reaching a junction, she scratched her head. Which way had they turned enroute? She hadn't been paying attention. There hadn't been any need...

"Maps!"

Looking down, she slapped her chest. Where was the cross-body phone bag? Damn. Another flaw in her plan. She left the pale grey pouch hanging on the back of the kitchen chair, along with her phone, credit and debit cards, a few pounds in cash, a comb, front door key, and a hanky.

She turned to look back down the road. What the hell was she going to do? She didn't want to go back. She couldn't call a taxi. Passing traffic was non-existent. So, she would be hiking. What does an hour's drive convert to in walking? Sixty miles? No, lots of country lanes. Say, forty miles... Twelve hours? Longer in sandals? Definitely more painful. Oh why, oh why, had she worn heels? She never usually did as she'd been put off them at an early age; the elderly neighbour (who babysat her as a child) had feet that looked like they were out of a horror movie. They were so bad, the poor woman could only wear open-toed orthopaedic sandals, so the deformed toes were on full display. As a five-year-old, it was terrifying having the old woman hobble after her, even though she was as kind as they came. Gemma's mother had explained it was because the lady had lived in high-heeled winklepickers in her younger years. It had put her right off. Sod fashion, she was going to look after her feet. She kicked off the offending sandals.

"If I can find the main road, maybe I could hitch a ride?"

She studied the signpost. 'Petworth 6m' seemed the most promising. She picked up the sandals and strode off with renewed vigour. A keenness to get there before dark.

***

Not five minutes later, the birdsong made way to the chug chug of a vehicle. She turned. The sound was growing louder. Coming her way. It couldn't be Tim... unless he'd borrowed a vehicle from the farm.

A red tractor came around the corner. Its horn honked. Tim. She stood her ground, expecting him to stop. TOOT. TOOT. TOOT. Not Tim. She jumped out of the road onto the grass verge. The driver raised his hand in thanks as he passed, glancing twice in her direction.

The tractor stopped a short distance up the road. A man, in his late twenties or early thirties, opened the far side door and leant out.

"Are you OK?" he shouted.

"Yes, thank you."

"Are you sure? You don't look like you're dressed for hiking and you... well, look a bit worse for wear if you don't mind me saying?"

"I'm fine."

"Do you want a lift somewhere?"

She strolled up to the tractor. "That would be good, but are you sure you want to?" She pointed to her mucky trousers, half expecting him to drive off.

"Err... got generations of farming genes in me. Think I can cope!"

He held out his hand. She did a quick wipe of hers on her jeans, before reaching up and taking hold of the dirty hand. She couldn't complain—hers were much worse.

He hauled her up into the cab with ease. Those farming genes in play, no doubt.

"Sorry, not much room. You'll have to perch here."

"No problem. Thanks." She settled her left buttock onto the edge of his seat. As the tractor set off, she pushed her feet against the back of the footwell to keep her from falling.

He glanced at her, "I'm Matt."

"Gemma or Gem. Either's fine."

"Well, Gem, can I ask what happened?"

"Let's just say, I had to leave somewhere in a hurry."

He nodded towards the mess on her knees, "Not many dairy farms down these lanes. The Starlings?"

"Huh... yes."

"You're not Tim's fiancée, are you?"

"Ex-fiancée," she retorted, frowning.

"Ohh. Like that, is it?"

"Do you know him?"

"Yes."

"Well?"

"Err... we used to be best friends when we were kids. Kinda drifted apart when we got to university. Different interests. Different directions. You know how it is.... I heard he's doing alright. Barrister, isn't it?"

"Yes, that's right."

A sudden bounce of the vehicle made her slip. The man grabbed her thigh and pulled her back up. "Sorry. Massive pothole."

"Not your fault.... Thanks for the save."

His hand remained on her thigh, holding her securely in place. The contact seemed innocent: as though he hadn't realised. She could easily shrug him off but the moment for action had passed. Not that she felt awkward. His touch felt... well, exciting... arousing. She swallowed hard and focussed on the road ahead.

"So, what's the plan? Where do you want to get to?"

"Guildford ideally. If you could just drop me off at a main road, I can hitch."

"You're not serious, are you? Single girl hitching? I can't let you do that. I'll take you home."

His hand returned to the steering wheel to negotiate a corner.

"No, it's too far. It's like an hour each way. I can't impose on you like that."

"I don't think you'll have much luck blagging a ride." He scrunched his nose and laughed. "We'll go back to my place, swap vehicles, and then I'll drive you home. I insist."

"I left my bag at the Starlings'. Don't really want to go back and get it. If I could just borrow a smartphone or a computer for a minute, I can order a taxi."

"You might need to borrow my bathroom too, if you want a taxi to take you anywhere."

It was pointless arguing, and that did solve the problem of getting home, so silence reigned.

She studied his profile. Soft sun-bleached curls framed his tanned skin. The stubble of late afternoon was just emerging on his chin and was trying its hardest to hide the odd acne scar. His ring-free hands gripped the steering wheel. Rough and dirty. Working hands. In the mirror, his dark brown eyes twinkled. He wasn't drop-dead gorgeous like Tim, but she felt drawn to him all the same.

He looked happy. Relaxed. Content with his world. The term 'jolly farmer' fitted him perfectly. Given another twenty years of working outdoors in all weathers, he would no doubt acquire a ruddy complexion to match his jovial disposition. But her attraction to him wasn't due to his physical features; it just felt nice to have someone express concern for her.

She searched ahead for another pothole...

*Stop it. Why are you even thinking like that? You only broke up with Tim like two seconds ago. Get a grip. And, anyway, he's a farmer. Bound to hate vegans. It'll only end up another disaster. Stop it!*

"So... if you don't mind me asking... do you live with Tim?"

Ohh, another complication. Why on earth had she moved in with him? It seemed like a good idea at the time. Cheaper to run one place than two. Her flat, being the smaller property, was the sacrifice. She made a profit on the sale, after repaying the mortgage, but had spent that on re-doing the kitchen in Tim's house. Without a deposit, it would be difficult to get back on the ladder. She would have to ask Tim for the money back. No doubt, as a barrister, he would find some reason not to pay up.

"Yes... unfortunately."

"And you definitely think it's over?"

"Yes, as far as I'm concerned, it's over."

"As it happens, I've got a cottage on my farm that needs a tenant for a while if you're interested? Just got a few things to finish in the kitchen, then it'll be ready."

"Err..."

"No livestock on my farm, if you're wondering," his head swivelled to give a cheeky grin. He was teasing her. She smiled back. It felt good to share a joke after what had been a very stressful afternoon.

She relaxed against his arm, "Umm... yes, wouldn't mind a look. If you're sure?"

"Yeah. Need a tenant. Was going to instruct an agent, so you'll save me a few quid if you take it."

"Can I have a look now?"

"Err... new carpets. Can I stick you in a washing machine first?"

# ELEVEN

They stood on the doorstep, both staring beyond the open door. The hallway was tiled in a black and white checkerboard pattern in keeping with the age of the Victorian farmhouse. Though spotlessly clean, the tiles were well-worn; a slight indentation marking the route along the passage to the kitchen at the far end. But, like the cottage, he had invested in new carpets for his own home. A cream-coloured, short pile offering adorned the staircase. Its chemical 'new' smell fought with her own recently acquired powerful odour.

"I could carry you?"

"Yeah. Probably best."

He scooped her up in his arms, as though she weighed no more than a piece of fluff, and carried her over the threshold. As they headed up the stairs, his muscles warmed her body. A physique honed from working the land. Unlike slim Tim who would struggle to carry her up the first step. Not that her fiancé—ex-fiancé that is—wasn't fit; he jogged regularly, cycled occasionally, but had no interest in gyms or lifting weights so lacked arm muscle. It never bothered her. Muscle-bound types were not really her thing. Still, the closeness, the tautness, stirred something deep within. A warming. A tingle. She gazed at his face. Was he feeling the same?

He knocked open the bathroom door with his shoulder and placed her down in the walk-in shower. Almost eye to eye, he studied her face, chewing on his lip. She stared at his mouth, her heart pounding. Their eyes met...

"Err..." He stepped away to open a cupboard and retrieved a wicker laundry basket, "Chuck your clothes in here and put it on the landing. I'll stick them in the machine." He handed her a towel, "I'll find you something to wear."

"Thank you. But just bung them in a plastic bag, there's no need to wash them."

"No, they're really stinky and I don't think I've got a plastic bag here. I'll wash them. I insist."

Before she could protest further, he hurried from the room, shutting the door behind him. She stared at the stripped pine. Was he coming back? She wanted him to. The fast-spreading tingle was urging her body on. Her breathing grew heavy. Her ear tilted towards the door. Silence. No clomp clomp clomp of someone descending the stairs. Not a whisper. Was he still behind the door?

A floorboard creaked. Footsteps, muffled by thick carpet, faded down the stairs. He had been behind the door. Shame he hadn't come back in... ripped off her clothes... his clothes...

She shook her head. "I need a cold shower." This was stupid. How could she even contemplate having sex five seconds after a split? She needed a break from men. A long break. Then be choosy. Very choosy. Make sure they're compatible in every way... including diet. She would not be making the same mistake again. Far too often, she had moved in with a man only to regret it.

She hooked the towel over the back of a chair. Unbuttoned her blouse, slipped it off, and dropped it in the basket.

Her hand cupped her chin. Dan. He had to be the record. Met at a party at the start of her final year of uni. The disorganized twit didn't have any lodgings lined up. Stayed the night and never left. The two of them squashed into her tiny study bedroom among piles of his dirty clothes and smelly pizza boxes. How she ever put up with it? Still, doubling-up proved a great cost-saving exercise, though the lack of personal space was probably what drove them apart. That and Dan's drug-taking. It was a good thing the final year ended early because of exams, otherwise the constant fighting might have ended in a murder. Probably hers.

Trousers next. Her nose scrunched. Gross.

Josh. Must have been about eighteen months after Dan. That was a fun holiday, hiking with Louise in the Peak District. The icing on the cake was bumping into Josh, an old classmate, halfway up Kinder Scout. She moved in with the civil servant on their return to Sussex. What was that? A week? She shook her head. Terrible. But she'd been desperate to get out of her parents' home. She chuckled. Feeble excuse. The relationship lasted a couple of months before she discovered the turd was cheating on her. She then went through a lean patch which lasted three years. There'd been the odd date, but nothing that went beyond that.

Bra. Looked clean. She sniffed the cup. Poo.

Then she met Yousef. Lovely Yousef. Now in her own flat, he moved in with her after a couple of dates. That had all gone wrong because Yousef treated her like a bad secret for fear of upsetting his Muslim family. She put up with it for a while because she was very fond of the junior doctor. But it became obvious the relationship wasn't going anywhere when his parents started putting pressure on him to get married... and he wasn't even thinking of her as being in the frame!

And then there was Tim. She packed her suitcases just three weeks after their first meeting.

Remembering past experiences, she had expressed doubts. But Tim countered, "View it as a trial arrangement. If it doesn't work out, you've still got your flat to go back to." He was very persuasive. Her objections didn't stand a chance. She sold the flat two months later. Another three months on, she was regretting it.

As she dropped her knickers into the basket, the landing creaked. She stood still. Would he knock? Ask to come in? Walk in and sweep her off her feet? The footsteps retreated down the stairs. The bang of a door marked the beginning of silence.

She stepped in the shower. Turned it to its coldest setting. She gasped as the deluge of icy water hit. The perfect solution to the heat she was feeling in more ways than one. Grabbing the soap bar out of the tray, she scrubbed away all the trials and tribulations of the day. Unable to spot any shampoo in the modern bathroom, she made do with the soap. Hair frothed, she stood straight, face turned up, and let the water spray... rinsing away her troubles... dousing her desires...

# TWELVE

Matt closed the front door. He stopped still. What the hell just happened? He almost kissed her—another man's girlfriend. Yes, she claimed it was over between them, but maybe it was just a lovers' tiff. They would sort things out and get back together. It would be unnecessarily complicated if he got involved. Especially as he knew the man and his family. And having been on the receiving end of such treatment himself, he knew how bad it felt to be cheated on. It had happened to him twice. The only serious relationships in his life had both ended with him being dumped in preference for someone else. No, he was not going to be the man who stole another's girl. He would wait until he was sure it was over between them.

He bit his lip hard as he got in the jeep and started the engine. There was something about her that he found totally engaging. She had spirit. She wanted to sort things out for herself. He liked a woman who didn't mind getting her hands dirty... and her feet... and her legs. Were they freckles on her face or mud? He smiled. He would shortly find out what had happened at the Starlings'. With any luck, Tim was in a worse state.

***

Matt drove into the farmyard. Mrs Starling was washing a car. Brand new by the look of it. And sporty. It had to be Tim's. The barrister was supervising from the doorway. Matt parked by the sheds. Gripping hard on the steering wheel, he growled in the throat. A car! The sod's first priority was a car! His fiancée was wandering the quiet country lanes in bare feet. Anything could've happened to her. She certainly didn't seem to have any qualms over accepting lifts from strangers. Or taking a shower in their house! But all Tim worried about was his poor mother missing a spot on his prized possession.

He leapt out of the jeep and slammed the door to get their attention. "Hi, Jenny."

Redirecting the hose to the ground, the grey-haired woman turned and smiled, "Hi, Matt." She wiped her water-splashed face with the crook of her elbow. The front of her rose-patterned dress bore the dark stain of water. The farmer usually wore t-shirts and jeans, so this was a dress for special occasions. A dress for meeting Gemma. "Just let me finish this and I'll make you a cup of tea."

"No, no, please don't worry about me. Not stopping for long. Just want a word with Tim."

Her brow shot up. She glanced at her son, then nodded, "I'll leave you alone to chat." She went back to hosing the car.

Matt walked over to where Tim stood; well out of reach of the spray.

"Hi, Matt. How ya doing?"

"OK. You?"

"Fine. Except for this." His hand spread outwards to indicate the poo-smeared car. He didn't seem bothered that his girlfriend was missing. Maybe it really was over between them?

"Is that Gemma's handiwork?"

Tim's head flinched back, "How do you know Gem?"

"Just met her. She's back at my house. I've come to get her bag. Then I'll give her a lift home."

"No need. I'll pick her up in a bit when my car's ready. God knows what she was thinking."

"Are you sure you shouldn't just leave her be for now? She's pretty angry at the moment. She seems to think it's over between you."

"No idea where she got that from. She's been in a funny mood all day. Stress of meeting the future in-laws, me thinks. Made a great first impression, that's for sure. I'll pick her up shortly." Pausing to look at his pride and joy, he bit on his lip. "Is she still filthy?"

"She's having a shower."

"Good."

He was more worried about his car than her. But that was Tim for you. Why would he expect anything less? The man was selfish and uncaring. Always had been. Always would be. If she had any sense, she would make the separation permanent. He stood in silence, next to Tim, for a few moments. He racked his brains for a conversation piece, but there was nothing. Nothing polite anyway. When they were kids, the chatter had been non-stop. But as adults, there was nothing to say without falling into another argument. The fallout was just too great. "See you around," was all Matt could muster before he leapt off the doorstep and went to help the drenched Mrs Starling.

# THIRTEEN

Shit! She slapped the shower valve shut. How much water had she wasted? In a heatwave too.

She stepped out, grabbed the towel, and dried herself.

After wrapping the blue fluffiness around her, she opened the door a crack. Good. The farmer had left a carefully folded pile on a chair just outside. Grabbing the clothes, she retreated back into the bathroom and placed them on the chair.

She held up the dress by the shoulder straps. She'd presumed he was single but was clearly wrong. Her hands dropped, sagging the dress on the bathmat. Her stomach tightened, "Aw." She whacked her palm against her forehead. *Stop it!*

What was his girlfriend going to think? Her bloke had brought some strange woman into their house for a shower, and lent her some of her clothes? If she caught her like this...

She dressed quickly. The clothes were more feminine than she would've chosen, but the lacy bra and knickers, and floral dress fitted her perfectly. The ensemble was completed by ballet-style shoes and a thin cardigan for the cool evening air.

She stepped onto the landing and stood still, listening. The house quiet except for the gentle rumble of a washing machine.

"Hi?"

Receiving no response, she headed downstairs to the hallway.

"Anyone there?"

The house remained silent, so she wandered into the sitting room. Despite the modern bathroom and new stair carpet, the renovations had evidently not got this far. The black-painted wood flooring was partially covered with a thread-bare rug. Each vying for the title of 'most worn'. The olive-green paint on the walls grubby, especially round the light switch. In an alcove, to the right of the Victorian fireplace, a collection of photos adorned chipped shelving. Passing a tatty oversized sofa and mug-stained coffee table, she snuck across the room for a closer look. A couple of portraits stood out. One was of the farmer and a woman, both in skiing gear, in front of a snow-covered mountain. The other was a wedding shot of the same smiling couple.

"Married... no chance then," she mumbled. "For heaven's sake, just stop it, will you."

The front door latch rattled. She hurried to the hall to find Matt dropping his keys on the console table.

"Sorry, Matt. Wasn't being nosy, just looking for you."

"That's OK. I've got a bit of an admission to make myself."

"Yeah?"

"Yeah.... I popped down the road to get your bag..." He held it out to her.

"Thank you."

"...Thought I was doing you a favour, but not so sure now." He grimaced, "Tim's coming to pick you up shortly. Sorry."

"Oh... It's OK. I've got to get home somehow. And I'm going to bump into him there anyway. Not really anywhere else I can go at such short notice."

He nodded. "Is it a nice house?"

"Very posh. Not really my thing. Never felt at home there. Reeks of his ex." She laughed, "Right down to the G-string we found under the bed this morning."

No laughter came from the man standing in front of her. Instead, he frowned, "Are you sure they were his ex's?"

"Well, they weren't mine." She laughed again but then realised what he was getting at. It was a bit much. She knew Tim. He would never... "What are you insinuating?"

"Well, are you sure he's not been playing away?" His nose twitched, "At home."

"Err... he doesn't have the time."

"Bit odd you found some knickers... that weren't yours?"

"Definitely not mine. It's just neither of us had thought to hoover under the bed. They were very dusty so been there a long time." Why she felt the need to defend Tim, she could not fathom. Call it residual loyalty or something, but whatever it was, she did not like the accusation he had cheated on her.

"Do you ever go away on your own? You know, like stay away, overnight?"

If she weren't so attracted to the man, she would've told him to piss off. The relentless inquisition was not appreciated, but she couldn't bring herself to swear at her knight in shining armour. And it was hard to ignore those dreamy brown eyes glistening with concern as they interrogated her face. Hypnotised by the golden fireworks exploding from his pupils, her features softened, "Um... yes, I go to Wales to see my parents every other weekend."

"Never with Tim?"

"He's come a couple of times, but he's usually..."
She grimaced, "...too busy."

There was an awkward silence.

"Sorry, I didn't mean to upset you, but I know what he's like. Better to know now than after years of marriage."

She swallowed, fighting the tears. "Doesn't matter anyway. I'm leaving, remember," she mumbled.

His hand rested on her shoulder, "Well, my cottage is available any time if you need it. I can always put a microwave and fridge in the lounge area until the kitchen's done."

Pushing the thoughts of Tim's possible infidelity to the back of her mind, she endeavoured to sound more upbeat and in control, "Thanks, that's very kind of you, but it's probably better for me to find somewhere closer to work."

"Well, it's there, even if you just need it for a few days. Doubt it'll be much fun living with your ex."

"Err... I'll let you know."

"I'll give you my number."

She delved in her bag for her phone. As she set up the new contact, he watched open-mouthed. She passed the phone to him, "Can you tap your number in, please." His eyes remained transfixed on her left hand as he took the phone from her.

He tapped away. "I'll send myself a text to check I've entered it correctly." She raised her eyebrows but said nothing. The noise of the text message sending was followed by a ding in Matt's pocket. He pulled his phone out. "Yep. Remembered it correctly." She bit her lip. So obvious, but it was flattering to know he wanted her number even though she had no intention of being his bit on the side. He held out her phone. Despite being right-handed, she used the left to take it, knuckle side up, curious to confirm his fascination was with her engagement ring. Yep, that was the culprit. It was a ginormous ruby, but she couldn't imagine such a masculine rough and ready sort of bloke being that into jewellery. She tucked the phone in her bag, then spread her fingers out to display the gem. Raising her eyebrows, her head tilted.

"Looks like my gran's."

"It's antique, so maybe it is." She tugged it off her finger, "Here, have a look."

He examined the band, "Yes, it is. The inscription is theirs. Mabel & Sid. 14.05.1960." He stroked the jewel with his thumb, "Huh. Never thought I'd see this again."

"Was it stolen?"

"No. I gave it to a girlfriend. She wouldn't give it back when we broke up."

"Tim bought it at a jeweller in Guildford, so she must have sold it at some point."

He stared at her, then nodded. After rubbing his fingers over the ruby one last time, he held the ring back out to her.

She pushed his hand away, "No. You keep it. It's yours."

"Not really. I gave it to her. I checked the legal position when she wouldn't give it back. It was an unconditional gift, so rightfully hers to do with as she pleased."

"But it's a family heirloom and I want you to have it. I've got no use for it anymore. And it was an unconditional gift to me so, as you say, I can do with it what I like. And I want to give it to you."

"But—"

"I insist."

"Let me give you something for it then."

"No. Didn't cost me anything, so I don't want anything."

"You might change your mind if you knew how much it's worth."

"Don't tell me. I don't want to know."

He stared at her for what seemed an exorbitant length of time. "This is awkward. I do want it—I was very close to my grandparents, so it means a lot—but I feel guilty about taking it from you. Are you sure?"

"Yes. Positive. It's back where it belongs."

The doorbell rang so she grabbed the ring from him and shoved it under the pile of post on the console table. They exchanged a smile at her quick thinking. Matt mouthed "Thanks" before he went to answer the door.

# FOURTEEN

"Nice dress."

"Yeah, thought you might like it," she grumbled as the car sped along the highway towards Guildford. It had not gone unnoticed, he had cleaned the car before coming to get her. Had he even bothered looking for her after her grand exit?

"God, you are in a right mood.... PMT?"

"Why does there have to be a biological reason? Why can't I just be fed up with you? It's over between us. I'm leaving as soon as I can find somewhere else to live."

"Are you sure it's not—"

"For heaven's sake!"

"Don't get so bloody stroppy with me. I'm the one who should be cross. What you did to my car. It's unacceptable."

"You deserved it."

"I don't know how you worked that out. I didn't do anything."

"Exactly!"

The rest of the journey was conducted in total silence. She occupied herself by staring aimlessly out of the side window. The last thing she wanted to do was catch Tim's eye. He would try to smile his way out of her bad books, so she was determined not to give him the opportunity. At one point, he tried to get a rise out of her by driving extra fast. She hated that. But she resisted the temptation to complain and stuck to watching the trees go by. He soon gave up, signifying the rarity of his capitulation with an overly loud sigh and a poke on her hip to get her attention.

He failed.

*** 

Tim sprang out of the car. Clunked his door shut. She fiddled with her bag. Smoothed the dress. Leant back against the seat and puffed out a blast of air.

He rapped on his window, "You coming?"

Her body slouched. Now he was no longer behind the wheel, there was nothing to stop the inevitable confrontation. But she couldn't sit here forever—much as she'd like to—so, here goes...

Her chest tightened as she climbed out slowly. She stood tall, hand on the door frame.

Tim peered over the coupe and showcased his trademark grin before breaking the silence, "It was kinda funny."

She slammed the door shut, "I don't think so."

"Oh, Gemmie, you look so pretty in that dress." He jogged around the car and, flashing a broad smile, held his arms wide, "Give us a cuddle."

She glared, then stormed off towards the house. As she rummaged in her bag for her key, she glanced back. Tim was still standing where she left him. Staring in the direction of the wheel arch, his posture was stooped. Motionless. She'd never seen him so sad before. A lump stuck in her throat. She hadn't thought about how he was feeling. This was a man who wanted to marry her and here she was tearing his world apart. She was on the point of

running over to hug him, when he pulled a tissue
out of his trouser pocket and started rubbing away
at a mucky spot on his treasured car.

She groaned and went back to unlocking the door.
Once inside, she kicked the door shut and fled to the
sanctuary of a spare bedroom.

# FIFTEEN

"Are you coming?"

"No. I'm staying in bed."

"You're the one who lost it. It should be you digging around in the shit for it."

"I don't need it anymore. If you want it, you have to look for it."

Rolling onto her side, she hauled the duvet over her head and stuffed the corner into her mouth to stifle the giggle that was desperate to get out. When Tim noticed the ring was missing from her finger, she told him it must have come off in the farmyard when she fell over. No way was she going to tell him, she gave it to Matt. It would be Tim's worst nightmare to search through cow dung, but serves him right. If he had stuck up for her in the first place, she wouldn't have had to traipse through that disgusting sludge. It was a fitting punishment for him. Shame she wouldn't be there to film the event, but she didn't want to get roped into the pointless hunt herself. In any case, she couldn't bear facing his parents again.

Tim sighed. "So, you're not changing your mind?"

"No."

"About leaving me?"

"No."

"I can't understand it. I know we have our disagreements about politics and ecology, but we get on great, don't we?"

She poked her head from the covers. He was standing by the guest room door, jangling his car keys in one hand.

"I don't think you really love me. I'm doing you a favour."

"A favour? Can't see how you worked that out. I'll have to find a replacement. Go through all that dating stuff again. I haven't got time for it. Work's manic at the moment." One side of his nose wrinkled, "And that's not likely to change."

"You make me sound like some sort of chattel."

"I'm invested in this relationship."

Her head shuddered at his matter-of-fact declaration. "And that's supposed to convince me to stay?"

"The sex is fantastic. You'll be hard-pressed to find someone as good."

Her head shook as she smiled. The man's modesty... just did not exist. Mind you, he wasn't lying performance-wise. But to claim uniqueness was a bit much.

"Not enough. Need to be in love."

"Maybe you just need a holiday. I should be able to get a few days off if I work extra late for a bit. How about the South of France?"

"I don't like flying. Don't like the heat. Don't like sitting by a pool all day doing nothing. If you don't know these things by now, there's no hope for us. Anyway, I don't need a holiday, I need a clean break."

"A holiday on your own?"

"Not a holiday. A permanent break. A new start for both of us."

"You're being ridiculous."

"Go away." She pulled the duvet back over her head.

"I'm going... but only because Dad needs to clean the yard, and once he's done that, the ring will be gone forever. You sure you won't come and help us look?"

"No."

"We'll talk more when I get back. Maybe you could come out from under the duvet before then. Get dressed. Have something to eat. So you're ready for a proper discussion."

"Nothing to talk about."

A loud sigh preceded, "Well, I've gotta go... err... I love you."

The door of the spare room slammed shut; the sound muffled by the duvet. She threw the stifling covers off the bed and stared at the door. Why did he have to say that now? Now she was leaving him. Not once had he uttered those words before. Not even when he asked her to marry him (as evidenced by the videos) had those special words crossed his lips. She rolled her eyes. A ploy to get her back in his arms. To wiggle his way back into favour. Well, it wasn't going to work. She grabbed her phone off the bedside table, tapped the microphone symbol in the browser, then spoke clearly, "Rental properties Guildford."

# Sixteen

Matt studied the attractive woman across the table. She was fiddling with her mobile. It was his fault. He hadn't been the most entertaining of dates. His mind was elsewhere.

"Do you want coffee?"

She looked up with a start, as though she'd forgotten he was there. "No, I'm fine."

"I'll get the bill then."

She nodded and went back to her phone.

He should never have agreed to this date in the first place. His mum had set it up for him. She didn't like seeing her son on his own. Nearly a year since the Bella debacle, his mother was constantly badgering him to start dating again. Tonight's nomination, Ruth, was the daughter of a neighbour of hers. Her job was something in marketing. He hadn't been bothered to probe further. All he could think about was Gemma. He'd had no calls from her about the cottage. He sent a text to say her clothes were ready. The reply back was short and to the point: «*Thanks. I'll pick them up soon.*» He even popped over to the Starlings' and asked if Tim and Gemma were still together. Gerald, Tim's father, had used a long list of expletives to basically say yes, they were, and he was not happy about it. "Bloody bean-loving bean counter."

Obviously, there was more to the story than just a falling out with Tim. He'd love to know more, but tact was required when Gerald was involved. Jenny was harder to read. She fussed over the teapot rather than join in the conversation. Nothing new there. She tended to keep her opinions to herself when they were in direct opposition to her husband's. His best option was to probe his own mother, Jenny's best friend, for the details. But whether he could do that without revealing his personal interest in Gemma to his busybody parent was a big unknown.

He'd even considered driving over to Guildford. Take her clothes as an excuse. Try to persuade her to leave Tim. She could do so much better than that cad. But there was no way of knowing if Tim would be there. If he were, it would seriously restrict what he could say to Gemma. Persuading her to leave Tim would be a non-starter. So, he would have to wait until she came over. Fingers crossed, on her own.

Of course, persuading her to leave Tim was one thing. Persuading her to date himself was a whole other matter. He was a step down in all departments. Looks. Clothes. Money. House. Vehicle. The only thing going for him was he was honest and decent, and treated other people with respect. Unlike Tim, he would never cheat on a girlfriend or use a woman for sex. What he yearned for was stability in a relationship. One that would stand the test of time. One like his own parents had, until his father was so cruelly taken away from them. Had he set his sights too high with Gemma? She was in a different class. A natural beauty. Intelligent. Thoughtful. Generous.

Mind you, Bella had been a natural beauty too. Not that she ever showed it to the world. It had been his privilege alone to see her stripped of make-up, though even that was restricted to after a shower or in bed. When she left him for his cousin, it was a real kick in the gut. Mind you, with hindsight, his relative had done him a favour. Blinded by Bella's good looks and sophisticated ways, like an obedient sheep, he'd spent what little money he had on jewellery and clothes for her. He'd started renovating the farmhouse at her insistence; she was not going to live in a 'shit-hole' as she called it. Admittedly, the house looked like it was about to fall down at any minute. He had no idea when work was last done on the family home. Not in his lifetime as far as he could remember. His dad once commented on the tractor wallpaper in his childhood bedroom as being a Grandad Sid improvement. Some of the furniture had also been hand-built by the industrious Sid. God knows how the man found the time. All he'd managed so far was paint the bedrooms, refurbish the bathroom, and get the upstairs carpeted. All in the middle of the night. The house tended to be low down on the list of a farmer's priorities, so he had needed that kick up the butt from the bossy Bella to get on with it. Things had kinda ground to a halt since she left. The downstairs remained untouched, as did the outside. If she had not left, it would all be done by now. A small price to pay for a lucky escape.

But then again, perhaps the house had a lucky escape as well. It would have broken his heart to rip out Grandad's hand-built kitchen with its wonky doors and well-worn worktops. History engrained into the oranged-by-time pine. To dump Gran's cosy sofa: the epitome of family togetherness. Snuggled together on a cold winter's night, heat bellowing out from a blazing fire, he envisioned Gemma leaning against his shoulder, staring dreamily at the flickering flames. Infant children clambering over them. Jumping off the sofa arms into an imaginary sea. Shrieks of laughter and giggles as they evaded the shark circling the coffee table—their dog or maybe a cat?

Why couldn't he have that? Why couldn't he have Gemma? After all, beautiful Bella had stuck around for two years before she left him for a richer, better-looking man. So, if she was not averse to a poor ugly sod like him then maybe travel in the opposite direction wasn't so impossible. It might have been in his acne-ridden youth, but now? He'd definitely improved with age. His nose and ears were no longer out of proportion to the rest of his face. His teeth had been fixed after some cajoling by Bella. Ditching the crew cut of his youth for a longer shaggier style at university had done wonders. More by luck than judgement—with no mum around to badger him, he just gave up on going to the barbers. But the hippy look had led to his first proper girlfriend, Kate, and she wasn't bad looking either. So, maybe he did have a chance with Gemma. But that chance was about zero unless he did something about it.

The bill was paid in silence. Ruth did not look up from her phone nor offer to split the cost. He didn't blame her. He owed her for wasting her time.

He drove her home in silence. There was no invite for a coffee. No kiss goodnight. No suggestion of a second date.

"Sorry," he winced as she got out of the car.

She shook her head, opened her mouth to speak, but then decided against it. Shut the car door and walked up the drive.

He rested his head against the steering wheel. How can someone affect you so badly? Someone you'd only met once. The briefest of encounters, yet you cannot stop thinking about her. He fumbled for his phone and sent a text, «*Hi Gem. Please pick up your clothes soon. Don't bring Tim. Want to talk about the ring.*»

# SEVENTEEN

The black velvet cube remained untouched on the kitchen island.

"Aren't you going to open it?"

"No. I don't want it."

"Don't be so ungrateful. It's so not like you, Gem. You should have kept that appointment yesterday. You need to talk to someone and get your head sorted." His finger nudged the box closer to her.

She pushed it away, "I don't want it."

"But I couldn't find the old one. A replacement is the best I can do."

"I don't want either ring. It's over, Tim. Why can't you understand that?"

"No, I'm not prepared to accept that. You're having some sort of mental breakdown. You need to go and see that psychiatrist. I've rearranged the appointment for Tuesday afternoon. Don't miss it this time, Gem. Otherwise, I'll have to take you myself."

He picked up the box and opened it. Taking out the new ring, he waved the diamond in front of her face, "Here look. Upgrade." The solitaire caught the sun coming through the window and dazzled her. She blinked several times as he grabbed her hand

and pushed the platinum band on her finger. "See, perfect.... Right, I'm off. I'm going to the London office at lunchtime, so I'll be late back. Don't forget to book time off for Tuesday pm."

He left the room and the front door banged shut a minute later. She exhaled a huge breath, then picked up her mug. She sipped the black coffee. Cold like the atmosphere. The Kindle, lying next to her empty cereal bowl, had switched off through lack of attention. This week had been a challenge to her resolve, but by saying as little as possible she had avoided being drawn into long arguments. By feigning engrossment in a book, she'd evaded that disarming smile. By sleeping in the spare bedroom, all temptation had been avoided. And Tim hadn't tried to encroach. Pending her trip to the shrink, he was giving her space. He called it 'thinking time'. Namely, thinking about how wonderful he was and the fantastic life he could provide. She played along. No way was she going to reveal her real thoughts: alternative accommodation and a new start. Hopefully, she would be luckier today and out by next week. This weekend could prove a nightmare, but Tim would be tired after his busy week so would probably lie in until late morning. That would give her the chance to escape to Louise's while he was still sleeping. Make a weekend of it and not come back until late Sunday night.

She took off the ring, put it back in the box, and walked to the bin. The lid raised in response to a wave of her hand. She held the velvet cube over the rubbish. Chewed her lip. The thing looked expensive. Bought by Tim, it probably was. She didn't recognise the jeweller's name, so boutique rather than high street? She withdrew her hand. She wasn't going to be mean like that farmer's ex-fiancée, especially as she'd already cost Tim one ring; she would let him get a refund. She opened a drawer and stuffed the box under the tea towels.

\*\*\*

Taking a swig of water from a reusable bottle, she followed the estate agent into the third flat of her Friday lunch hour tour.

OMG. This studio flat was more claustrophobic than the last one. Stunk of fresh paint. And, being in the eaves, baking hot.

"Bathroom over there," the agent nodded to the right as he headed to the sole window. "Just a shower. No bath."

She walked to the door at the end of the row of kitchen units and stuck her head in. Good job she was slim.

"No basin?"

"Kitchen sink."

She glanced round the main room. "Why's it more expensive than the last one?"

"Nice view."

She wandered over to the dormer. Guildford Cathedral was just visible in the distance: a twentieth-century red-brick construction perched on a hill overlooking the sprawling town. Hardly picturesque when compared to the works of Sir Christopher Wren et al. But in estate agent world it was a view worth having, though strictly standing only. At seat level, all she would see was blank walls.

"I was hoping for some outside space," she reiterated the wish imparted to the four other agents during that week. All had been negative in their response. All four lunchbreaks wasted on futile tours, and it didn't look like today's would yield any better results. It would seem space either comes with mold or a greater monthly cost. On her salary, she could afford the higher rent but that would mean no savings to put by for her dream. So, she was going to have to rough it for a few years—well, more than a few—if that smallholding was going to remain in sight.

"You won't get a garden on your budget."

"Balcony?"

"They get snapped up pretty quick. I can let you know when one comes available, but I've no idea when that'll be."

"I really need something straight away."

"Well, this is ten square foot bigger than the last one." He said it as though it was a plus point. But a lot of the footage was under the slope of the wonky old roof, so the usable space was considerably smaller than the other flats viewed that hour. At least, it was spotless and there was no sign of black mold. Unless it was covered by the new paint job? She stared out of the window to think.

Of course, there was one alternative. But was it worth the commute? Was it worth the risk of bumping into the Starlings? And was it worth the agony of living next door to a married man who you fancied something rotten? To see him daily, knowing you could never have him. Torture. The upside was the beautiful countryside in which it was set. She hadn't got round to seeing the cottage in the end, yet it sounded idyllic. Definitely worth a look. Even if it were just for a few months, that would give her time to find something better in Guildford. And being out in the countryside for the summer was preferable to being stuck in a place like this.

"So, what d'ya think?"

"Err... I'll have to think about it. I'll give you a call next week."

"Might be gone by then."

She nodded, "I'll take the risk."

# EIGHTEEN

Monday at the office was busy but, having completed the accounts she was working on by 5.15pm, she bunked off early. It was rare for Tim to be home before 10pm, so there was no need to inform her ex she would be late back. To do so would only result in questions she was not prepared to answer.

Matt had sent several texts over the last week reminding her to collect her clothes from Willow Farm. Her heart fluttered every time his name appeared on the screen, but the messages were all very perfunctory and to the point. Anyway, the man was married so it was ridiculous to have a crush on him. She was behaving like a teenager. Even looked him up on Facebook. His business account was easy to find, but she drew the line at contacting him or posting a comment in case his wife raised an eyebrow. Instead, she stared dreamily at the photo of him standing by his red tractor whenever she had the chance.

After grabbing the bag of borrowed clothes off the passenger seat, she stepped out of her electric car. As her trainers hit the concrete surface, she remembered Matt's comment on having no livestock. The courtyard was nice and clean as a result. Nothing like the pooey Starlings'. As nobody was around, she went for a nose in a nearby barn. A long table stretched across one end, dotted with the odd vegetable leaf and sprinkle of soil. Wooden crates stamped with the words 'Willow Farm Organics' were stacked to one side.

She smiled at the third word. Dating an organic vegetable farmer wouldn't be such a hardship. If he were single, that was... which he wasn't. Shame. Dreaming of a sudden divorce, she picked up a wilted leaf and sniffed the fronds.

"Carrot," the deep voice made her jump.

She nodded, blushing. The heat spread from head to toe. She flapped her hand in front of her face, "Hot, isn't it?"

Matt nodded, "Do you want a cold drink?"

"No, I'm fine, thanks. I... I see you're an organic farm." A thumbs up accompanied her closed-lipped grin.

"Are you into all that too?"

"Yes. Very much so."

"What about Tim?"

"No... despite my best efforts."

"Didn't think he would be," he mumbled. "Still trying?"

"No. Lost cause in all senses."

"So, you've left him then?"

"Not yet. But I'm leaving as soon as I can sort out somewhere to live. That's what I came to see you about. Is that cottage still on offer?"

"Absolutely. Come on, I'll show you around." She held out the bag of clothes. He took them. "Thanks. Yours are in the house. I'll get them when we come back." He dropped the bag onto the table before trudging off down the side of the barn. She bounced after him.

"What sort of stuff do you grow?"

"The usual staples. Carrots, 'tatoes, beetroot... all sorts. Some fruit. Apples and pears mostly... and trees."

"Trees? For sale?"

"No. Woodland. Rewilding some of my land. Hoping it will be an added attraction for holidaymakers as well as wildlife."

"Holidaymakers?"

"Yes. That's why I've got a cottage free. Converting a barn into three self-catering holiday lets, but I doubt anyone will want to stay while work is ongoing. Hence, my offer."

Her voice dropped, "Right."

"If the noise is too much, I'll do it while you're at work."

"Oh no, make as much noise as you like, whenever you like. You're doing me a favour after all."

"But you looked worried just then?"

"Not because of the noise. Because I might not get to stay here for long."

"Don't worry. It'll be a while yet before they're all finished. Doubt I'll be looking for any bookings before next summer. So, you can have it until at least then."

"That'll be great. Thank you so much."

They passed through an open gate onto a stony track.

"This is the old orchard."

"It's beautiful." She waved away a bee as they wandered through rows of gnarled trees underplanted with grasses and wildflowers.

Matt nodded to the left, "Beehives down there. Apples, pears and quinces."

"Don't think I've ever eaten a quince."

"Best for jelly. Too bitter to eat raw."

"Oh, right."

"You can help yourself to any fruit or veg. Well, for yourself that is." His cheeks dimpled, "Not if you're planning on feeding the world."

"Understood. Thanks."

They walked into a courtyard—a mishmash of worn brick pavers and cracked concrete—surrounded by a u-shaped brick and flint-cobble barn. A skip stood to the left, brimming over with rotten wood and rubble. Next to that were neatly stacked roof tiles. Reclaimed by the looks of them. Clearly destined for the roof on the left of the courtyard which was currently protected by blue plastic sheeting. The rest of the barn was sporting its new hat proudly.

"Right, here we are."

"So pretty."

"Thank you. Used to be cow sheds when it was my parents' farm."

"Lucky cows.... Your parents retired?"

"Dad died. Trampled by a cow."

She stopped in her tracks, "Ooooo, nasty." A few steps on, Matt halted to face her. "Sorry to hear that. Sounds awful."

"It was a while back. Time heals, as they say. Though Mum still finds it hard sometimes."

Gemma nodded. "Does she live with you, here on the farm?"

"No, she retired to the coast, but comes up and helps me on packing days when she's not travelling the world on cruise liners... or should I say, destroying the world?"

"Yep. Destroying. I'm with you on that."

"I can't persuade her not to go on them. She thinks it's her time to enjoy herself. Which I agree with, but there are greener ways to have fun. But if I nag too much, she reminds me of all the trees she has helped me to plant. As far as she's concerned, that makes her carbon neutral. The fact I would plant those trees anyway doesn't come into it. Stubborn woman."

Gemma smiled. The more she found out about him, the more she liked. Organic farming. Re-wilding. Environmentally aware. Shame he wasn't single. They recommenced the stroll across the courtyard.

"You said she helps you with packing?"

Matt kicked at a loose brick, "Must sort this yard out sometime. Err, yes. I do veg box deliveries. Locally. She helps me with that. Gave up on the livestock after Dad's death."

She stood still. *Cows... muck... Tim.* As Matt reached the door to the right-hand section of the 'U', she called out, "Matt..."

"Yes."

She walked over, "You said you used to be friends with Tim?"

He searched through a bunch of keys, "That's right. Until uni."

"Is there any reason for him being such a dirt-phobe? Well, not dirt, shit to be more precise. Sorry for the language."

"It is what it is. Shit's fine."

"Being brought up on a dairy farm, you would think he'd be fine with a bit of poo. But he's totally paranoid. The amount of soap he gets through after having a crap.... Sorry, language again." Matt laughed. "Just seems strange for a farmer's son."

"He fell in a slurry pit when he was thirteen."

"Oh, what!"

"I know... pretty disgusting. Luckily, it'd been recently emptied so it was only a few feet deep. But still, he was covered in muck and swallowed a load. Passed out from the toxic gases. It made him very ill. He was in hospital for ages being pumped full of antibiotics."

She mumbled, "He never told me."

"After that, it was hard to get him out of the house. Before, the pair of us used to run wild. We had two whole farms to get up to no good on. Afterwards, we had to pick our routes carefully. Avoid anywhere livestock had been. Of course, having milking sheds right on his doorstep didn't help." He raised his eyebrows, "You know what that's like."

"Yeah.... No wonder he didn't chase after me.... No wonder he hates Louise coming round. Ohhh, what I did to his car. I feel awful now. It must have been his worst nightmare to clean it."

"His mum did it for him."

Her mouth fell open. How could you respond to that? Her stomach clenched, "You're kidding?"

"Nope. Saw her washing it."

"Oh, gawd." She grimaced, "Just had an awful thought."

"Yeah?"

"I told Tim I dropped the ring in the yard. He went to look for it. Which was as I hoped—bit mean, but he deserved it. But now I suspect he didn't get his hands dirty at all. Got his parents to search?"

"Probably."

"Damn. Don't mind if it was his dad... but his mum?" She pouted. "How chivalrous is Mr Starling Senior?"

"On a scale of one to ten... zero."

"Ooo, I feel really guilty." She liked Mrs Starling. Jenny had been friendly and welcoming, unlike Tim's grumpy father. Given her a guided tour of the farmhouse. Prepared that massive tea, which—because of Tim—she hadn't been able to eat.

"Don't be. It's her own fault if she helped. She shouldn't be such a doormat."

She stared at Matt's feet. True, Jenny hadn't intervened during that fateful event. Had not told her husband to behave. Gemma hadn't paid her much attention during the milk battle but, if anything, the elderly woman had looked horrified... or was it terrified?

"Who's Louise?"

"My best friend. She unblocks drains for a living. Tim has to take a million showers after she's visited. That's like after he's steam-cleaned the whole house. I feel terrible. I encouraged her to give him lots of hugs and kisses."

"I wouldn't feel too guilty about it," sneered Matt.

"How did he manage to fall in? Surely, there's fences to stop that happening?"

"He was showing off to a girl, standing on top of the fence, pretending to jump in. She got annoyed and shoved the fence and he toppled. She didn't mean for him to fall. She just wanted him to stop messing about. Still, might go some way to explain why he treats women so bad."

Her body tensed, "He's never hit me."

"Abuse doesn't have to be violent. It can be psychological."

She thought aloud, "He never lets me have a say when there's a decision to be made... but that's just because he's a control freak..." Matt raised his eyebrows at her but didn't comment. "...and when we're discussing politics or something, he always has to win the argument.... But he is a barrister, so not surprising really."

"It shouldn't be about winning..."

"Try telling him that."

"...You can respect someone else's opinion even if you don't agree with it."

She went quiet. Best not mention: Tim always criticised what she was wearing; constantly tried to get her to eat meat and dairy; laughed off her ambitions; rarely paid her any compliments... unless he was showing off to friends or colleagues. Was Matt saying Tim was mentally abusing her? Tim's insistence of a fragile state of mind. The need for psychiatric care. Was that gaslighting? She shivered. It had never occurred to her, but the more she thought about it, the more it made sense. But there was a reason behind it—the slurry pit. Maybe Tim was the one needing counselling, not her?

Matt unlocked the door of the cottage, "Um... so this is it." He tapped a white painted door as he passed by, "Cloakroom." Then stopped. "Open plan kitchen and living area. I'll prioritize getting the kitchen finished. Just give me a couple of weeks and it'll be done."

He waited for her to survey the unfurnished room. The smell of new paint and floor varnish mingled in the air, irritating her sensitive nose. The carcasses for the kitchen units were lined up in a row about a foot away from the back wall, awaiting installation. Underneath was a dust sheet attempting to protect a beautiful oak floor. Leaning against a wall to the left of a log burner, a collection of reclaimed wood; the flaky paint, scuffed and gouged. Fingers crossed, he wasn't going to sand all that character away. Patio doors overlooked the courtyard, with just a narrow coat-hanging space (with shoe rack underneath) separating them from what she now realised was the front door.

"I'm going to make the cupboard doors and worktop out of this old wood here. If you don't like the ramshackle look, I can paint it whatever colour you like."

"Ramshackle's fine by me." She rubbed her knuckle over her nose. "Aaachoo!"

"Bless you.... I only painted it yesterday, hence the stink. I'll leave the windows open. Not likely to get any unwelcome visitors as there's no direct access from the road. You'll have to park at the farmhouse and take the path we took today. Is that a problem?"

"Not at all. I like a walk."

"I've got an old fridge somewhere." He walked across the oak floorboards to the far corner of the room, "I can put it over here. I can probably find you some furniture and cooking stuff. I'm going to have to get some eventually anyway."

She smiled. "I've got a few bits in storage, so should be OK apart from a bed and a sofa."

"What about a microwave?"

"Yeah, got one, thanks."

"Great. Bed and sofa it is.... Sorry, was that a yes or no to the fridge?"

"Yes, please."

He nodded. "Just the one bedroom through here. Ensuite with shower. No bath, I'm afraid."

She tugged off her trainers to mosey across the new jute carpet. Stuck her head around the ensuite door, "Nice." Then headed to the white-painted patio doors that also overlooked the courtyard. "It's perfect as it is. Thank you."

"That's OK. Happy to help. Any questions?"

"Err, how much is the rent?"

"It might be noisy at times until I finish all the cottages, so shall we say covered by the ring? Just pay for the services."

"Gosh, that's generous of you. Are you sure?"

He nodded. "Unless you want the ring back?"

"No. Definitely not."

"Is it mutual? Your breakup, that is?"

"No, he's in denial. Thinks I'm having a mental breakdown. Even booked me in with a counsellor..." Matt frowned. "...Extremely annoying that he won't take me seriously. I try and tell him why I'm leaving him—they're good reasons—but he just laughs, and says it's always been like that between us, so what's the problem?" The engorged vein on Matt's temple twitched. She was giving him more evidence of Tim's... psychological abuse? The words knotted her stomach. It was hard to take, that she, Gemma Williams, graduate, accountant, and successful career woman, had fallen victim to domestic cruelty for a second time. It never occurred to her before.

With Dan, it had been so in-your-face. Literally. And she had fought back. Hell, most of the time, she started the battle by chucking a pizza box at his head, so fed up with his mess. To her shame, she had let him get away with that old excuse: "You started it." But it could never justify his vicious response. She'd been a fool not to chuck him out at the first sign of trouble. But she was twenty-one, he was her first live-in boyfriend, and she couldn't bear the thought of all those 'I told you so's from friends, horrified she had let him move in so quickly in the first place (She never told her parents about Dan as she could only imagine their likely reaction).

But with Tim... They had fun together. Laughed together. Played together. He never once hurt her. When she lobbed that yoghurt at him there was no fear. When he hurled it back... just anticipation of the sexual encounter to come. Yet...

Matt broke the awkward silence, "So, what is the problem? Sorry, am I being too nosey?"

"No, it's fine. Nice to have someone willing to listen. He's not, that's for sure." She drew a deep breath. "Basically, we've got nothing in common. I'm an eco-friendly, vegan socialist. He's a climate change denier, meat-eating capitalist. He's obsessed with having the latest gadgets, clothes, cars, whatever. I try to be eco-friendly and re-use or recycle... alien concepts to Tim. We don't even like the same movies. And I want a family. He doesn't."

"He can't have kids. Well, not without a reversal op."

"What?"

"He had a vasectomy while at uni. Didn't want to be trapped by some girl getting pregnant while sowing his oats. And he sure was sowing them far and wide."

She frowned, "He never told me he'd had the snip. And he's been using a condom right from the start because I'm kind of organic to the extreme. Don't like to take drugs if at all possible and the sound of an IUD... eeew... bit squeamish and don't fancy something unnatural permanently inside me. Does that make sense?"

"Yeah. I see where you're coming from."

"So, he's been using a condom even though he didn't have to. Why would he do that?"

"Maybe he didn't want you to know he can't have kids. Might have put you off going out with him."

She shook her head. "That's very deceitful."

"Yes, I agree. Trust is very important in a relationship. You won't get it with him. He's not a nice person. You're better off without him." He scratched his head, "I'm finding it hard to see how you ever got together."

"Me too."

"Definitely over then?"

"Definitely."

"But he won't like it?"

"No. Apparently, I'm cheap to run!"

"Speaking as someone who's permanently broke, that's kinda my sort of girl too."

"Yeah, but that was a reason he gave for wanting me to stay. No mention of love or feelings. Just cheap!"

"Harsh. But do you love him?"

"I thought I did. Now I'm not so sure.... I certainly don't love him right now. It's over as far as I'm concerned. If he doesn't like it... well, tough."

"Stick to your guns. Don't let him wriggle his way back into favour."

"Oh, I'm not going to. He can take a running jump."

# NINETEEN

Her plan to leave without a scene failed at the first hurdle. Tim had taken a rare day off work to make sure she kept the appointment he so 'thoughtfully' re-arranged. So, what with that annoyance and his presence, there was no way she would be able to keep calm. She just wanted to be out of the house as quick as possible and away from him and his judgemental stare.

Her blood boiling, she muttered, "Psychiatrist. How dare he!" She shoved her left hand in amongst the clothes, took a step to the right, bunching up her work suits. A clothes hanger pinged off the lower rail and clattered on the hardwood floor of the walk-in wardrobe. Gemma kicked away the wooden triangle and stuffed in her other hand to continue with the grand clothes grab; the whole rail swamping her arms as she struggled through the doorway... a doorway partially blocked by a scowling Tim. Lips pursed, he let her pass. She plonked the collection of jackets, shirts and trousers into the suitcase that lay open on the bed, swept the overhangs within the confines of the black case, then headed back into the wardrobe to empty her two designated drawers.

Crouching to floor level, she yanked open the first. Footsteps entered behind her. *Ignore him. Pig.* She scooped the contents into her arms. A rattle of hangers caught her ear. She glanced behind. Chucked the bras and knickers back into the drawer, some missing the target, and sprang to her feet. Hands on hips, she glowered, "Don't put them back. I'm leaving."

"Don't be silly."

She waited until he had organised the suits and blouses neatly along the rail, before grabbing them and heading for the door. This time he blocked her way. A tussle for ownership of her wardrobe ensued. Tim won. He threw the clothes to the back of the wardrobe, "Stop being such a silly bitch. Think about me for a change."

"I'm always thinking about you—"

"Why are you leaving then?"

"Give me a chance to finish, will you."

"Go on then. I'm waiting." He stood, arms crossed, blocking her way to the scattered clothes.

"How about you think about me for a change?"

"I think about you all the time." He winked.

"I don't mean like that. I mean like let me have a say in things."

"OK. Not a problem. You tidy up in here. I'll put the suitcases away."

"No. I'm leaving, Tim. I'm not changing my mind."

"You're not making any sense. I'll do anything you want. Just tell me. This is sortable. There's no reason for you to leave."

"Just let me go, Tim. That's all I want from you."

"What the hell is wrong with you? Why would you throw all this away?" He waved his arms around to indicate the house. "Why on earth would you dump me? Nobody dumps me. It doesn't make any sense. I'll call that counsellor. Get her to come over here so you can have a chat."

"I don't want a bloody chat. I just want out. Why can't you get that into your thick head?"

"You're the one who's being stupid."

"Arggghhhh!" she screamed right into his face, then dodged around to the clothes. As she scrambled to collect up her belongings, the door slammed shut. She turned just as the key clicked in the lock. "Tim! Tim!" She ran to the door. "You can't lock me in here. Let me out!" Bang bang. "Let me out, Tim. Right now." Bang bang.

"No. You can bloody well stay there until you stop being a stupid bitch."

"You can't keep me in here forever. I'll call the police." There was silence from the other side of the door. "I'm texting Louise." She spoke out loud as she pretended to type, "Please call the police to Tim's house if I don't text you again in fifteen minutes. There, sent it." Of course, this plan would only work if he didn't spot her phone on the bed. Was anything covering it? She had a feeling it was under the suitcase lid. God help her if a notification came in and ruined things with a loud ping. "It won't do your career any good, let alone your hopes to be a politician. Domestic abuse. False imprisonment. I WILL press charges if you don't let me out RIGHT NOW."

The lock unclicked.

*** 

Tim watched in silence as she packed her bags. She sneaked the phone from under the case and tucked the device in the rear pocket of her jeans. He grabbed it. She tried to grab it back.

He held the mobile high above her head, "What's the PIN?"

"Like I'm going to tell you." He grabbed her hand and tried to force her index finger onto the fingerprint scanner as she struggled to get free. "It won't work. I turned it off." She hadn't, but the lie worked a treat and he relented. She taunted, "You're wasting time. Must be less than five minutes to go now. Do you really want a criminal record?"

He said nothing as he zipped the larger suitcase, then carried it down the stairs and out to her car. She followed, carrying a second smaller case, a washbag, and a used bath towel. She unlocked the boot remotely and he lifted the lid and loaded both cases.

"Where are you going?"

She glared at him. No way was she telling him that. He would only follow her there and cause a scene.

"Well, when you've calmed down, give me a call and I'll pick you up. I'll pay for anything you need. Holiday. Counselling. How about combining the two? Go to a retreat somewhere. There's a posh one round here somewhere that celebrities go to. I'll pay."

Her nostrils flared, "You're unbelievable sometimes, Tim. I'm not ill. I've finally come to my senses."

Tim's brow furrowed. Shaking his head, a smirk grew.

He still did not get it. He still thought she was going to come back after a short break. But, for once, he didn't have a comeback. Instead, he opened the car door for her to climb in. As she settled behind the wheel, he pulled the seat belt out, leant across her, and clicked it into the slot. As he retreated, he went to kiss her, but she quickly turned her head so all he got was a mouthful of hair.

"I do love you, Gemmie. Remember that before you ruin both our lives."

# TWENTY

Gemma felt emotionally battered after yesterday. There had been a massive argument, where Tim had called her every name under the sun. He accused her of ruining his life, being stupid and not thinking straight. She had screamed back, calling him a selfish, inconsiderate pig and worse. And that was even before they had that final fight in the bedroom.

She deserved a lie-in after all that (and she wouldn't be able to concentrate on work anyway), so she'd called the office and asked for a few days holiday to take her up to the weekend; being too honest to feign sickness. The HR lady had pressed for more information as it was such short notice, so she gave the briefest explanation possible: split up with her fiancé and needed to sort out new living arrangements. She ended up giving her new address, but not before Priya promised it would never be given out to anyone, especially not Tim.

She lay in the bed with just a white cotton sheet over her. Despite the early hour, it looked like it was going to be another hot day. May and June had been exceptionally warm and dry. Now early July, the summer had been a scorcher so far. Which was nice as long as she didn't dwell on why the climate of Southern Europe had travelled so far north. She left the patio doors open throughout the night such was the uncomfortable heat. The unlined linen curtains occasionally billowed in a gentle breeze to reveal glimpses of her new landlord sawing planks of wood in the courtyard. Dressed simply in denim shorts, a tight t-shirt, and a pair of work boots, his muscles strained his sleeves to bursting point as he worked. He disappeared into the neighbouring cottage every now and again with the cut wood, his absence accompanied by bursts of banging. Entranced, she watched his coming and going for a good half hour, before he reappeared, this time shirt in hand. He stood still and used the grey top to wipe the sweat off his ripped torso and then his neck. He threw the t-shirt onto his toolbox. Resumed his sawing. Disappeared. Banging echoed around the courtyard. Reappeared. The curtain wafted outwards for a change, catching his eye. He returned her gaze, smiled and waved. She lifted one hand from under the thin sheet and waved back. He went back to work. Sawing... disappeared... hammering... reappeared. But this time, he walked over to her patio doors.

Holding the curtain back with one hand, his cheeks dimpled in a mischievous smile, "What rate do you think I should charge for the show?"

"Premium."

"You should charge too, you know."

"Err?"

"Sorry, that came out wrong."

"I'd say. Not a very politically correct thing to say to a woman lying in bed."

"I agree. Sorry. Out of practice with this chatting up malarkey."

"Well, your wife probably wouldn't appreciate it."

"Err... I'm not married."

"Divorced?"

"No."

Her stomach shrunk. Death was such a difficult subject to broach, but she had to ask. She spoke quietly, "Widower?"

His brow furrowed, "No. Single."

"Single? But the photos in your house? They're wedding photos."

"Not me. Twin brother."

"Oh." She chuckled. "I thought it was you. Thought you were unavailable."

"No, definitely available... if you're interested?"

She gave him the quick once over. "I'd say." Grinned and laughed.

"Would it be politically incorrect of me to come over and climb into bed with you?"

"Yes... but don't let that stop you."

She lifted the sheet revealing a glimpse of her naked form.

After kicking off his boots, he strode to the bed. Quickly pulled off his shorts to reveal black trunks, and climbed in, tugging the cover over them.

He smelt of sweat and dust. If it were anyone else, she would've turned her nose away at the stink, but this labourer's scent was curiously alluring. Like a drug, she wanted more. Placing her arm around his torso, she drew him in for that first kiss. A soft sensual kiss that grew more fervent.

He broke away, "I'm afraid I haven't got any condoms with me."

"You remembered what I said then?"

"Yep. But not a problem, there are other ways..." with that he disappeared under the cover.

# TWENTY-ONE

His hand stroked her bare shoulder as she lay sleeping across his torso. Her soft breath brushed the hairs of his chest in an intermittent breeze. Her warm body rose and fell in time with his own. She was way out of his league. Like someone else had been. But this girl was different. More down to earth. He gently tapped the freckles on her nose. No make-up—bonus! Yes, she had been trapped in Tim's lair, but she'd come to her senses and escaped. And by some miracle, she had chosen him. Now all he had to do was make sure she stayed. He'd done a rubbish job on that account in the past.

He met his first love, Kate, a few weeks into his second year at university. He studied agriculture and horticulture. She, computer science. They were inseparable. Two years after graduating, Kate got a great job offer in New Zealand. He'd been all set to go with her. Even had a job lined up for himself. Then his dad died. There was no way he could leave his mum in her distraught state, let alone expect her to deal with the farm. He had to stay. They got engaged quietly with no fuss, and the relationship continued on Skype for another five months... until Kate announced she had met someone else and was already living with him. Took him ages to get over that.

Then there was Bella who left him for his cousin. The annoying thing was, he introduced the pair at his own birthday party. With hindsight, he should have realised something was up. He noticed Bella's eyes wandering over to the other man during the barbecue and then there'd been her absence for a good half hour. When she finally returned, she was all hot and flustered. An odd smell about her too. She claimed to have got stuck in the toilet. It didn't connect until she left him six weeks later. It was the smell of another man. She'd had sex with him at his own party. Probably in the loo. What followed was six weeks of numerous girls' nights out. Even a girls' weekend away in Paris. 'Discussing her friend's wedding plans' had been her stock excuse. He'd been a total muppet not to suspect. What hurt more than anything was the deceit. Why hadn't she just left him as soon as her attention turned elsewhere? He suspected he'd been kept as a fallback in case things didn't work out with the new guy. Later events seemed to confirm that view.

Yes, he had to do better this time.

This was not how he planned their union. His intention had been to wine and dine Gemma. Impress her with his conversation. Of course, the silver-tongued Tim would be a hard act to follow. The wealthy barrister would have taken her to the best restaurants. Holidayed in luxury hotels in exotic locations. If she expected that of him, he'd be in trouble. But she said she was trying to live an eco-friendly lifestyle so maybe he should just be himself. Take her to the places he loved. Do the things he enjoyed. If she enjoyed them too, that bode well.

He'd never done anything like that before; an intimate act before even one date. He always took it slow with a woman. Bided his time. Made sure she was perfect, before even suggesting a coupling of bodies. Hence the distinct lack of notches on his bedpost. His mother gave him constant grief over his hesitancy, "You need to get a move on. You'll be left on the shelf." But he'd been burnt twice, so things needed to be right. They were with Gemma. For him anyway. It was hard to know what she was thinking. Maybe he was just the rebound guy? His biggest fear was she might still go back to Tim.

He had needed to show her he was interested. That he had skills. Whether jumping into bed with her was the right way to do it... His lips pursed. She might think it was just a one-night stand or, worse, he was taking advantage of her current state of mind. He must take her on a date. ASAP. Show her he was serious and a better prospect than Tim.

Her body shifted. Eyes open, she smiled, then rolled off onto her back, "I'm starving."

He leant over, "Me too," and proceeded to nibble her plump lips.

Her hand gently pushed against his chest. He backed away, inches from her mouth.

She giggled, "Not a vegetarian then?"

"No. Vegan." He dipped towards her lips but stopped at the wide-eye stare. "What?"

"You're a vegan?"

"Yes. You seem surprised?"

"I didn't think farmers were."

"Didn't I mention it before?"

"Um... you said something about no livestock."

"Yeah. Because I'm vegan. Is that a problem?"

"No! It's bloody fantastic! I love you!"

With that, she pressed her mouth to his...

# TWENTY-TWO

Gnarled limbs stretched to infinity. Skywards, a thicket of unruly bottle-green blocked the sunlight. The soil, at their knobbly feet, barren as though all life had scarpered.

"What d'ya think?"

Gemma scanned the ancient yew trees. "I think I'd be scared witless if it were dark."

He laughed, "It is a bit spooky."

"How old are they?"

"Some of them are supposed to be two thousand years old."

"You're joking. That's ridiculous. That's like Roman times, isn't it?"

"My history's not great, but yes, think so."

Her hand caressed the thick craggy bark, "To think a Roman soldier might have rested here, leaning against this tree. It would've, of course, been a lot smaller then." She gazed at the contorted branches overhead, "I can't believe I've never heard of this place. It's not like it's a million miles from Horsham."

"Is that where you're from originally?"

"Yeah, that's where I was born and brought up. Mum was born there too." She chuckled, "Dad's an alien invader from Wales." Looping two hands over a branch, she hung, knees bent, ankles crossed. "I lived in Horsham until I moved in with Tim. Well, except for when I was at uni in Canterbury. What's this place called again?"

"Kingley Vale."

He smiled. Hell, he couldn't stop grinning other than to talk. He must relax those cheek muscles a tad otherwise she'll be thinking she's walked into a horror movie.

She smiled back. "I guess it was too far from Horsham for a day trip, but too close for a holiday. That mystery band of land around your area, you never visit."

He laughed, "If you say so."

She dropped to the ground. "Hoist me up. I want to climb to the top."

He lifted her so she could clamber onto the lowest branch. She crawled along the limb, then rocketed up the trunk.

He'd chosen well. One of his favourite walks. And Gemma was enjoying herself. The doubts of that morning began to dissipate. They had plenty in common. The morning had sped by in chatter and laughter, ever since they abandoned the bed for a well-earned breakfast. His second of the day. They had showered together. Prepared a picnic together. Went and bought condoms together. Lots. And now they were climbing trees together. There was no embarrassment. No reticence. It was free and easy between them, like the oldest of friends, but with added benefits.

He hauled himself onto the branch and followed her into the canopy. She was perched high on the thinnest of branches. For safety's sake he remained on a lower bough, but to be honest, right now, floating seemed a distinct possibility. Talk about cloud nine... more like cloud ninety. His arm slowly encircled her waist. She draped hers over his shoulder, then kissed the top of his head.

"Top of the world," she exclaimed.

"Not quite. Climbing up there next," he pointed to the hill behind them.

"Picnic there?"

"Yes. Perfect spot. Great view over Chichester and the coast."

"I might be too busy looking at something else," she teased.

He gazed into her emerald eyes and smiled, "Me too."

# TWENTY-THREE

They ate the picnic sitting cross-legged on a tartan car blanket, face-to-face on the grassy hilltop burial mound. He returned her gaze as she studied his features. The fine crow's feet to the side of his eyes; no doubt the result of a life outdoors. The small pockmarks on his forehead and cheeks; evidence of a teenage affliction. Another scar, too large to be acne, on his neck.

She touched her own neck in the same place, "How did you get this?"

"Had a mole removed."

"Cancerous?"

"No, thank god. It was getting itchy, so had to go. They did a biopsy, but it was fine. Downside of working in the fields. I'm much more liberal with the sun cream now." His brow lifted, "Had my warning."

She nodded and took another bite of apple. Her free hand pointed at his scarred knee.

"Tripped over while drunk. Less said, the better." They both chuckled. "My turn. No earrings?"

She quickly swallowed her mouthful. "Self-mutilation."

He laughed. "You better keep that opinion to yourself. You'll be upsetting half the world's population.... I guess you don't like tattoos either?"

"No... and make-up. I'm 100% natural."

"I love that. My ex was a bit of a make-up fiend. Couldn't kiss her without getting covered in it. Made a right mess in the bed if she didn't remove it."

"Do you miss her?"

Gazing into her eyes, he spoke softly, touching deep into her soul, "Not anymore."

Keeping eye contact, her mouth dropped open. "Er... If you were still with her, what would've happened with us when we met?"

"Very hypothetical. Let me think.... I'm probably too well behaved to have an affair, so I guess—if we had kids—I would just feel duty-bound to stick with her and be thoroughly miserable for the rest of my life."

"I would be miserable too. We would just be meeting at social events, going ohhh if only.... Then when we're like seventy and your wife has died of cancer or something, we can finally be together and live happily ever after."

"What about Tim?"

"What about him?"

"Well, he's the only person we both know, so we would only be at the same gatherings if you had stuck with him."

"Umm... I murdered him when I was fifty. Just got out of prison in time to meet you again at your wife's funeral."

"You spin a good yarn, Gem. Ever thought about writing a book?"

She shook her head, "Doesn't appeal. Involves too much tapping away on the computer. Much rather be running wild!" She held out her apple. He demolished half in one bite. "My turn?"

He nodded; his mouth too full to reply.

"What sort of books do you like?"

Munching the fruit, his head rocked to and fro. He swallowed. "To be honest, I don't have much time for reading anything but farming magazines. You?"

"Romance." He laughed and, nodding his head, glanced towards the nearest footpath. His gaze returned to her. "I could lend you my Kindle so you can read some."

"Thank you. That's very kind of you," he replied with formality. They both chuckled.

"How come you're a vegan?"

His eyes widened. "Probably the same reasons you are. Animal welfare. Environment. Health."

"Yeah, that just about covers it. I guess that's why you gave up the livestock when you took over the farm?" He nodded. "When you told me that, I thought it was because of what happened to your dad."

"Couldn't face the evil cows," he joked. "No, I always felt uneasy about the dairy farm. You know, forcing the mums to have babies just so they can produce milk. They make a hell of a racket when you separate them. Hated it. We also had pigs in two massive sheds. It was horrendous. Not just the noise, but the smell." He stuck out his tongue in disgust. "I'm not saying Dad didn't look after them. He had high welfare standards, but still..." He shook his head, "...just didn't like it. Felt like opening the doors and releasing them into the wild."

"Why didn't you?"

"Parents. Neighbours. Two thousand pigs invading the local village. Can you imagine it? I'd be a pariah." He laughed, "Probably disowned."

Smiling, she took another bite of the juicy red fruit and then went back to gawping at his muscular frame.

He laughed, "There's a great view over there, you know."

She giggled, "There's a better view here."

He leant forward and pushed her apple-holding hand away from her mouth. He kissed her with enough force to make her fall onto her back. The apple dropped and bumped down the hill. She fumbled for his fly and undid the button.

He stopped her with his hand, "Not sure that's a good idea. This is a popular dog-walking spot."

She brushed him away, "No one about at the moment." Down went the zip.

He glanced around as she plunged her hand into his khaki combat shorts. She stroked over the thin fabric before slipping her hand inside his trunks. He groaned and reached for the rucksack. With her free hand, she helped him tug it closer and unzip the pocket containing the condoms. Just as she was pulling the packet out, a large black dog leapt on Matt's arm.

"Get off," he exclaimed, pushing the unwelcome visitor away.

Wagging its tail, the Labrador bounced around them. Approached. Jumped away. Returned to stuff its nose in the bag.

Matt lifted the bag above his head, "Shoo... shoo."

The dog scampered away, before bounding back and snapping the box right out of Gemma's hand. The missile of black fur shot off down the footpath into the scrub.

Matt jumped up, quickly did up his fly, and chased after the thief. He disappeared behind the high gorse bushes.

She sat up and placed a hand over her mouth. *Please don't come this way, dog owner.* How embarrassing that would be. She fondled the edge of the rug. If the worst came to the worst, she could yank it over her head. What was she thinking anyway? She only left Tim yesterday and here she was about to have sex with her new landlord. Before they'd even properly started dating. Usually, she waited until she was sure the relationship was heading somewhere before going that far. Admittedly, that was often not very long. She was always overly positive with a new bloke. Always thought he was 'the one' and rushed into things. She was like a character in a film or tv drama. Meet someone. Strip off. Have wild crazy sex. Usually in a ridiculously uncomfortable or inappropriate place. At least this hilltop was soft... but still massively inappropriate. The dog had proved that.

She must slow things down. Take her time. Not make the same mistakes as in the past. Make sure he definitely was 'the one'. *But he is. Isn't he?* She tugged on her ear lobe. *Do I want to spend the rest of my life with him? Yes. Do I love him? Yes. Is he the most gorgeous creature to ever walk on this earth? Yes. Do I miss him and worry like mad when he's not with me?* She looked towards the scrub. There was still no sign of Matt returning. She had a pit in her stomach. An unease. Maybe he'd fallen down the steep hill? Maybe the dog had turned nasty? Maybe the owner was some sort of knife-wielding mugger? She stood up and ran to the chalky pathway.

A sigh escaped her lips. Matt waved as he jogged towards her. He held up the condoms victoriously as he got closer.

"Well done."

"They're a bit chewed."

The box was shredded and sodden with saliva. He pulled out a couple of squares from between the tears. Slimy toothmarks pitted the surface.

"Eewww. You're not sticking them in me like that."

"No, don't worry. No intention of doing so. Let's go home. We won't be disturbed there."

\*\*\*

They lay sprawled over the bed. Hot and sweaty. Exhausted and spent. Tim's claim to being the ace in tatters. Daring and adventurous replaced by caring and sensual. Selfishness replaced by selflessness. She shouldn't have pressed Matt to perform in a public area. It wasn't his style. A fumble in a field, a quickie against a wall, wouldn't work for him. He wanted time to explore and titillate. Drive his woman crazy with desire before the erotic lovemaking even began.

"So, Mr Sex God, how come you're single?"

"Been taking a break. Last relationship ended badly. Found out my girlfriend was having an affair with my cousin."

"Was she stupid or something?"

"Better prospect. More money. Flash car. Big house. Not a poverty-stricken farmer like myself."

"Money isn't everything—"

"Glad you think that cos I ain't got any."

"Can't buy you happiness."

"Think she found that out the hard way."

"Oh?"

"Yeah... he dumped her for someone else about six months later. She turned up on my doorstep in tears, pleading for me to take her back."

"Did you?"

"No fear. Told her no chance. I wasn't interested anymore, and I wasn't going to be her fall guy until she ran off with the next rich bastard that came along."

"And what about your cousin? Are you speaking?"

His eyes narrowed. "As little as possible," he grumbled. "Can we talk about something else?"

She wasn't going to force the issue. The two men had fallen out and it was not her place to suggest a reconciliation, especially as she didn't even know the other guy. He sure didn't sound very nice, running off with his relative's girlfriend and then chucking her six months down the line. If she were a nosey so and so, she might have pressed for more info. But the subject had upset Matt and she needed to cheer him up.

Her hand clasped his manhood, "Or perhaps 'do' something else?"

# TWENTY-FOUR

She laughed, "Stop staring. You're making me all self-conscious."

"I like it. It suits you."

She swept her grubby hand through the short pixie cut that Tim would have hated, "You don't think it's too drastic?"

Matt stepped over the row of beetroot, to stand in front of her, and gently tweaked a stray lock on her temple, "Not at all. Looks great. And much more practical for working in the fields. Is that why you did it?" His pink-stained finger caressed its way down her cheek to her chin.

"Not really. I've had it short before. Before Tim." Matt kissed her softly. "I wanted it cut off because it was just annoying me..." He kissed her again. "...always falling in my face." Their lips met for the third time. "And now it's summer, it's getting all hot and sticky. As you say, much more sensible for farm work." The fourth time was longer and involved tongues.

He broke away, "I really appreciate your help with this, you know."

"That's OK. I'm enjoying myself. Much more fun than being stuck in the office."

Pulling up two handfuls of veg as he stepped back over the row, he asked, "So, how come you're an accountant when you so clearly love getting your hands dirty?"

She yanked a beetroot out of the ground and stood straight. Ripping off the dead leaves, she faced Matt, "It wasn't my intention."

"No?"

"I studied ecology at uni. Got a plum graduate job at a company that specialises in ecological surveys on development sites. I blew it... got sacked for insurrection."

He froze, eyes wide. His head jerked. "Please explain. I'm intrigued."

"About three months in, I found some Great Crested Newts on a proposed site for a major housing development. I put it in my report. My boss wanted me to remove it. His argument was, we've saved enough bloody newts across the country already; losing one site wouldn't matter. I refused to take it out. It was our job to report what was there. The consequences were not for us to worry about. Anyway, I was removed from that job and sent on another." She paused for breath.

"Same problem again?"

"No. When I read the final report for the first job—about a week later—he had bloomin' well gone and altered it. I was fuming..."

"I bet you were."

"...I reported it to the planning authority. Needless to say, that was the end of my employment there."

"And put you off working in that field?" He took the beetroot from her and dropped it in the crate.

"No. I tried to get another job. There's a lot of competition for graduate placements in that profession, but I applied for the next year's intake and also sent my CV to various companies on the off-chance. I don't know whether it was because I was on some sort of blacklist or because I'd been sacked, but I wasn't even getting interviews."

"So, why accountancy?"

"I had experience from working in my parents' practice during the summer holidays whilst at college and uni. And worked for them full time for about ten months after the sacking. You know, while I was still hopeful of getting back into ecology. But that didn't happen and, once I had accepted that, it was relatively easy to find an accountancy job."

"And do you enjoy it?"

"I don't dislike it. Keeps me busy, so I'm not sitting there thinking 'Oh, I wish I was looking for bats', but I'd much rather be outside doing stuff like this." She waved the wilted leaves in the air before chucking them on the ground.

"I'd offer you a job, but I think you're beyond my pay scale."

"How much are you offering?"

"Err... it might have to be voluntary. Cashflow's a bit tight right now what with the renovations. I fully admit to being rubbish with money. It seems to go out faster than it comes in. I took out a mortgage on the house to pay for the work on the cottages, which is giving me nightmares. I know it'll pay off eventually once I've got holidaymakers staying but, at the moment, I'm scraping pennies each month to make the repayments."

"Have you asked for a payment holiday?"

"Now, see, this shows how rubbish I am with money. Hadn't even entered my head that you could do that."

"Worth a try?"

"What do I do? Just ask the bank?"

"They'll probably want figures. Current earnings, forecasts... that sort of thing."

"Yeah, this is where I'm going to come unstuck. My books are a mess. Even I can see they don't make any sense."

"Why do you say that?"

"Well, the bank balance in the software is showing an overdraft of something ridiculous, like a hundred and fifty thousand—that might be a bit of an exaggeration, but not far off—whereas my actual bank statement is only about three thousand overdrawn."

"Yes, that does seem a bit odd... unless you've got loads of outstanding cheques... or one massive one. Do you want me to take a look?"

"Do you mind?"

"Not at all."

"You might have to wait a bit for payment."

"Oh, I wasn't planning on charging. You've done loads for me after all, what with the cottage and free veg."

He smiled, "I love you... not just for the free labour, you understand?"

Her stomach fluttered. How long had it taken Tim to utter those words? Forever. And even when he had, it was doubtful he meant it. They were just words to her ex: something to say to get what he wanted. But with Matt, it was genuine. She could see it in his eyes. The way they glistened with joy as they gazed upon her. She could see it in his smile. The way his dimples crinkled to reveal a glimpse of teeth. She could hear it in his voice. The soft deep tone aimed directly into her heart, filling it with elation.

"I love you too."

# TWENTY-FIVE

"Sorted," Gemma announced as Matt re-entered his farm office.

"So, am I bankrupt?"

"No. Just stupid," she giggled.

He rolled his eyes as he walked towards her chair, "Cheers." He threw her a smile as he leant over her shoulder to peer at the computer screen. "So, what did I do?"

"You seem to have had a few weeks when you decided to abandon decimal points on expenses. Like 'one eight point zero zero' was entered as 'one eight zero zero' and so on."

"Right. I did have to replace a dodgy keyboard a while back. Think it was January? Maybe Feb. Anyway, some of the keys weren't working, so probably happened then." He smiled cheekily, "I think that absolves me from any blame."

"Ahh, but you didn't spot the errors," she ribbed, laughing.

"True. Guilty as charged. What do I need to do to correct it?"

Stunned by his capitulation, she stared at the screen. Tim would never have admitted his guilt. Well, Tim would never have seen it as his fault in the first place. It was a nice feeling to win an argument for a change, though you could hardly call it that. Just a friendly exchange of views. She loved the fact Matt didn't turn everything into a war of words...

"Gem? Are you there?"

"Oh, sorry," she giggled, blushing. "Away with the fairies."

Eyes twinkling, he chuckled. "Do I dare ask?" She shook her head. He raised his eyebrows but pressed no further, "So, what do I need to do to correct it?"

"I've done that. All reconciles to the penny now."

"You're a star, Gem. Can't thank you enough." He hugged her. "Right, seeing as my solvency has now been confirmed, I can afford to splash the cash on a meal out as a thank you." He teased, "Unless you'd rather be paid, that is?"

"No, dinner's a great idea. Do I need to dress up?"

"No, you're beautiful just as you are. I, on the other hand, am a stinking, sweaty, mud-covered mess... so I'll be taking a shower." He stood straight and formally held out his hand, bowing slightly, "You are of course more than welcome to join me."

She took his hand, "I humbly accept your kind invitation."

\*\*\*

After a shower and sex combo, getting dressed... frantically stripping off, making love again, re-showering, and re-dressing, they finally made it to the car. They took her electric vehicle as it was cleaner and would be easier to park than Matt's jeep.

They drove into Chichester, parked in a multi-story, then walked into the city centre. It was still only 5pm, so they strolled around the cathedral, then headed to an art gallery, which stayed open late on Saturdays according to its website. After viewing some abstract paintings, Matt expressed a desire to have a go himself. Gemma nodded in agreement, "Go for it. I might join you." A new hobby to share, along with the interest in architecture and art, the love of walking and horticulture, the green mentality and passion for nature. She had finally found someone to share all aspects of her life with. It was too good to be true. She mustn't get carried away. Be sensible. Take her time to get to know him inside and out, and make sure he's being honest with her.

Hand-in-hand they made their way to the restaurant. She was pleased to see it catered solely for vegans—no need to search the menu for the miserly offerings she always had to put up with when out with Tim.

Scraping the final bits of pudding from the plate, she glanced at Matt. He sat upright. His closed-lip grin inane.

"What?"

"I feel the need to make a little speech."

"Oh... right." She dropped the spoon and sat back with a jolt. He couldn't possibly be about to propose, could he? They'd only been together for not much more than a week. Tonight was only their second proper date if you didn't count dinners at the farm. She didn't want to be in the same situation as when Tim proposed. At least, she wasn't drunk this time, so could stand her ground and ask for time to consider.

Her silence was his cue, "I know it's early days... but it feels so right. You feel so right. I'm so comfortable in your company... not in a bad, like, take you for granted way.... I just know I can tell you everything and anything without fear of judgement. But most of all, I hate it when I'm not with you. I worry something awful might happen to you. An unfounded fear, but I can't help it. I guess what I'm saying is, I'm head over heels in love with you, Gem. I think we were meant to be together. You've got to admit, it was a strange set of circumstances that made our paths collide. It's got to be destiny, fate, whatever you want to call it..."

Her stomach tightened. He would be devastated if she turned him down. And she didn't want to. She loved him. But then again, she thought she loved Dan, Josh, Yousef... even Tim... until they showed their true colours. Given another couple of weeks, she might hate Matt's guts too. Time was what she needed.

"...I guess, what I'm asking is..." She braced. Here it comes. "...will you move in with me?"

A brief laugh escaped her lips. But there was no relief. She actually felt... well... disappointed. She shuddered. *Get a grip, girl. You don't want to get married.* But live with him? Yeah, why not? She loved him. Wanted to spend the rest of her life with him.... but... she rubbed the back of her neck...

Matt tapped continuously on the base of his wine glass. The absurd grin gone; replaced by a severe case of lip-biting.

She swallowed. "Surely it's too soon?"

"I thought you moved in with Tim after a couple of weeks?"

"I think it was three, actually. But whatever it was, it kinda proves my point. Too soon."

"But we're sleeping together every night. When you're not at work, you spend all your time with me. It's like we're living together already, but just splitting our time between two homes. One that doesn't even have a fully functioning kitchen. It seems a bit daft."

"I know, but still... it's hard to explain."

"Try me. I'm listening."

"It just feels as though I'm about to make the same mistake all over again. I want this to work. I really do. But I don't want to rush into things too quickly. I've done that far too many times and it's always ended badly."

"Things are never quick enough for true love. That's what we've got here. I've never been more sure of anything. Why waste time dilly-dallying around? I want to be with you forever. Don't you want to be with me?"

"Yes, course I do. I love you. I just need some time to make sure."

"But you say you love me. So surely you're certain already?" She remained silent. She didn't know how to word it without offending the man she loved. "Oh..." He sat back. "...you mean sure of my love for you?"

She grimaced. "Sorry. I've been hurt before. Thought everything was hunky-dory, only to find out it wasn't. I've been cheated on. I've been rolled over for an arranged marriage. I've even been beaten up. With Tim, my opinion never counted. He was turning me into a doormat, but it wasn't an obvious in-your-face sort of thing. It was little things... sort of insidious? Is that the right term? I don't know. I'm not even sure he was doing it intentionally, but he seemed to be taking over more and more of my life. Then he was trying to make out I was having a breakdown when all I wanted to do was leave him." A tear trickled down her cheek.

He leant forward, "I'm so sorry, Gem, sweetheart. I didn't realise. But I promise you, I'm not any of those men. I will love and cherish you. Value you as my equal. Maybe put you on a pedestal and worship, but I would never ever hurt you." Lips closed, he smiled, then pushed his napkin towards her, "Here, have this. It's clean."

She took the serviette, wiped her eyes, and blew her nose.

"We'll wait. If that's what you need, we'll wait until you're sure."

"Thank you. You're not offended, are you?" He didn't answer. "Please don't be. I do love you. More than anyone before. Way more. More than I ever thought possible." She reached her hand across the table. "I love you, Matt. I'm totally in love with you."

He nodded. His eyes glistened in the accumulating moisture. He bit his lip, before placing his hand over hers and giving a gentle squeeze, "I love you too."

# TWENTY-SIX

Matt pulled on yesterday's trunks and jeans, followed by the grubby t-shirt. After sniffing the socks, he stuffed them in his pockets and slipped the trainers onto his bare feet. He didn't bother tying the laces. Swivelling in his sitting position on the edge of the bed, he gazed at the sleeping woman who preoccupied his mind, day and night. Gemma still had another hour before she needed to get up to go to work, so he kissed her gently on the head and tiptoed out of the room through the patio doors.

Outside, the sun fought a battle with the early morning haze. The mist was winning so far, but by lunchtime it would be another scorching hot day. Passing through the orchard, he paused to pick up a handful of the June drops still lying scattered amongst the grass.

"Arggghh!" he screamed, hurling the fruits hard into the trees. They bounced and cracked through the branches, knocking a few of their relatives to the ground.

Why would she not move in with him? It was ridiculous that one of them always had to return to their home in the morning, to shower and redress ready for the day ahead. He'd even taken a change of clothes to the barn one evening, only to be frowned upon. She relented, but for "Just this once. Don't do it again."

It was daft that they either cooked in one house or the other:

"Matt, have you got any cumin?"

"Yes, I'll just nip home and get it."

And shared the shopping:

"Gem, do you want me to get you anything at the supermarket?"

"Oh, yes. Loo rolls, please."

Sucking in his lips, he had crossed out the '1' next to toilet rolls and replaced it with a '2'.

Daft.

Yes, it had only been two weeks, but some things were meant to be. Why could she not see that? How could she doubt his love for her? Maybe he needed to show it more. Make a grander display of affection. He'd held off from going too over-the-top for fear it would look contrived and forced. But just being himself was clearly not working. Rose petals. Champagne. A weekend away. It would have to be Paris—synonymous with romance.

Entering the farmhouse, he headed straight for the office, plonked himself in the chair, and switched on the computer. He typed 'short breaks in paris' in the search box. Sixty-nine million results. He sat back. His hands dropped from the keyboard to his lap. What the hell was he thinking? This wasn't what Gem would want. She wouldn't enjoy staying in a hotel however luxurious it was. She wouldn't enjoy traipsing around the city streets, breathing in the foul air of traffic. Yes, she might appreciate a trip to the Louvre to see the art, but the crowds she would do anything to miss. No, he knew her. He knew what made her tick.

He left the room and headed to the understairs cupboard. A hard yank unstuck the door. He switched on the light; it flickered then blew out with a pop! One filament bulb he'd forgotten to upgrade.

Never mind. He'd sort that out another time. He stared into the dark. It was in there somewhere. Probably right at the back; it had been a long time since it had seen the light of day. A trip to Cornwall while in the sixth form. Tim, Mike, Ash, and himself. Before Tim and he had fallen out. Nerdy Kate had never been that interested. Bella? A trip to Paris was more her style. But for Gemma—perfect.

The hoover was removed first, followed by the ironing board. He crouched to enter, brushing away a cobweb that tickled his face. The next obstacle was a pile of farming magazines, browned and crinkled with age. A front cover, showing the latest milking equipment, raised a chuckle as he hauled them out. He checked the date: April 1952. New destiny: the recycling bin (after a good browse). An ancient portable gas heater was rolled out, rattling as it bumped over the threshold. His dad had talked about huddling around the contraption before central heating was installed in the farmhouse. That would have to go in the skip; it would probably blow up if you lit it now. Two board games from his childhood were balanced on the top: Monopoly and Game of Life. His mum was the biggest cheat ever. Banker—more like bank robber. He chuckled. He would keep the games for his and Gemma's kids. Granny will have to behave. He brushed off the thick layer of dust. Good job the cupboard had avoided Bella's meticulous spring cleaning, which would have resulted in these heirlooms being chucked. He ventured back in, retrieving three moldy car rugs, more magazines, an antique wooden clothes horse, a torn umbrella, and an empty cardboard box for a top-of-the-range laptop he'd never owned. He scratched his head. Bella? They would all be tossed except the clothes horse which could have a new home in one of the holiday cottages. Finally, he dragged out a musty cylindrical bag and carried it out into the back garden.

It took a bit of wrestling to get it out of the tube, but careful examination and reconstruction revealed it to be still in one piece.

Perfect.

# TWENTY-SEVEN

The office phone rang making Gemma jump. She'd been concentrating on the job in hand, trying to work out what the hell the client had done with his posting of the HP purchase of a car. She scratched her head as she picked up the receiver.

"Gem here."

"Gemma, there's a Tim Starling to see you in reception."

"Tell him to piss off."

There was a lengthy silence, before the receptionist spoke again, "I don't think the partners will be very happy if I say that to a client."

"He's not a client. He's my ex and I don't want to talk to him. Tell him to go away."

"Hang on."

Tim and Sophie's exchange was muffled, presumably by a hand over the mouthpiece. Sophie was trying to persuade him to leave. Tim's grumbling was hard to make out, until he shouted, "I'm staying put. And I'll be staying here until she talks to me."

"Did you hear that? He won't go until you've come down and talked to him."

"He can stay there forever for all I care. I'm not coming down." She slammed down the phone. Her hand went to her mouth. That was rude. Sophie had done nothing to deserve such treatment. She quickly emailed a grovelling apology to her beleaguered colleague.

She glanced at the clock on her computer. It was already 1.20pm. Lunchtime. So engrossed in her work, she hadn't noticed the time. And she'd missed the sandwich guy. Her stomach rumbled. She'd have to go out to buy lunch. That required a trip through reception. The only other route would set off the fire alarm. She looked around the open-plan office. It was half empty. Those present were already munching on their lunches, but what about those who weren't? She stood up, walked out to the mini-kitchen, and opened the fridge. There was a packet of chicken sandwiches, a BLT baguette, and a banana. She picked up the banana. Stared at the yellow skin. What was she doing? She wasn't a thief. She dropped the fruit back in the fridge and closed the door. She would just have to starve. *No. Hang on. Why should I go without, just to avoid him?* She went back to her desk, grabbed her bag, then headed to the stairwell.

At first, there was a spring in her step. A newfound confidence. But that waned as she descended closer to the inevitable confrontation point. By the time she reached the ground floor, she was doing a good impression of a tortoise. Clasping the fire door's handle, she braced. *I've just got to walk past. Don't look at him. Don't say anything.* She tugged the door open and headed into the unknown.

She strode into the reception area. Nothing was going to stop her getting through this challenge. Not Tim. Not anyone. Her green eyes remained fixed on her destination. The front door was the path to freedom. *I can do this.* In the corner of her eye, Sophie was standing by the visitor seating holding a cup of coffee. The receptionist turned to see who had entered. Behind Sophie, Tim relaxed in one of his favourite poses: his arm across the back of the cushioned bench and his right ankle resting upon his left knee. He jumped to his feet, knocking the coffee in Sophie's hand. The steaming liquid spilt down the poor woman's skirt, momentarily distracting Tim. Despite the temptation to go to her colleague's aid, Gemma remained resolute. If she stopped, she would never get away. She had to go on. She realigned her eyesight to her means of escape.

"Gem! Thank god you've seen sense..." Tim's voice trailed off.

Eyes ahead she exited the building. The door didn't bang shut as per usual. *Keep walking. Don't look back.*

"Gem! Please!"

He caught up and grabbed her arm, jerking her to a halt, "We need to talk."

"Nothing to say."

"Well, I have."

"I don't want to hear it. Go away." She shrugged her arm, but he held firm. "This is harassment. I'll go to the police if you don't let go right now."

He let go. She'd hit the nail on the head with her threat. There was no way he would risk police action. His job was far too important to him.

Scurrying away, she resisted the urge to glance behind until reaching the pedestrian crossing. Thankfully, he still stood where she had left him, though his dogged stare was unnerving. His hand swept over the side of his glossy hair before giving a hesitant wave.

She frowned and stepped into the road.

TOOT! TOOT!

# TWENTY-EIGHT

Unsettled by her lunchtime experience, she scowled at the computer screen. Why couldn't he just leave her alone? It was over. Surely, he could see that now she had moved out. You couldn't get much clearer than that... unless she went and told him she had a new boyfriend. But if she told Tim that, he'd be wanting details and if they weren't forthcoming, she wouldn't put it past him to follow her. Last thing she wanted was to drag Matt into all this. The two men had history. There must be more to the end of their friendship than the 'drifted apart' claimed by Matt. After all, her new fella never said anything nice about Tim. It was obvious he didn't like him. And Tim had never mentioned Matt to her in all the time she'd been with him. But, if they had fallen out as young adults, maybe his silence wasn't so strange. There were plenty of old school friends she had lost contact with, and she didn't go round chatting about them to all and sundry. Anyway, regardless of what caused it, there was still bad blood between them, and she wasn't about to stir it up, especially as Tim's parents were neighbours of Matt. So, informing Tim of her new relationship was out of the question.

Anyway, she'd moved out. None of her life was any of his business anymore. Stuff him!

With all that swirling in her head, there was little point staying late to catch up with the work she had failed to do that afternoon, so she left work promptly at 5.30pm and headed for the multi-storey carpark.

\*\*\*

She tugged the seat belt across her body and snapped it into place. The passenger door opened a crack. She flew at the door and grabbed the handle, but it slipped from her hand as the intruder yanked. Head and shoulders out of sight, the man's black-suited frame stepped close to the threshold. Heart racing, her trembling fingers fumbled to get the seat belt undone. *Undo will you.* The sicko swivelled to reverse in, bum first. She shook the buckle. *Undo!* Two large hands were placed over hers. She struggled to free herself from the hot sweaty prison, but the fingers dug in tight. Visions of the horror to come swept through. Rape. Murder. Her stomach shrunk in a nauseous bubble. Close to heaving, she looked up at the face of her assailant.

Tim.

She collapsed back in the seat and breathed deep. "You scared the living daylights out of me."

"Sorry, but I really need to talk to you. You left me no choice."

"You could choose to just leave me alone. I'm serious about going to the police if you keep this up. I'm taking notes." It was a lie that she had recorded anything so far, but she was going to from now on. As soon as she got home, she would make copious notes on today's events. And the wardrobe incident to boot.

"Gem, I love you. I want you back. You can't be happy on your own. I'm not. I miss your silly eccentricities. The, shall we say, entertaining discussions. I'll even put up with your weird haircut, I'm so desperate for a shag."

She remained quiet. She wasn't going to tell him of her new boyfriend as there was no way to predict how he would react.

"Please, Gemmie. Come home."

"I want you to get out of my car, right now."

His usual cool self was rattled for a moment, "Stop being so fucking childish."

"It's you who's behaving like a baby."

"You can be such a bitch at times..." He flashed her his best smile, "...but I still love you."

"Tim... please just go. It's over. I'm not changing my mind."

"Are you hungry? We could go and get some dinner together and you can tell me what I've done wrong."

"You haven't done anything wrong—except stalk me. We're just too different. Long term it's just not going to work."

"It's about the babies, isn't it? I suppose we could have one or two if that's what you really want."

She stared into his eyes. As far as she could remember, this was the first compromise he'd ever offered. A tinge of pity hit her gut. Maybe she'd been too hard on him. Should have given him more of a chance? He'd never treated her badly unlike some previous boyfriends she could mention. So, he liked to get his own way, but he never hit her to get it. Their disagreements never ended in a shouting match or fight, but rather a ripping off of clothes and some hard thrusting. And she was sure he'd never cheated on her, despite Matt's assertions. On the whole, he'd been a total gentleman... well, until she finished with him. Except for bamboozling her into an engagement... and that incident at his parents' house when he hadn't stuck up for her. But he thought both were just a bit of fun. Then she'd lost the plot. Pent up anger from the forced engagement exploded... and that was that. Harsh, but she had Matt now and Matt was her dream man.

"It's not just that. It's our whole outlook on life. You're never going to be a vegan..."

"I could try," he interrupted.

"...or live off-grid in the wilderness."

"That would be something for you to compromise on. You can't have it all your own way."

"But that's the point. I can without you."

He sighed.

"I am sorry, Tim. I never meant to hurt you, but it's over. You're just wasting your time trying to convince me otherwise."

He remained quiet. It was unlike him not have the final say. An indication he was more badly affected than she imagined. Her lips pressed together. She felt terrible, but to offer solace would only encourage him. Thankfully, he opened the door and climbed out in silence. She sighed. Shifted in her seat to get comfy.

Holding the door, he leant back in, "I'm not giving up, Gem. I'll give you a few weeks to come to your senses, then we'll talk again."

She didn't comment but waited for the door to close. Grabbing the steering wheel, she screamed silently, baring her teeth. Why couldn't he just leave her alone? She thumped the wheel. Then started the car and reversed out of the space. How did he find her car? Had he searched the whole carpark before she arrived, or maybe just followed her in? "Whatever—unacceptable," she griped. "How dare he give me a fright like that."

She sped around the corner, then down the ramp. Tim—on foot—was at the bottom of the slope. Her top teeth bit hard on her lower lip. Her foot pressed on the pedal. The car sped down the slope. What are you doing? She swerved around the oblivious man and drove on, her heart pounding. You bloomin' idiot. You've escaped a life sentence with him. Don't do one for him. He's not worth it.

# TWENTY-NINE

The key rattled against the lock. Slipped to the side, adding to the scratches on the shabby paintwork. She closed her eyes. Breathed deep. Stop shaking, will you. It was only Tim. But what if it hadn't been? What if it were a rapist? Or Tim had attacked her? Hadn't she read that most rapes were by people you know? Murders too. She very nearly committed one herself—just because Tim was intent on speaking again, when all she wanted was the harassment to be over so she could concentrate on her new life with Matt. Opening her eyes, she sniffed. Squeezed her fist over the keys, "OK, you can do it." Still trembling, she used her left index finger as a guide and shoved the key in. Turned until the lock clunked. Pushed open the door and stepped inside.

As she closed the front door, Matt appeared in the hallway. She ran into his arms and started to sob.

"What's wrong?"

"I... he..." She buried her face into his neck.

"Gem, you're worrying me. What happened?" He helped her into the sitting room to sit down on the sofa. He cuddled her tight. "Has someone... err... hurt you?"

"Tim..." she blubbered unable to finish the sentence.

"He's not..." He gulped. "...r-raped you, has he?" His muscles froze, clamping her in his embrace. In her ear, the thud thud thud of his heart quickened.

She struggled free. Placed her hand on his chest, "No, no. Just cornered me in my car, in the carpark. And earlier at lunchtime too."

"Did he threaten you?"

"No, it was nothing like that. He just gave me a fright cos he jumped in the car, and I didn't know it was him straight away. He tried to persuade me to go back to him."

"But you're not going to, are you?"

"No. Definitely not. I love you."

"Good.... I love you too." There was a silence. "I might have to have a word with him."

"No, I don't want you getting in a fight. I can handle it. It's my problem."

"You're saying that like it's not over?"

"He said he'll be back in a few weeks to talk again."

"Does he know you're living with me now?"

"No. Thought it best not to say I was in a new relationship."

"Might come to his senses if he knew."

"But I don't want him coming here causing trouble. It's bad enough him turning up at work. But, at least, he doesn't know where I'm living now and I want to keep it that way, so please keep out of it. I'll deal with it. He won't do anything stupid because his job's too important to him."

"I hope you're right."

"It's stopped him doing stuff before."

"Jeez, Gem. What the hell's been going on? I thought you said he never hit you?"

She shook her head, "Oh, he didn't. Nothing like that."

"Then what?" She bit her lip. He wasn't going to like it. "What did he do?"

"Er..." She grimaced, "He locked me in the walk-in wardrobe when I was packing to leave.... He only let me out when I threatened to call the police."

Matt closed his eyes and rubbed his hands over his face. "Unbelievable. The bastard. If he comes anywhere near you, or phones, or anything, then you tell me straight away. You shouldn't have to deal with this on your own. In fact, I insist you don't."

"I don't want you to fall out with his parents."

"Don't worry about that. You're more important." He cupped his hands over her cheeks, "You are the most important thing in my life. I'm here for you, forever."

# THIRTY

The droplets battered against the windowpane. Finally, a good dose of rain. His crops were in desperate need of the downpour, for sure. He pulled out his hanky and stuffed it into a gap where the frame had warped, putting an end to the gurgling and spluttering. God, he needed to get on with the exterior painting. Strip off all the old flaky layers. Primer. Two coats. Do it this summer. Before things got draughty. He stared at the slate-grey sky. He'd need some dry weather. His crops needed wet. He puffed. Dilemma.

He glanced at his watch. His mouth twisted. Still only 6pm. Gemma wouldn't get back from work for another half hour. Or was that her now? Out of sight, a car growled along the lane but, no, it was too noisy for Gem's electric motor.

The red hatchback swung into the farmyard. He walked out of the sitting room and into the hallway. Opened the front door ready for the unexpected guest.

"Hi, Mum."

"Hi, Matty-moo."

"Awww, please don't call me that. You know I hate it."

He helped her take off her wet raincoat, then draped the dripping article over the stair newel post.

"But you're my little boy."

"Not so little."

She smiled. "How's things? You've been unusually brief with your phone calls and messages recently. I'm suspicious there might be something you're not telling me?" Her brow lifted in query.

"No, just didn't want to disturb you while you were away. How was it?"

"Oh, it was fantastic. The Fjords were amazing. You should go there yourself sometime..." She looked him directly in the eye, "...with a girl?"

He remained tight-lipped. As much as he wanted to tell her he had found the love of his life, there was a complication. His mother's close relationship with the Starlings meant he could not risk revealing he was now with Tim's ex. It was very much to the front of his mind how upset Gemma had been yesterday after her encounter in the carpark. Last thing he wanted was Tim to show up here and cause her more distress. Or, even worse, persuade her to go back to him. She still hadn't agreed to move in with himself, so that could only mean she still had doubts about their long-term future.

"I'll make some tea."

"Changing the subject's not going to work, Matty-moo. You can't fool your mum."

He ignored her and walked off into the kitchen, "Have you got photos?"

"I was going to ask you the same."

He laughed as he filled the kettle, "What of? Wonky veg?"

"You're impossible. I might have to camp here until I find out the truth." The chair scraped over the tiled floor as she sat down at the kitchen table. After a good rummage in her oversized handbag, she pulled out her phone. "Right. Photos of Norway. Here we are."

Glancing at his watch, he spooned the tea leaves into the teapot. 6.15pm. What the hell was he going to do if Gem turned up? When Gem turned up. There was no way he could get rid of his mum in fifteen minutes. She would know he was up to something. She'd sit in her car until she knew what... and then she'd be planning the wedding!

"OK. Let's see them." He sat down at the rickety kitchen table that had lived in the farmhouse for as long as he could remember. Even longer than his dad could—if he were still alive. An heirloom carefully crafted by his grandad, Sid, for his bride, Mabel. Bit of a weird wedding gift, but definitely well-used and much-loved. He took hold of the phone and started to scroll through the photos, "Wow, they're fantastic. What was the ship like?"

"Oh, wonderful. Though I think I'm twice the weight." Her voice rose as she battled for supremacy with the noisy kettle, "Food was amazing and so much of it." The kettle conceded defeat with a loud click. "Impossible to say no."

"I won't offer you any cake then," he joked, heading back to the counter to pour the hot water into the antique brown betty teapot.

"Oh, please don't tempt me. No food until Christmas for me."

After replacing the chipped lid, he grabbed two mugs from the shelf above. All three items he set in the middle of the kitchen table, before retrieving a carton of oat milk from the fridge. His mother frowned at the milk substitute as she poured out the tea, "I should have stopped off at the Starlings' first. Got some nice milk to go with my tea."

Matt ignored her again. They'd had this conversation many a time over the years. The woman could not understand why he had to go the whole hog and become a vegan. Now, if he were a vegetarian, he could still enjoy the lovely fresh milk from down the road. They were both intractable on the subject, so it was pointless to revisit.

"She still hasn't returned, you know?"

"Who?"

"Tim's fiancée. Jenny says he's going spare with worry." She sipped her tea. "They've no idea where she's living now, and she's blocked his calls. He did manage to talk to her yesterday, at her workplace, so that's something."

"Is he still hoping to get back with her?"

"Absolutely. Love of his life."

"But not hers?"

"He's certain she's just having a bit of a meltdown over the wedding. He's regretting booking it for Christmas. She was very upset when he told her. Thinks he should have left it until next summer."

"Maybe she just doesn't want to marry him?"

"They were very happy."

"According to Tim."

"Yes, but you'd know, wouldn't you, if there were problems..."

"I didn't."

"...Jenny says everything was hunky-dory between them." She chuckled, "Gerald even caught them at it at the farm, in Tim's bedroom. So, they were very much in love. Couldn't keep their hands off each other. It's just after the engagement, she got all stressed out and disagreeable. One minute she was fine, the next... well, you know what happened at Jenny and Gerald's, don't you?"

He nodded, "She was pretty mad at him when I picked her up. Seemed set on leaving him."

She gulped several mouthfuls. "Mental breakdowns can make you say and do odd things."

"So, that's what he thinks it is, a mental breakdown?"

"Yes. Jenny says he's going to enquire about getting her sectioned."

He balked at his mother's words, "Bit extreme. Surely it's not justified."

"The poor girl needs help, Matthew. I'm sure you would do the same if your girlfriend was losing it."

"I'm not convinced she is though. People walk out on relationships all the time." He shrugged, "Why can't it be that. It just wasn't working for her."

"Don't be silly, Matt. Tim knows this girl better than anyone. You're letting your past affect your judgement. I know Kate and Bella treated you badly, but true love does exist. I had it with your father. Tim has it with Gemma. The sooner she gets help, the better." She looked towards the hallway, "Is that a car?"

"I've got someone living in one of the barns now. It's probably her."

His mum's eyes narrowed, "Her?"

He picked up the teapot to pour her another cup.

Her hand shot over the mug, "Not for me. I want to know more about this woman. How old? Single? Pretty?"

He remained tight-lipped and crossed his fingers under the table. With any luck, Gemma would go to her place first, but that was doubtful. They liked a kiss and a cuddle, if not more, as soon as she got back from work.

The front door opened, and the bedraggled female staggered in backwards, shaking her umbrella.

His mum's brow furrowed, "Does she have a key?"

"Err... no, I unlocked it for you."

Gemma balanced the half-open umbrella on the doormat, then turned. "Oh, you've got a guest. Hi." She kicked off her shoes and walked towards them.

He would have to act quick to avoid a kiss. And he'd have to bank on his mother not recognising Gem. If Jenny Starling had shown her any photos of the 'happy' betrothed couple, he was in trouble.

"Hi, there. This is my mother, Sue. Mum, this is my tenant, Ge-raldine."

Gemma threw him a look. He stared back, wide-eyed like a rabbit stuck in headlights. Would she play along? Or was he doomed? The awful moment seemed to last an eternity, but then

Gemma held out her hand to shake his mother's, "Sorry to disturb you. I was just hoping to borrow a can opener for my supper."

*Phew!*

Double phew: his mum was smiling at the new acquaintance, so he'd gotten away with that too.

"Why don't you join us, dear. I'm sure Matt can rustle up something. He's a very good cook."

If he were not already in a relationship with Gemma, he could have throttled his mother. Matchmaking at its finest. Would she ever give up?

"Err…"

Matt quickly intervened, "Thought you were on a starvation diet, Mum."

"Yes. Silly me. I forgot. I'll make my exit and leave you two young ones to have a nice meal."

She stood, "Nice to meet you, Geraldine. Enjoy your meal. Don't let him chicken out."

*Unbelievable!*

He walked his mother to the door and helped her put on her coat. They kissed each other on both cheeks, then his mum whispered, "Give me a call tomorrow. I want to hear how it went."

"I'm her landlord."

"You just have to take the opportunities when they arrive, Matty-moo. Otherwise, you'll be on your own for the rest of your life. She seems nice. Very pretty. Take that chance, son. It might lead somewhere good."

He smiled and nodded. It already had unless he'd blown it with this evening's deceit. He closed the door behind her and turned to face the music.

Gemma was standing, hands on hips, in the kitchen doorway. Growling. "I've been the secret girlfriend before, you know. I didn't like it then. And I don't like it now."

"I can explain."

"It better be good. And it better not be a lie. I've had that an' all."

"She's very close to the Starlings. She'll probably go and drop in on them now. If she knew you were Tim's ex, there's no way she could keep it a secret. She's a total chatterbox. Loves to poke her nose where it's not wanted. You noticed that, surely?"

She nodded, "She did seem rather keen to set us up together."

"Total busybody. Well-meaning but an absolute nightmare. Anyway, you don't want Tim turning up here, do you?"

"No. I never want to see him, or anyone related to him, ever again."

He stopped in his tracks, "Err... well, you don't tell my mum who you are then."

Her smile was guilty. Not half as guilty as he was feeling right now. She stepped towards him, "Sorry, I doubted you."

He took her in his arms, "My fault. I should've warned you about my mother and we could've planned ahead."

He held her tight. He didn't want to ever let go, for fear she might not return. How on earth was he going to tell her? He thought she knew. He racked his brains. Hadn't he mentioned it? He must have done, surely? But even if he had, it clearly hadn't registered in her brain. How would she react if she found out... when she found out? He couldn't keep it a secret forever. But he'd already gone past the point when he should have said something. Now, she'd be fuming. He could lose her. What the hell was he going to do?

# THIRTY-ONE

Gemma's eyes drifted to the trees that ran along one side of the field. Their unabashed greenery put the scorched brown grass to shame. The leaves twinkled in the evening sun, flickering in response to a gentle breeze. Above, the sky was clear and blue, only marred by the flight of an occasional seagull. Beyond the khaki tent, a shallow rocky stream trickled its way towards the coast. A beautiful setting for a campsite. Even better, they had the place all to themselves. Matt had contacted one of his farmer friends to ask if they could borrow a quiet out-of-the-way field for the weekend. They'd come up trumps with this one.

Catching her toe on a rope as she walked around the tent, she tripped. Her hand shot onto the faded fabric to steady herself. "Whoops!" She cringed, fingers on mouth.

Matt stopped hammering stakes at the back end of the unsteady structure and looked up, "What have you done?"

"Little bit of a rip," she giggled.

Walking around the tent, he carefully stepped over the slack guy ropes to join her, "Little?"

"Sorreee."

"Don't worry about it. It's old. Surprised it came out of the bag in one piece, to be honest. We'll just have to hope it doesn't rain."

She laughed. That was funny coming from Matt. Until yesterday, he'd been positively fretting over the drought conditions. The storm had alleviated his immediate concerns, though his preference was for regular showers rather than the odd deluge. At the moment, it was touch and go as to whether his crops were going to reach a standard that justified the premium paid for organic vegetables. And he couldn't afford to drop his prices.

"I'll rephrase that. Hope it does 'not' rain here in Dorset. Send all the clouds to Sussex."

"I wouldn't mind a bit of a cooling sprinkle. I'm boiled."

"Beach isn't far. Let's finish putting the tent up first, then we can go for a swim."

"What about the rip?"

His eyebrows raised above those smiling eyes, "Window?"

"Yep. We definitely need one of those."

Her strong man went back to effortlessly hammering the stakes into the baked-hard ground. Abandoning her own attempts to push the pegs in by hand, she busied herself by tightening the guy ropes. Now and again, she peeked at the tanned and muscular body that was concentrating so hard on its task. A sweat stain ran down the back of his t-shirt despite the lack of exertion. His shorts strained as he knelt, revealing a builder's bum. "Farmer's bum," she muttered under her breath. She licked her dry lips. Then shuddered back into activity when Matt stood up. He walked to the jeep, dropped the mallet in the back, then took a swig of water from a bottle. He waved the reusable container in her direction. She shook her head. Went back to tightening the ropes, noticing Matt was doing exactly what she'd done just moments ago—ogle. She smiled, blushing, then scrambled into the tent to smooth out the groundsheet.

"Pass me the sleeping bags, Matt."

"Hang on. I'll unzip them so we can have one on top and one underneath."

A protracted zzzzzzz...zpp, then another, reverberated through the tent fabric like a busy bee on a mission. The quilted fabric was pushed through the flap to her. She laid them out as Matt suggested.

"Gem," Matt's muffled voice came through the side of the tent.

"Yes?"

"Have a look out the new window."

She half-stood in the cramped space, lifted aside the torn fabric and poked her head out. "Whooaa!" she laughed. "Great view." She glanced around, "Watch out, someone's coming!"

"Shit!" Matt bolted round the tent and dived in the doorway, flinging his naked body onto the sleeping bags.

She laughed, "Didn't know you could move so fast."

He rolled onto his back, "Something tells me I've been had. There wasn't anyone, was there?"

She giggled as she sat astride the muscular frame. "No, but it got you where I want you, didn't it?"

# THIRTY-TWO

A joyous weekend. Two days of long walks—hand-in-hand—along the coast, interrupted with cooling dips in the sea. Picnics for lunch and cooking over an open fire for their evening meals. They talked about her dream of off-grid living. Matt hadn't poo-pooed the notion like Tim. Her new fella was definitely up for the adventure. He particularly liked the idea of not having to deal with customers or worry about large-scale crop failures. The Dorset countryside also gave her a chance to show off her survival skills: lighting fires without matches, foraging, bathing in the stream, weeing in the woods. Matt was impressed. Tim would've thought her a disgusting animal.

Lying flat on her back, her hands trailed through the clover, "I want to stay here forever."

"Me too," Matt agreed, plonking down beside her. He puffed.

"What?"

"I can't stay away from the farm for more than a few days. We have to leave early tomorrow morning." He grimaced, "Sorry."

"Yeah, and I've got work on Tuesday. Bummer." She rolled onto her side. "Got anything special for our final supper?"

"I thought we could bung some rice and beans in the saucepan with the leftover veg. Not very special, is it?"

"Sounds yummy." She jumped to her feet. "I'll start the fire. You get the food."

\*\*\*

The rice and bean concoction was enhanced by an overdose of chilli: Matt surprised her with a hug from behind, sending a dollop of the powder into the pan. They managed to scoop out some, but clearly not enough. The meal was eye-watering hot and required copious amounts of cold beer as an accompaniment. Extremely drunk and suffering from uncontrollable giggles, they crawled into the tent for a somewhat fumbled attempt at lovemaking. Getting the condom out of the wrapper proved a challenge in itself, let alone putting the thing on. The drunken encounter wasn't up to its usual high standard and the effects of the alcohol delayed Matt's final crescendo until she'd almost fallen asleep.

In the small hours, awoken by his lips upon hers, the sex was slow and sensuous. With their eyes transfixed upon one another, they showed their love. She knew then, if he were to ask her again, she wouldn't hesitate to move in with him.

Matt extricated himself and was now sitting on top of the sleeping bag, facing away from her. He was taking longer than usual to remove the condom. She shifted from the wet spot. *Wet spot?* Her hand shot to her groin. A trickle dribbled down her buttock.

"Matt, I'm more drippy than usual. Is everything OK?"

His silence was disconcerting.

He faced her, "It's broken. Sorry."

The tension left her body in a breath. A yearned-for baby with the man she loved. What could be more wonderful than that? The grin almost broke out but she pressed her lips together. What if Matt felt differently? They'd only been together two and a half weeks, so there was no way he'd be wanting to have a baby yet. Ridiculous to even think he might.

"No worries. I can find a chemist first thing tomorrow if you..." Her voice trailed off. She was going to say 'if you like' but it seemed inappropriate to put the ball in his court and ask him to make that decision. Possibly even harmful to their relationship.

"Morning-after pill?"

"Yeah."

"Is that vegan?"

"No idea."

"I wouldn't expect you to take it if it isn't."

She swallowed hard, "But that would mean an abortion?"

"Not necessarily."

Her face scrunched. He couldn't possibly mean adoption. Could he? Surely, he wouldn't expect her to go through a whole pregnancy and then give up her much wanted and loved baby. That couldn't be right.

"If I'm not pregnant?"

He remained silent.

"Oh..." her heart shrunk, "...you've had the snip too."

"No, no, definitely not. I want kids." His eyes ran over her face, searching for clues. He already knew she wanted a family, so he could be seeking a timescale. Sucking in her cheeks, she gave nothing away; not wanting to frighten him off. It worked. Too well. "Err... not necessarily right now."

She couldn't resist, "When were you thinking?"

He hesitated. "Well, when were you?"

"Err..."

Talk about awkward silence. There was no way she could say 'now' without jeopardising her relationship with this so-perfect man. But he was asking her 'when' as though it was given that they would have a family together. It was just the timing. What did he want? Her turn to search his face for a clue. He was biting his bottom lip. A furrowed brow framed his chestnut eyes. Unfortunately, there was no date etched on his pupils. No cursive form to his acne scars. And no whisper of a year from his sexy mouth.

They stared at each other. Someone would have to say something soon. She remained quiet, determined it would be him.

"This seems to be one of those moments when neither wants to admit to their feelings first.... I'll go first if you like?"

She nodded.

He flopped down next to her, pulling the cover up to his hips; leaving both their bodies half exposed to the humid night air. Staring at the stars through the flapping section of torn tent, he took a deep breath. "I knew for certain—pretty soon after we first got together—that you are 'the one' for me. I want to spend the rest of my life with you, Gem. Grow old together. Compare wrinkles. See who can hobble the fastest—"

She laughed. "Wheelchair races!"

He rolled onto his side to face her, "As far as I'm concerned, a baby would be icing. I don't want you to take the morning-after pill. I want to go with the flow... if it happens... great."

"What if it doesn't?"

"Keep trying? I want that icing." She smiled but said nothing. "But what about you? You haven't said what you want yet." His brow crinkled, "I haven't blown it between us, have I?"

"No. Don't worry. We're on the same page. I want what you want."

His eyebrows raised, "Phew!" He snuggled close, putting his arm around her. He stilled, face upturned to the roof, but eyes wandering.

"What is it?"

He turned to her, "Would you like that ring back? Or is that too weird?"

"I don't know. I love the fact it was your gran's, but then again, I don't want to be reminded of who gave it to me first.... I'll have to think about it."

"So, is that a yes or a no?"

"Thinking about it."

"I'm not sure you're getting my drift..." Her brow scrunched. He looked equally confused. "Er... not the ring... the proposal?"

"Oh! Yes! Sorry, didn't make the connection. But yes! Definitely, yes!"

# THIRTY-THREE

Gemma scratched at the burnt crust on the flat-looking loaf. Was it possible to disguise the nuking? Cover with icing and pretend it's a cake? Or a biscuit? Turn it into bread-and-butter pudding? Or just feed it to the ducks? She tapped the top with a knife. No, they'd break their beaks. Well, that was the best part of a day wasted. Her first attempt at making vegan bread. Probably her last. Unless she could get some tips from the expert. She'd ask Matt where she went wrong later, once he'd returned to the house... and finished laughing.

She moved in on Monday; the day of their return from Dorset. Now Sunday, she already felt at home in the cosy farmhouse. The four days back at work a chore, she left Guildford each day at 5.30pm promptly and rushed home to be with Matt. Wanting to be with him all the time, a moment away was too long.

Returning to the sink to finish the washing up, she gazed out the window while swishing the water around a mixing bowl. Matt wasn't in sight. He was working in the potato field beyond the far hedge. She would go and help him once she'd finished tidying the kitchen. Take him a sandwich made with her disastrous bread. He'd be amused even if it proved inedible.

The engagement ring sparkled on the sill in front of her, carefully placed as far away from the sink as possible. She accepted the gold band on Tuesday with a rather unromantic, "I'll take that ring if it's still on offer." That it meant so much to Matt, overrode the reservations over its recent history. She wanted to make him happy, and her discomfort was a small price to pay. His smile beamed as he placed it ceremoniously on her finger. To her amusement, he finished off with a "Thank you." Of course, it was totally impractical for pretty much every task she could think of. She'd already ripped one tea towel, pulled a thread on her favourite trousers, scratched her smartphone, and nearly pulled her scalp off when the thing caught in her hair. But despite the hazard, there was a fondness for the item. Its sentimental value to Matt warmed her heart and, within a day or two, any association with Tim had disappeared from her mind. She often slid the ring off, just to read the inscription and gaze at the sweet little hearts. Something she'd never done during her short engagement to Tim. Her priority then was to just get rid of the thing.

She'd asked Matt if he had any photos of his grandparents. He promised to dig some out, but he hadn't got round to it yet. Mabel was top of her list for a daughter's name, but not wanting to jinx anything she hadn't mentioned it to Matt yet. Sidney seemed more like a girl's name to her, so another possibility. For a boy, she fancied something to reflect her Welsh heritage. Maybe Rhys, like her own paternal grandfather, or something way out there, like Gruffydd or Huwcyn. Though that might be a hard sell to a thoroughbred Englishman.

The doorbell rang, interrupting her daydream. She quickly dried her hands, pushed the ring back on her finger, and went out into the hallway. She opened the front door expecting a delivery man, but was confronted by the one person she did not want to see: Tim.

He flinched back, then froze, mouth open. Tim speechless—that was a first. But it didn't last long.

"Gem! What the fuck are you doing in Matt's house?"

She bit the bullet, "I live here." There seemed little point in denying the fact when she'd been caught in situ. And the Starlings were bound to get the information soon enough from Mrs Begood. Matt had arranged to have lunch with his mum next week, so he could tell her about their engagement and apologise for the white lie he had fed her previously. He wanted to speak to her alone, which Gemma was happy to go along with, given the speed at which things had happened.

"You're with Matt?"

"Yes."

Eyes narrowing, his jaw twisted. "Hmm, didn't think my cousin was one for revenge. Gotta hand it to him, he's done great—I'm well pissed off."

Her brow furrowed, "Cousin?"

"Yeah. Didn't you know? Matt's my cousin."

"Err..." She racked her brains. Matt had mentioned a cousin. It was he who had run off with his ex. But he never said that cousin was Tim. Or named his former fiancée. And he never said Tim Starling was a cousin or even that he was related to the Starlings. Why would he not mention that? "...no."

"Classic." He guffawed. "Mr Nice Guy, not such a goody-two-shoes after all. I think I'll go congratulate him on coming over to the dark side. Where is he?"

"Out in the fields," she mumbled.

"Where abouts?"

She couldn't think straight, couldn't speak. "Err..."

"Never mind. Sure I can find him. See you later."

He strode off across the yard to the track that led through the fields. She closed the door quietly, trying to process the conversation. Collapsed back against the wall as her stomach emigrated to New Zealand. A solitary tear trickled down her cheek. Legs jelly, she slid to the floor. No wonder it had been so easy for Matt to retrieve her bag; the Starlings were family. He'd been well keen to know all about her relationship with Tim. And he'd positively encouraged her to leave him. All the disparaging remarks. Insinuating Tim was cheating on her. That G-string probably was Bella's, just as Tim had claimed. And Matt knew it! It all made sense. Tim was the cousin Matt's ex had run off with. And now Matt was getting revenge by bedding her. Even the insistence on washing her clothes, the first time they met, was a ruse to get her back to his house and give him a second chance of hooking up. The cottage—just another plot to get into her bed. Flaunting his body in front of her when he could have easily done his sawing elsewhere. Why else would he lie to his mother about her identity? He obviously didn't want Mrs Begood to know he was up to no good. And that would be why he didn't want her to come to lunch with them next week; talking about their engagement wasn't even on the agenda. He was even trying to get her pregnant, so Tim would never want her back. No wonder he was so keen to seal the deal. *The bastard. How could he?*

She tugged off the ring and stared at the ruby. The realisation hit her like a ton of bricks, "Bloody shitty aarghhh toe-rag!" Tim hadn't bought the jewellery in Guildford. For some reason or other, the ring had been left with him by Bella when he threw her out. Talk about cheapskate. He'd just given her what he had to hand. Both of them! She hurled the ring down the hallway. It bounced off the tiled floor, spun into the kitchen, and wedged itself under the fridge door.

Her head spinning, she ran upstairs to the spare room, grabbed her suitcases, and dragged them into the main bedroom. She flung the biggest case on the bed and unzipped it. Blinking away the

tears, she spun to face the chest of drawers. She
yanked on the top pair of handles, jumping back
as the drawer crashed to the floor. She scooped
up the contents and dumped them into the case.
Then rifled through the wardrobe, again flinging
her clothes into the bag. Once a sufficient pile had
accumulated, she squashed down the contents and
zipped the case. The smaller suitcase she wheeled
into the bathroom and chucked in her toiletries and
towels. A bottle of shampoo burst open, spilling its
mint-green contents over her belongings. "Arghhh!"
She smashed the refillable onto the floor, splattering
the slippery liquid everywhere.

***

The staircase was too narrow to carry both suitcases,
so she kicked the larger one off the top of the
landing. It bounced down the stairs and crashed into
the front door opposite. She didn't bat an eyelid at
the massive gouge in the paintwork as she rushed
past into the sitting room.

First stop was the coffee table, where she grabbed
the Williamses' family photo album. The one she
and Matt had shared a laugh over the previous
evening. Then she dropped to the floor to rifle
through the Blu-rays stacked against the ancient
chest of drawers (used as a tv stand), searching for
her own. She piled eight on top of the album, then
picked the whole lot up. As she stood, her eyes fell
on the wedding photograph on the shelf. She shifted
her collection of possessions into one arm, picked
up the picture, and examined it closely. It definitely
looked like Matt. Same hairstyle. Same pockmarked
skin. Her brow furrowed. Did the identical twin
even exist? Or was it just another lie to add to all
the others? What she needed was a group photo.
She left the room to abandon her pile by the front

door. Then returned to rampage through the room, tipping out the drawers of the coffee table and chest. Her hands brushed through the contents, scattering them across the rug. Some paperwork shot off under the sofa. A pen rolled across the floor and hit the pile of logs stacked next to the fireplace. But she didn't care; she had found what she was looking for: framed in off-white cardboard and embossed with a gold band that met at a cluster of hearts at the top. She studied the photo. There he was, in the middle, with his bride. She searched through the guests, pointing at each one in turn; to be sure no one was missed. There was not anyone even close in looks.

There was NO twin.

# THIRTY-FOUR

A smiling Matt was loading the first maincrop potatoes onto the trailer. A great crop despite the hot weather. He couldn't wait to get back to the house to cook some up and serve them to Gem for her approval. Perhaps oven-baked with a dollop of the chilli leftover from their camping trip? Maybe not. He wanted her to taste the potatoes. Simply roasted in rosemary and olive oil with no accompaniment to detract from the flavours? He quite fancied a big plate of chips with lashings of homemade tomato sauce himself. Perhaps not the gastronomic experience he was aiming for...

As he heaved up a crate, his eyes flicked across the field. "Shit." His cousin was hopping across the dry lumpy mud towards him. Tim on dirt was a bad sign in itself. But there was no sign of Gem so, with any luck, he hadn't been to the house. Or she had the sense not to answer the door. Good thing her car was parked in a barn... but were the doors shut? He shoved the crate onto the trailer and dusted off his hands. He stood still and faced his rival. *If he'd seen her...*

The lean six-foot-two man strode right up to him. The fist shot out, smashed into his left eye, and...

\*\*\*

"Ow, ow, ow." The pain broke through the fogginess. He tried to open his eyes, but only one was willing. The other was swollen, congealed, and sending daggers through his brain. What had happened? He remembered Tim walking up to him, but then nothing. But even in his swimmy state, he could join the dots. "Gem!"

He staggered to his feet... stumbled across the fields... threw up on the track...

He lurched into the farmhouse, "GEM... GEM!"

Silence.

He glanced in the sitting room. A mess. Ran upstairs. Spinning into the bedroom, dizziness hit and he dropped to all fours. Drawers were emptied over the floor. Discarded clothes lay dishevelled across the bed. His stomach churned. Using the doorframe, he hauled himself to his feet. "Water." He tottered to the bathroom. Slipped upon entry. Slid to the sink. Gulped the water straight from the tap, then soaked his flannel. He pressed the cold terrycloth to his eye. Perched on the edge of the bathtub and took out his phone.

He called Gem.

He called Tim, though it pained him to think she may have left with his cousin.

Neither answered.

He tried again and again. Sent texts. Left messages. Eventually a text from Tim: «*Stop harassing me*»

«*Just tell me, is Gem with you?*»

«*Not yet*»

What the hell did that mean? Was Tim still hoping for a reconciliation? Was she on her way to him? He texted Tim again, but his number was now blocked.

Facebook? Being only a business user of the app, he had never thought to connect with Gem before. Finding her profile was easy enough, but her account was private so he flung off a friend request, not particularly hopeful of approval. He downloaded Instagram. Same result. He couldn't find her at all in LinkedIn. This was getting him nowhere and probably wouldn't reveal her current location anyway.

He removed the compress. Soaked red, he dropped it in the bath. He ran to the kitchen, retrieved the first aid kit from the cupboard, and strapped a cotton wool pad against his bloody eye with a bandage. He grabbed his keys and dashed out of the house, slamming the door behind him. Jumped in the jeep and headed off towards Guildford.

# THIRTY-FIVE

Gemma's phone rang on the seat next to her, taunting her in her misery. She'd been driving aimlessly around the countryside for at least two hours now, cursing Matt. Cursing Tim. Cursing men in general. She fumbled for the tissue on her lap. Wiped her eyes. Blew her nose. Then chucked the soggy mess in the passenger footwell.

Sniffing, she pulled into a lay-by and rummaged around the glove box for more tissues. The phone rang again. She picked it up and read the name. Swiped to reject. Then tapped on the missed calls history: Matt, Matt, Matt, Matt, Matt... The text messages weren't much better; pleas for her to answer his calls.

She got out of the car, walked around the bonnet to the verge, and hurled the phone far into the scrubby bushes. Fists on hips, she snorted. "That'll teach him."

The phone rang yet again; this time muffled by its new surroundings.

"BASTARD!"

She marched back to the car. Slammed the door shut and settled back in her seat. Both hands gripping the steering wheel, she stared at the road in front. Where to head to? Where the hell was she, anyway? She glanced at the verge. Perhaps she'd been a bit hasty with throwing her phone away. Should have just blocked his number. She reached for the door handle. Her hand slapped back on the wheel, "SOD IT!" She couldn't be arsed with scrambling about in the bushes. In any case, there wasn't anything to stop him using a different number. No, best off without it.

She started the car and checked the battery display. A quarter charge left. Find the nearest town and locate a hotel. Start looking for a job and a place to live tomorrow.

"Buy a new phone."

# THIRTY-SIX

There were no cars in the driveway when Matt pulled in. He rang the doorbell several times, but no one came. He tried to get round the back of the house, but the side gate was locked. Placing his ear against the wood, he listened. Not a sound. He peered in the garage window. No cars there either. No one was home.

He sat back down in his jeep. Maybe Tim had gone to his parents? He found the number in his contacts and called them.

"Hi, Matt."

"Hi, Jenny. Is Tim there?"

"No. He was here for lunch but left ages ago. Did he not pop in to see you?"

"Um... briefly."

"So, you're going for a drink sometime?"

"Err... I need to speak to him about that." Talk about digging a hole, but he couldn't bring himself to say what had really happened to his sweet gentle auntie.

"Don't you have his number?"

"Err... no." Another fib to add to the pit, but telling her Tim had blocked him from calling would require too much explanation.

"I'll text it to you."

"Thanks."

"Don't be a stranger, Matt. Pop by sometime."

"Will do. Maybe next week?"

"That would be nice."

"OK. Bye." He ended the call somewhat abruptly. He didn't have the time to get drawn into a lengthy conversation and Jenny was almost as bad as his mum for chatting.

*Where the hell are they?* Tim couldn't have whisked Gem off to some luxury hotel, could he? A treat to woo her. Celebrate their reuniting. Matt banged his head hard onto the steering wheel at the thought of them in bed together. A pain shot through his injured eye, so he sat back up to think. It was Sunday. Tim would have work tomorrow. They both would. Tim was always busy. Gem was in the middle of an important audit. So, unlikely they could stay away more than a night. They would have to come back to Tim's house at some point. Gem might have her clothes with her, but Tim would need his suit.

A knock on the window made him jump. A policeman. He wound down the glass.

"We've had a report of someone acting suspiciously."

"Oh, probably me. Sorry. I'm just looking for my cousin. This is his house, but he doesn't appear to be in."

In front of the car, the policeman's colleague was checking his number plate whilst making a call.

"Your name?"

"Matthew Begood."

The man called to his colleague, "Matthew Begood?" The policewoman nodded back. "What happened to your eye?"

"Just an accident. Tripped over."

"Right. You might want to get it looked at. There's blood dripping all down your neck. Anyway, I suggest you move along, the neighbours are getting agitated. I would strongly advise you head for the hospital."

"Will do."

Matt waited for the police car to pull away before reversing out of the drive. He drove around the block four times before parking at the far end of the road. He could see Tim's driveway with his one good eye. Now it was just a matter of waiting. He couldn't decide whether he wanted Gem to arrive with his cousin or not. He didn't want her to be back with Tim, but at least he would know where she was. At least he could talk to her. Find out what lies Tim had fed her to make her leave so abruptly. His gut tightened as a thought hit him: maybe he had taken her by force. After all, Tim had once locked her in his walk-in wardrobe. And he'd frightened her the other day in town, so it wasn't beyond the realms of possibility. But, duress or not, why waste time emptying the drawers downstairs? Taking her clothes was understandable. But what on earth had they been looking for in the sitting room?

***

By 11pm the daylight had faded away to be replaced by the artificial glow of streetlamps. His left eye stung and itched. He restrained from rubbing, but he was beginning to regret not taking the policeman's advice. He would've had plenty of time to visit A&E but, of course, he didn't know that at the time.

The road lit up behind him, ignited by LED headlamps. A sleek coupe purred past and swung into Tim's drive. Matt edged his jeep closer and parked opposite. He wanted to know if Gem was with him before he made his move.

Tim got out first. Illuminated by the security light, he seemed cheerful and full of life as he darted around the back of the car to open the passenger door. Matt's heart sank.

The elegant legs swung out. They were almost as dark as the night and ended in extremely high heels. This wasn't Gemma. Matt exhaled. The tall, graceful woman exited the car. Tim shut the door, took her hand, and led her to the house. They kissed passionately on the doorstep whilst Tim fumbled with his keys; trying to open the door without taking his mouth off his lover.

Matt had to concede, Tim had great taste in women. Shame he treated them like shit. This one could be a catwalk model. Stunningly beautiful, pencil slim and equal to Tim in height. Like bees to a honeypot, his cousin never had any problems attracting women. Even at school, girls had fluttered about Tim trying to get his attention, whilst he himself had been the ugly spotty friend. The few girlfriends he had, during his teenage years, were the sidekicks of Tim's latest love. Feelings didn't come into it. It was probably why he always found it so difficult to start a new relationship; he always needed reassurance the person was with him for the right reasons. With Gem, it had been different. He was so head over heels in love with her, there hadn't been any reticence. Once he was sure she had left Tim, he had acted... and fast. A bit too much like Tim for his liking, but it had been an unstoppable force driving him on.

The lovers entered the house, still attached by the lips. Tim flung the woman against the wall, pulled up her dress. Matt turned away, "Close the door, man." Glanced back to see the door swing shut.

Gem had been adamant Tim would never cheat on her. But he knew different. The man had no morals. No concern for the feelings of others. If he wanted something, or someone, he took it. So, it wouldn't be surprising if Tim's association with this woman predated his breakup with Gem. The owner of the knickers? He was prepared to concede that particular G-string could well be Bella's. They certainly sounded like the sort of thing she would wear. But that didn't get Tim off the hook.

Anyway, that wasn't his problem. Gem wasn't here. Not even Tim would be such a cad as to bring another woman home with one already there... unless there was something funny going on. Could there be? He hadn't known Gem that long. No, he couldn't believe that. That was stupid. She had committed to him. Wanted to have his baby. And there was never any suggestion of her being into kinky shit. So, where the hell was she? Maybe she'd gone to her friend's. What was her name? Lisa? Louisa? Tim would know. He might know her address too.

***

He rang the doorbell. His hand went to his mouth. Perhaps this wasn't such a good idea. Tim wouldn't be happy with him interrupting his shenanigans. He stepped well away from the door. Having one usable eye left, he couldn't afford to lose that as well.

The door opened.

"What the fuck! I told you to stop harassing me."

"I'm just trying to find Gem."

"She's not here."

"Do you know where she is?" Tim started to close the door. Matt pushed back. "Please, Tim. Just give me some of her friends' details. Her parents?" Tim pushed harder. "Please. I'm begging you. Just the girl who does the drains. Just her phone number."

"Why should I? You ruined it for me."

"She'd already left you."

"Thanks to you."

"She was unhappy. I didn't do anything until it was over between you." He rammed his knee against the oak. His foot, now beyond the threshold, was in a precarious position.

Tim screamed in his face, "You didn't bloody well hang around though, did you? In there like a bloody shot. Didn't give me a chance to sort things out. All she needed was a bit of counselling, then we would've been back on track."

"There wasn't anything wrong with her."

"How would you know? You'd only just met her."

Matt paused. It was pointless arguing with the barrister. This is what Gem had been up against. He breathed deep, removed his leg but kept his hand pressed against the wood. Keeping his tone low, he pleaded, "I just need a phone number, Tim. And it looks like you've moved on, so please just give me something to go on."

"Spying on me, were you?" He waved his hand over his shoulder towards the staircase, "This means nothing. Just something to occupy me until I get Gem back. So, if there's any phone numbers to ring, I'll be ringing them. So, fuck off!"

With that, he slammed the door shut.

Matt traipsed back to his vehicle. He knew when he was beat. He would have to spend tomorrow visiting all the accountancy practices in Guildford. That was the trouble with new relationships—you didn't have all the details.

As he studied the map app for the best route to the local A&E, a taxi drew up outside Tim's. For a moment, he thought it was Gemma arriving and was about to leap out of the car. But then the striking woman left Tim's house, slamming the door behind her. Holding the straps of her high heels in one hand, she stomped barefoot down the drive, scowling. Opening the cab door, she turned towards the house and gave it the finger.

Matt smiled. That was something at least.

# THIRTY-SEVEN

Matt arrived back home at 4.10pm, smelling of yesterday's potatoes with added sweat. His clothes dishevelled and crumpled from the couple of hours of restless sleep in the A&E waiting room. He had finally seen the doctor at about four in the morning. A mirror was held up for him to view his bloodshot eyeball. A right mess. Until that point, he hadn't noticed the blood all over his cheek and down his neck, or the reddish-brown stains on his t-shirt. The hospital staff must have thought him a tramp who'd been in a fight. After careful examination, the doctor proclaimed, "Shouldn't be any lasting damage." She cleaned out the split above his eye, put in half a dozen stitches, and replaced the bandage with something more professional-looking. The dressing was the only clean thing on him.

His fingers scraped through his greasy hair as he stood in the doorway, staring into nothing, replaying the events of the last twenty-four hours or so. After getting sorted at the hospital, he had waited in a carpark until 9am before traipsing around Guildford. The time spent waiting in his jeep used productively, searching the internet for accountancy practices and putting them in some sort of order of size. PLC audits meant she must be employed by a substantial business. At lunchtime, he finally struck lucky—if you could call it that. The receptionist had heard of Gemma, but she hadn't turned up for work that day or even phoned in sick. Her boss was not happy. The only emergency contact they had for her was Tim. Fat lot of good that was to him.

He then went to the police station to report her missing. That went down like a ton of bricks:

"So, she left with a suitcase packed with clothes?"

"Yes."

"You do realise if we chased up every man or woman who has run out on their partner, we'd have no time to do anything else?"

He left before he got charged for wasting police time.

Now he was home. An empty house. No smiling, laughing Gemma to greet him after a hard day working in the fields. No one to cook for and share a meal. No one to playfully flick water over while they washed up together. No one to make love to.

Tears in his eyes, he slouched into the kitchen, grabbed the nearest glass off the dish rack and filled it with water from the tap. He rinsed out his stale mouth before gulping down the rest. What he really needed was a proper drink. He spun round. A beer. A cold one. Just four steps to the fridge, he grabbed the handle and tugged. The brain-slicing squeal made him wince. "Ow." He pressed his hand against his stitches. Shut the door and picked the offending article off the tiled floor. He placed the ring on the countertop and stared at the ruby. If only he had said it then; back when they had first met. Told her who Tim had got the ring from, maybe he wouldn't be in this mess right now.

He slumped down against the pine worktop, his head coming to rest on his lower arms, and wept.

# THIRTY-EIGHT

Reluctantly, Matt opened the front door. He didn't want to talk to her. He said as much over the phone, not half-an-hour ago, when she called to ask why he wasn't at the pub. He had totally forgotten about the lunch date with his mother. The one where he intended to come clean over his relationship with Gemma and who exactly she was. He was banking on their engagement pleasing her so much, she wouldn't dwell on the Tim aspect of Gem's past.

Her mouth dropped open as she studied his face. "You look a right state, Matty-moo. What happened to your eye?"

"I got thumped."

"By who?"

He blasted the air from his mouth. "Let's sit down." He headed for the kitchen. Shame there wasn't a longer route. His mum followed. He cleared the three beer bottles from the table and dropped them in the sink. He turned back. She handed him the dirty plate, frowning. "Do you want something to eat?"

"No. I want to know what's been going on?"

He dragged out a chair for her, then another for himself, opposite.

She sat down, "So, who hit you?"

"Tim."

Her brow furrowed, "Tim? Why?"

"He found out Gemma was here."

"His fiancée was here?"

"Ex-fiancée."

"Why was she here?"

"Why d'ya think?"

"Oh! Matthew, you haven't stolen his girlfriend, have you?"

"Ex-girlfriend. And no, she'd already left him."

"But she only disappeared a month ago. When did you start dating her?"

"About then."

"So, you started dating his girlfriend..."

"Ex-girlfriend."

"...straight after she left him?"

"Yes."

"And she moved in?"

"Yes."

"When?"

"She moved into one of the barn cottages first."

"With Geraldine?"

"Err, she is Geraldine."

"I thought Tim's fiancée was called Gemma."

"Ex-fiancée. Yes, she's called Gemma. Geraldine is Gemma."

"So, I tried to set you up on a date with someone you were already seeing?"

"Yes."

She grabbed a farming magazine off the table and whacked him over the head, "Why the bloomin' secrecy?"

"I didn't want Tim to find out she was here. He'd been harassing her. Going to her office and stuff."

"Well, he's upset. Jenny says he's desperate to find her."

"She doesn't want to get back with him."

"So, where is she now?"

"She's left. Tim said something to her. I don't know what exactly, I wasn't present."

"So, is she back with Tim now?"

"No. She's disappeared…. I can't find her, Mum. I don't know what to do. I love her."

"You might be better off without her. Sounds a bit flippity. What sort of woman leaves a man and the next day takes up with another?"

"It's not like that. We're in love. The forever kind of love. There was chemistry right from our first meeting. I want to spend the rest of my life with her. I just can't bloody well find her."

"Don't swear, Matthew. Have you tried her parents?"

"I don't have any details other than they live in Wales."

"Directory enquiries?"

"I've tried that, but their surname is Williams, so that's like half the bloomin' population. I don't even know whereabouts in Wales they are."

His mother sat back to stare out of the window for a minute. "No idea how I'm going to explain this to Jenny and Gerald."

"Tim might have told them already."

"Are you going to press charges over your eye?"

"No."

"I'd stick by you if you did, you know. As they say, blood is thicker than water and they're not my blood relatives. They are yours though, so think carefully."

"I'm not going to. I've already decided."

She sighed, "I know you don't want to hear this, but I really think you should cut your losses. She wouldn't have left if she truly loved you."

Best not mention they'd got engaged and were trying for a baby. His mother was still holding the magazine. "I'm sure it was a misunderstanding."

"Still, I'm not sure I like the sound of this girl. She moved in with Tim pretty quick too. I think it was like a week or two after they met. Serial… manizer. Is that even a word? How can you possibly ever trust a girl like that? No, I think both you and Tim are better off without her. You'll get over her. You've survived breakups before... of relationships that lasted much longer."

"You don't understand. I've never felt this way before. Kate and Bella were nothing in comparison to this. I'm not giving up until I find her. If I have to knock on every door in Wales, I will."

"It's a right mess, Matthew. That's what it is, a right mess! I think I'll pop round and see if I can catch Jenny on her own. See what she knows. See if she's still speaking to me." She glared at him. "You remember I'm off to Australia on Thursday?" He nodded. "I'll probably stay until the end of the year. Then I can help them pack ready for their move back. Will you be OK?"

He forced a nod. Partly because he didn't want her to worry and partly because he didn't want her to cancel her trip and stay if she was going to be so negative about Gem. He was on his own in this, but he would do whatever it took to get the love of his life back.

# THIRTY-NINE

The Juliet balcony of her rented flat provided an ideal location for breakfast. Bathed in the early morning sun, she tucked into the oat bran and strawberries. On her spoon was a squishy, moldy fruit. *Shame to waste it.* Grimacing, she forced herself to swallow the slimy berry. Then followed with mouthfuls of fresh fruit to clear the taste away.

The rest of the meal was eaten at a leisurely pace as she surveyed the street. Her block of brand-new apartments was situated at the end of a residential road of Victorian townhouses. She eyed the characterful neighbouring properties with envy. Most of them had been divided into flats and she would've loved to have rented one, but she'd been unable to find a tenancy at such short notice. So, she was stuck in this tiny studio apartment instead, for at least the six-month length of the lease.

Being Sunday, there was little activity except for the odd person walking their dog. As she swallowed the final mouthful of oat bran, nausea swept through. She rushed to the bathroom, but the food refused to re-emerge. She lay down on the cold tiles to wait until her stomach settled.

Three weeks had passed since she first drove into Reading. She'd been lucky to find a position as an audit senior within a few days of arrival. Checking over the records of listed companies wasn't her number one choice in the world of accountancy. In fact, she found it thoroughly boring. She'd much rather deal with small businesses, but needs must, so she'd gone ahead and accepted the offer. At least it would give an immediate income until she found something else. The position was temporary—cover for a lady on maternity leave. She snorted. Wouldn't it be ironic if she herself were pregnant? It was certainly a possibility. She and Matt were trying for a family, and it must be five or six weeks since her last period. That had been a bit of a blink and miss it affair which she'd put down to all the stress over leaving Tim. She scratched her head. After their walk at Kingley Vale but before they went to Chichester for that meal. So, sometime early July. If only she had her old phone, she could've checked her calendar. Of course, the missed period could all be down to angst. Just as July's had been unusually light due to Tim troubles, August's could have been non-existent because of Matt woes. Without warning, a surge of bile shot up her gullet. She gagged, spraying the floor with a lumpy concoction dotted with strawberry pink. She spewed out a few more acrid dribbles before relaxing onto her back.

"What if I am? Do I keep it?"

If she were going to stick to her new rule of no more men, then this might be her only chance of motherhood. Supporting herself was not a problem. She had an excellent CV and never had any problem finding work. She would have to take minimal maternity leave; wait until the baby's about to drop and go back after a few weeks. It would be hard financially until her child reached school age, what with the nursery fees. Then there would be the after-school club to pay for. Maybe she should go freelance? Set up her own practice and work from home. She's got the skills. She just needed the clients. She would have to continue with the temping until she had enough work of her own.

She crawled into the main room, dragged out the storage file from behind the sofa, and rifled through the sections.

"Ahh, here it is."

She pulled out the document—her agency employment contract—and read through the terms carefully, looking for any clause forbidding her to do her own work on the side. There was a clause preventing her from stealing clients from her employer and another blocking her from hijacking potential clients, but nothing about working for herself. She read it through a second time, just to be sure. Satisfied her plan wasn't thwarted, she stared out of the window. Once she had saved enough, she could buy that dream property. She grabbed her laptop off the sofa and plonked herself down in its place. She typed 'smallholdings for sale UK' in the browser and clicked on the most promising search result. The lowest price on the estate agent's website was £175k for four acres of pasture and a house 'with potential'. In other words, derelict. If she managed to save an optimistic £10k a year, that would take her seventeen odd years. But, if she continued with the accountancy work, she could get a mortgage. That would mean she would just need a deposit. Why, oh why did she ever pay for Tim's damn kitchen! If she scrimped and saved maybe she could raise the down payment in three or four years... assuming prices didn't rise too much in the meantime.

"I can do it. I'm a twenty-first-century woman. I don't need no man."

# FORTY

Louise hugged her in the doorway, before wandering around the small flat; checking it out for the first time. Gemma's best friend opened the door to the only cupboard. "Hmm," she frowned, confronted by a stack of white goods (washing machine and dryer) with a hoover squeezed in the gap to the side. "I was thinking this was the door to the bedroom but evidently not." Gemma chuckled. "So... where is the door to the bedroom?"

"There isn't one. Studio flat."

"But it's so tiny.... Is there a pull-down bed somewhere?" Her friend scanned the walls of the L-shaped room.

"Sofa bed," replied Gemma, giving a nod to the side as she flopped onto the seat.

"Oh, right. Makes sense seeing as there's no room for much else. It's tiny. But there's only one of you, I suppose?"

Gemma didn't answer. She hadn't reckoned on going into the big reveal this early on in their get together. She doubted her forthright friend would be that impressed with her getting into this predicament. And, if she were going to get a telling off, she would rather leave it until as late as possible.

Anyway, it was obvious what Louise was digging at, so there was no need to go into that right now.

"Someone new?"

"No," Gemma retorted, folding her arms, "and there's not going to be either. I've had enough of men. I'm staying single forever."

"Do you want a cat for your birthday?"

She laughed, "No, I do not."

Louise pulled out a dining chair and sat down opposite. "So, what happened with Matt? I thought he was the bee's knees. Mr Right."

Gemma slumped back into the cushions, "I thought so too. Turned out it was all a lie. He was just using me to get back at Tim."

"You don't half pick 'em, Gem. You know Tim still wants you back, don't you? He's being a right pest. Keeps phoning me."

"You won't tell him where I am, will you?"

"No, I've already promised you that. Dad's been fully instructed too, so Tim won't get anything out of him if he tries phoning our business line." She sucked in her cheeks. "Why don't you go back to him? He clearly loves you very much if he's willing to overlook your... err... transgression."

"I'm not interested in getting back with Tim."

"You were good together."

"He was stifling me."

"You shouldn't have let him boss you around. Any fella of mine would be out on his ear if he told me what to do. You could go back to him on condition he behaves. Lets you have a say in things." Gemma shook her head. "Why not? He was a lovely bloke apart from that and his OCD."

*Ha!* An opportunity to change the subject. "I found out what caused that."

"Yeah? What?"

"He fell in a slurry pit when he was a teenager. Made him really sick. He was in hospital for ages."

"Oooo, no wonder he treats me like the plague. He must think I don't shower or something."

"Probably thinks you don't shower enough. Once doesn't hack it for him. You need to be thoroughly sterilized, heat-treated, and soaked in bleach."

"Maybe I'll hold off on the hugs next time I see him. If I see him again, that is?" she framed her last sentence as a question. Then raised her eyebrows with a jerk of her head.

"You won't see him again. Ever. Can we change the subject, please?"

Louise sighed. "OK. What do you want to talk about?"

Gemma whispered, unsure of the likely reaction, "I'm having a baby." There was silence. "I'm pleased."

Her friend rubbed the back of her neck, "Well, congratulations then, I suppose. Tim's or Matt's?"

"Matt's."

"Have you told him?"

"No. Not going to."

"You shouldn't let him get out of paying child maintenance."

"I don't want his money and I don't want to see him ever again. If he knows he's got a kid, he might want access, maybe even custody. It would be a nightmare. Best he doesn't know."

"Do you want me to sound out Tim?"

"No, I do NOT want you to sound out Tim."

"He might still have you back. Raise the kid as his own."

Gemma snorted. "He doesn't want kids. Anyway, that's beside the point, I don't want him. Can you please drop it, Lou."

Her friend nodded. "What will you do?"

"I'll stay here until I've saved enough to buy a smallholding."

"Still sticking to your dream then?"

"Yes."

"What about your parents? Have you told them about the baby yet?"

"They're coming down for a few days next week. I'll tell them then."

"Maybe they'll ask you to go and live with them." Gemma grimaced. "I thought you loved your parents?"

"I do, but that doesn't mean I want to move back in with them. Would you want to move back in with your mum and dad?"

"No fear."

"We're both far too old to be living at home, anyway."

"Speak for yourself, Gem. I'm only twenty-eight. You're the one hitting the big three-o soon."

"Don't remind me."

"So, no to a cat. Cot? Pushchair?"

"What I'd really like is some books. James Herbert or Stephen King."

"Horror? That's a bit of a change for you. What happened to Romance?"

"It died a horrible death. Reading love stories is like rubbing salt in a wound; just makes me miserable. I never got my happy ending."

"You still might."

She glowered at Louise and bristled, "Not with Tim."

# FORTY-ONE

Matt drove through the country roads. His eyes were not turned by nature's artwork of orange, bronze and yellow. He did not see the Welsh Mountain sheep scampering along the edge of the moorland verges. The mountains of Snowdonia, looming high in the distance, held no interest to him. Not even a signpost caught his attention.

Arriving in a village, he parked in front of the Post Office, bumping his front wheel over the kerb. He didn't bother to straighten up, but jerked the handbrake hard and turned off the ignition. He picked up his mobile and, keeping it in his hand, jumped out of the jeep. He scanned the surroundings for pedestrians. The street was empty except for a rather scrappy-looking cat trotting along the pavement towards him. The moggy tried to gain favour by rubbing itself against his legs, but he didn't have the time nor inclination to respond to the overly friendly gesture. Instead, he pushed the annoyance away with his foot and headed into the Post Office, which turned out to be a general store as well.

There were just three people in the shop. Nearest was a stout woman of some years, dressed in a thick beige jumper, jeans, and walking boots. The rucksack on her back wobbled as she bent to examine a basket of red apples. She selected two, then walked to the sandwich section, where she commenced a debate with a man of similar age over which fillings to choose.

"Um, sorry to interrupt..." The couple turned to face him. "I'm looking for a woman called Gemma Williams. She's thirty years old but looks younger." He held up the photo displayed on his phone, "Have you seen her? Or know her family? Her parents live in Wales. Not sure where though."

He held his breath as the pair studied the portrait.

"Sorry, not seen her. We're holidaymakers so don't know anyone round here," the woman replied.

Exhaling, he nodded.

"The shop assistant might be more help," the well-spoken man suggested.

"Thanks. I'll ask her now."

He trudged away towards the till. A head of brunette hair bobbed up and down behind the counter accompanied by the clinking of bottles. For a second, his spirits lifted.

"Gemma?"

The girl jumped up, "Sorry, sir. What did you say?"

"Err, sorry. Thought you were someone else." He showed her his phone, "This girl here. Gemma Williams. Do you know her? Or of her?"

"No, 'fraid not. Can't think of a Gemma round here. Um... did you want to buy something?"

"Err..." His eyes flicked to the display behind the girl. "I'll have a bottle of that whisky on offer, please."

She pointed at the litre bottle, "This one?"

He nodded, then scanned further along the back wall, "And a pack of beer."

"What sort?"

"Any will do. I'll leave it up to you."

The girl picked a multipack of eighteen cans from the bottom shelf, and shoved them on the counter, "OK?"

Matt nodded, then grabbed a handful of chocolate and raisin cereal bars from a counter display, "These too."

As she rang up the items on the till, he gazed at the whisky, biting on his lower lip. Should he get another? She'd think him a drunk... but he wouldn't be coming back this way, so what did it matter?

"Actually, I'll take another bottle of this while I'm here."

The girl smiled and reached behind for a second bottle of spirits as he took out his wallet.

"Do you need a bag?"

"No, I'm fine. Car's outside."

"Card or cash?"

"Card."

She nudged the card reader towards him. He pushed his debit card into the slot and tapped in his PIN.

'CARD DECLINED' flashed on the screen, just as the holidaymakers came up behind him.

"Maybe you typed the PIN wrong?" suggested the assistant.

Matt tried again though he was pretty sure that wasn't the reason. "No, still not working.... I'll try my credit card."

The heat sweeping across his cheeks, he fumbled in his wallet for the replacement. He mentally crossed his fingers as he typed in the PIN. If this didn't work, he would be well and truly stuck in the middle of nowhere once his fuel ran out. He had no cash left to fall back on. His current account overdraft facility had just maxed out. His mother was still in Australia. He only had a small circle of close friends; none of who he felt comfortable calling upon for monetary assistance except for Ash.

But his oldest friend (discounting Tim) had his own money worries right now. The pub Ash bought on a whim two years ago was struggling to make a profit and was in desperate need of an overhaul to bring it up to date. Ash had asked him if he would like to invest in the business, to which he'd had to say no. He just didn't have the cash to do that as well as his own projects on the farm. So, asking Ash for a loan was out of the question and the landlord would be too busy to drive to Wales to rescue him in person.

That left his closest relatives—the Starlings. And they were still seething over him 'stealing' Tim's fiancée, despite the fact Gerald didn't even seem that keen on the vegan accountant. He had a massive argument with his uncle over that point. Both his aunt and Gerald would not accept his claim that Gemma had already left Tim before he made his move.

In his anger, he'd blasted Gerald, "You don't even like the girl. And if that's the case, you should be grateful for me spiriting her away—if that's what you're going to insist happened."

Gerald shouted back, "It's the principle of the thing—you do NOT make a move on your cousin's girlfriend whatever the circumstances."

"What about Tim and Bella? Never heard you complain about that!"

"In public! Don't think for one minute, I didn't give Tim an earful for that. My son's a total shit. Doesn't mean you have to be one too!"

They hadn't spoken since. Surprisingly, even the usually sociable Auntie Jenny hadn't broken the vow of silence. Matt suspected that was down to her husband rather than choice.

The upshot of it all was he had no one he could ask for help. And the machine was taking a ridiculously long time to approve his card...

"Connection's not very reliable," encouraged the girl.

He nodded, sucking in his lips. Made a pile of his purchases, despite the distinct possibility of having to return them to the shelves.

'APPROVED' appeared on the screen.

*Phew*. He sighed as the receipt printed. He duly took the slip, picked up the booze and bars, and turned to leave the shop.

"Have a good day, sir."

He left quickly, without responding. He was NOT having a good day and he couldn't see it getting any better. He'd not had a good day, a good week or a good month since Gemma left. He dumped his purchases onto the front passenger seat, negotiated the cat that was still loitering on the driver's side, and climbed in. He slammed the door shut, which frightened the cat; it shot off across the road and through a hedge.

He paused, hands on the wheel. The sky was starting to darken. Where to try next? Maybe one last pub before calling it a night. He tapped the maps icon on his phone. There was a hostelry about a mile further up the road. It did bed-and-breakfast too. Fingers crossed, they'd have a room free; he was fed up with sleeping in the jeep and he might not be welcome in the bar without a shower first.

***

He flopped onto the four-poster bed. King-sized, the springy mattress was perfect for a romantic break. Shuffling up to the pillows, he scanned the room. The quaintly battered furniture was at home in the olde worlde pub. Just the sort of thing Gemma loved: hundreds of years old and still in use. If she were there, they would have lit the open fire, dropped the duvet and multitude of cushions on the floor, and made love in the warmth of the flickering flames. But he was on his own. The dreaming only added to his misery.

He chucked the scatter cushions on the floor—what else was he supposed to do with them? Someone like Tim would have a fit upon realising such furnishings spent half their life on the carpet. A carpet stomped on by outdoor shoes to boot. Then the grubby cushions ended up against the next guest's nice clean linen. He seriously doubted they were washed between each occupant, if ever. Surprising Tim even ventured into hotels—he sneered—unless he took his own sheets. God, he hated that man. What lies did he feed Gem to make her leave so abruptly? There must be more to it than being his cousin.

Throat thickening, he swallowed. Crossed his arms over his thumping forehead. "Gemma... oh, Gemma... where are you?"

Before seeking refuge in the bedroom, he had visited the bar. Fought to order a pint and a burger from the beer-stained counter, before making the rounds. The place was crowded, but mainly with walkers on holiday. The tourists didn't welcome the unkempt man interrupting their cosy meals. Hardly glancing at the photo, they waved him away, with a "No, sorry." The few locals present had no knowledge of his love. Talk about searching for a needle in a haystack. She could be anywhere in Wales. Well, in fact, she might not even be in this part of the UK. He was relying on bumping into her parents or someone who knew the family.

When she first left, he tried working his way through the phone book. But that drew a blank. Maybe they were ex-directory? He didn't want to look at the phone bill. Certainly, the direct debit hadn't gone through, because of the red letters that had dropped on his doormat. He hadn't opened them. Nor had he checked his bank account for months. Business email and Facebook—he was too scared to view. He must have majorly pissed off all his customers. But that was the least of his worries right now. The only thing that mattered was finding Gemma and putting things right.

Rolling to the edge of the bed, he reached down to the whisky bottle smuggled in within his bag of clothes. He unscrewed the top and took a long swig. Rested the rim on his lips. If Gem were pregnant with his child... she would be starting to show by now. Might even be feeling movement. And he was missing it all. He gulped down three mouthfuls. "Gemma, Gemma, please come back to me. Please, come back." But his phone didn't ring. There was no rap at the door. A pebble didn't crack on the window. She wasn't coming. His lips trembled around the glass. The thought of never seeing her again... never feeling her soft body against his, never hearing that giggle... never seeing his child grow up... what life was that? Not one worth living. He knocked back the alcohol...

# FORTY-TWO

Her hand soothed the bump as the six-month-old alien within did a few somersaults before settling. An appendage now formed a little hummock on her right side. She prodded with her forefinger. The baby kicked back. She smiled. The short interruption over, Gemma went back to work; reconciling the bank receipts to the sales invoices listed out in the spreadsheet.

Her mini accountancy practice was going well. She'd gained quite a few new clients over the winter months as the tax return deadline of 31st January crept ever closer. She was keeping it a strictly online affair, so clients wouldn't be put off by her expanding tummy. This also meant she could easily relocate the business to another part of the country when the time came. The maternity cover job ceased two months ago, and she was now doing three days a week temping and four days her own work. She took no time off as she needed to make as much money as possible before the baby came.

Now mid-January, she had three months of relative quietness on the business front to look forward to, starting next month. The baby was due in the third week of April so, as long as she only took a couple of weeks leave, she would be back at work in plenty of time for the summer deluge. In the meantime, she had plenty of company accounts to get on with.

The doorbell sounded, startling her. There were few visitors to her Reading flat: just her parents and her best friend, Louise. She wasn't expecting any of them today and she hadn't ordered anything online. Maybe it was a delivery for one of the other flats?

She clicked on 'save', grabbed the multi-coloured crochet throw that was draped over the sofa, and went out into the communal corridor. She swaddled herself in the blanket before opening the front door. A blast of ice-cold air hit her, then rebounded in frostiness towards her visitor.

"Gemmie."

Tim gave one of his best smiles; rehearsed to within a millimetre of perfection. She remained quiet.

"Can I come in? It's cold out here." He stamped his feet and rubbed his gloved hands together to prove the point.

"I don't want to talk to you." She pushed the door, but he slapped his hand on the wood, bringing it to an abrupt halt.

"Gemma, please. I've come all this way. Just let me say my piece. Please," he pleaded.

Baring his gleaming teeth, he made the most forlorn face ever. She couldn't help but take pity.

"Five minutes. Then you leave."

He nodded.

She let go of the door and walked back into her flat. Both doors slammed behind her as she headed for the sofa. She turned. Tim removed his coat and started dusting off the snow. *Yeah, thanks, mate. Make me floor all wet.* Discarding the throw, she collapsed back into the comfy cushions and rested her hands on her protruding stomach.

How had he got her address? Her parents would never have given it out; she'd got that promise from them and they weren't ones to break their word. Tim arranged his wool coat over the back of the dining chair. Adjusted it twice. Smoothed out the sleeves. She drummed her fingers on her bulge. That left Louise. No, she could trust her. Who else knew where she had moved to? She'd given her parents' address to her old employer, so it wasn't them. That left Louise's dad?

"How did you find me?"

"Private detective," he answered as he sat on the chair to take off his shoes.

"Seriously?"

"He followed your parents from Wales last week. Worked a treat. Wish I thought of it sooner." He centred the shoes under the chair. Stood and finally looked in her direction. "Gem...ma..." his voice drifted off. His eyes remained fixed on her stomach. "You're pregnant?"

"Yes."

Mouth open, he stared. His voice cracked, "It's not mine, is it?"

"It can't be, can it," she bristled, crossing her arms.

He jerked back. "What?... Oh...." He rubbed the back of his neck. "Who told you? Matt?" She nodded. "God, he's really got it in for me." His mouth twisted as he studied the floor. He faced her again, "Is it his?" She nodded. "Does he know?"

She shook her head. "Please don't tell him. I don't want anything to do with him." He nodded before dropping into the sofa beside her. "Have you had any contact with him?"

"Not since the day you left."

"So, you've not seen him at any family get-togethers?"

"Nope."

"Not even at Christmas?"

"Nope."

"Don't you see your aunt over Christmas?"

"She was away. Anyway, why are you so bloody interested? Thought you were over him."

"I am. Just wondering if he said anything about me."

"Well, ain't seen him, so no idea."

"What about your parents?"

"Jeez, girl, stop nagging. They're not talking, thanks to you. Got it?"

"Oh."

He plonked his feet on the coffee table and stretched his arms up and over his head. *Make yourself at home, mate.*

"So..." She kicked off her slippers and put her feet up next to his. Wished she hadn't—her big toe was poking out. "Err... what did you want to say?"

Bringing his arms back down, he puffed his cheeks, then popped the air out. "I was hoping to persuade you to come back to me." He nodded towards her belly, "But that kind of changes everything. If it were mine, I might still consider it. But as it's not—no way am I bringing up someone else's stinking brat." There was an uncomfortable silence. "Then again, thinking about it, a family might be good for my political career. The selection committee said as much..." Not knowing what to say to that, she let him continue vocalising his rambling thoughts. "...It would have to be registered as mine, of course. Though, I suppose there might be some extra kudos for bringing up someone else's kid. Bit odd that it's my cousin's though, so probably best to keep quiet. Don't want a scandal. Can you keep your mouth shut, Gem?"

"I can hardly open it at the moment." He turned to face her. "There's one major flaw in your plan, Tim."

"What's that?"

"I don't want to get back with you."

His smile dazzled, "I can work on that."

She shook her head. "And you would have to be a proper dad. Change nappies. Read stories. Play silly buggers. And not complain about the messy finger marks all over your lovely house."

His bottom lip curled down, "Yuggh," but was soon replaced by a cheeky grin. With a mischievous glint in his eyes, he whispered in her ear, "Have you thought about adoption?"

She suppressed the laugh, pulling in her lips. Incorrigible Tim. A serious suggestion dressed up as a joke. The manipulative sod. If she exploded, he'd claim 'just teasing'. She knew his game... and it was bloomin' hilarious now she'd wised up. He nudged her. Her lips pressed harder as her body quaked.

He nudged again, "Go on, laugh. You know you want to."

"Do not."

He tickled her side.

She giggled, "Don't, Tim. I'll have to go to the loo."

"You're no fun anymore."

"Well, that's no concern of yours now, is it?"

"I don't know—"

"Just go, will you. It's over between us."

"But I only made the one mistake. You know, at my parents' house. And I was just having a laugh. I didn't mean any harm. Your reaction was way over the top."

"You just sat there laughing."

"It was funny."

"For you, maybe. It was plain awkward for me. You should've come to my rescue."

"What was I supposed to do?"

"I don't know. Tell your dad off. Get me some clean water. Something! Not just sit there having hysterics."

"I thought you handled it pretty well. Well, until you walked out. I wasn't laughing then, I can tell you."

She stopped herself from commenting on what happened next. His amusement at her traversing the muck strewn yard. His distinct lack of effort in chasing after her. Yes, she now knew why he hadn't negotiated the stinking sludge himself, but he could've gone back through the house and out the front door. Instead, he entertained himself further by filming her difficulties. There had been no support. No sympathy. No apology. And he still didn't get it. He never would, so pointless arguing further. She changed tact.

"You didn't tell me you'd had a vasectomy."

"I didn't think you wanted kids, so it wasn't relevant."

"But you didn't even say anything when I told you I did. If you're going to marry someone, you should at least give them all the facts. It's deceitful. What were you going to do when we started trying for a family? Pretend you were infertile?"

"I was never going to agree to having kids, so we would never have got to that stage."

Her fists clenched, digging her nails into her palms, "You don't realise, do you?"

"What?"

"That you never let me have a say in anything. Holidays, restaurants, day trips... wedding venue. Kids. It was always what you wanted; you never consulted me."

"I am a bit of a bossy so and so. You should have said something."

"I did. Plenty of times. You never listened."

"You should have been more forceful. Put your foot down."

"Don't make it out to be my fault. I shouldn't have to fight to be heard. You should have wanted me to have a say. It's supposed to be a partnership, not a dictatorship."

"That's a bit harsh. If you had said something, I would have changed."

She seriously doubted that, but didn't want to argue the point.

"Anyway, it wasn't just that. I was getting fed up with sorting out the rubbish. Annoyed with your excessive consumerism. Frustrated you wouldn't stop eating meat—or at least cut down. It was never going to last. We're just too different."

"But we had a great time, didn't we?"

"We did. But the cracks were beginning to show. You were starting to drive me nuts. And I think you would've got fed up with my quirks eventually too. Another few months and you would've been glad to see the back of me. It's probably because you still liked me when I left, that you haven't been able to let go."

"No closure."

"Yes."

"Umm, I think you're right. Now I see you like this, I find myself distinctly uninterested. Sorry."

She stared into his eyes, the capitulation and apology momentarily flooring her. "That's OK. I want you to move on. Find someone more compatible. True love." She smiled at him, "I never wanted to hurt you, you know. I just wanted out. I know I went about it in an odd way, but I couldn't get you to listen to me. It all kinda built up and I just had to get out before I got stuck in a marriage I didn't want. It's not that I regret our time together. I don't. I'll always have fond memories of you, except for maybe the stalking."

"Yeah. I'm sorry about that. It was unacceptable behaviour. It 'is' unacceptable behaviour. Kinda did it again today—I won't do it again. I'll say goodbye now and that'll be it. You won't see me again."

He heaved himself out of the sofa, stepped to the chair to put on his coat, then sat to tie his shoes. Gemma went over and stood in front of him. He got to his feet. She embraced him and he returned the hug, kissing her on the forehead, "Goodbye, Gemmie. Good luck with the baby."

She smiled at him, "Goodbye, Tim. Good luck with everything."

He walked out of the flat, closing the door behind him. She stood still, waiting for the familiar sound of the front door slamming, then wandered over to the window to watch Tim stride off. Maybe she'd been too harsh in her judgement. Maybe he hadn't realised she didn't appreciate his controlling nature. Maybe he really thought she was having a breakdown... because he cared. But whatever Tim felt, she would never go back to him. Lumbering her child with an unloving father was out of the question. And there wasn't one moment she had missed Tim since walking out on him. That was not true love. Matt, on the other hand, pervaded every thought. The dagger in her heart twisted relentlessly. His deceit drove the knife deep, yet she ached for his presence. His smile. His friendship. His body.

Tim crossed the road and climbed into a shiny red sports car. Yet another new motor. The engine growled as he sped away. Clearly not electric. She shook her head, sighing. He would never change. She was well out of it.

A tear trickled down her cheek. Not for Tim. For that lost love. The love that had been reciprocated with nothing but a performance worthy of an Oscar. She sniffed and headed back to the foldaway table her laptop sat upon. The only solution was to keep busy.

# Forty-three

She stared at the envelope. It had been a week since Tim's unexpected visit. He promised she would never hear from him again, but this envelope was adorned with his scrawly handwriting. She dropped it in the basket of paper recycling and went to make a cup of tea.

As the kettle boiled, she glanced at the letter... then again... and again. "Come and open me," it taunted. "You'll never know if you don't read me."

"Oh, sod it!"

She marched over, swiped the beast from the pile, and ripped the envelope open. She slid out the contents: a funny card congratulating her on being a prospective MILF. She laughed. Typical Tim.

"Ooo!" she plonked herself down in the nearest chair and held her breath. Kicking over, she exhaled and opened the card.

Inside was a brief message: 'Think I owe you this, plus an extra prezzie for you and baby. Buy some socks. All the best, Tim.'

She unfolded the blue piece of paper that had fallen onto her lap. A cheque. In the age of digital banking, it had been a long time since she'd seen one of those. It was made out to Gemma Williams.

The sum: thirty grand. Presumably twenty-six for the kitchen plus a very generous present.

She smiled. Her dream had just become within touching distance.

# FORTY-FOUR

Gemma's arm linked through her mother's, as they studied the properties on offer in the estate agent's window. It was going to be tough finding something suitable. She had the thirty grand from Tim for a deposit. She'd also managed to save a bit more from work over the last six months, but she intended to keep this back for baby expenses, an emergency fund, and any renovations the new property might require. Her bank would lend up to £120k as long as her parents guaranteed the repayments. The mortgage advisor was worried she might not return to work after having the baby, despite Gemma telling him she would have to; she didn't have any choice over the matter. She needed an income to repay the mortgage. No way was she going to default, whether her parents acted as guarantors or not, for to do so would end her dream completely.

The window display showcased a selection of cottages and terraced houses situated in the local town and surrounding villages. There was one property with a sizeable garden of two acres, but the mansion that accompanied the plot put it way out of her price bracket. She sighed.

"Let's ask inside," her mum suggested.

The bell chimed as they stepped across the threshold.

In a distinctive Welsh accent, the female estate agent asked, "Buying or selling?"

"Buying."

"Budget?"

"£150k"

The agent raised her eyebrows, "A flat then?"

"No. Smallholding. I'm not fussy about the house. It can be falling down or non-existent. As long as I can live on the property, I'm perfectly happy in a caravan, or even a tent." Her mother glanced at her as though she were barking. The agent managed to keep a straight face buy sucking in her lips. "I just want land more than anything. Space to grow fruit and veg. Bit of woodland. And a water source—preferably natural."

"Well, don't have a problem with natural water sources in Wales. Just have to look up." The agent chuckled at her own joke. Then sat back. She tapped her lips. "Not sure I can help at the moment. No, hang on..."

The agent searched through her filing tray and slid out a sheet, which she placed on the desk in front of them.

"This has just come to us, so haven't got the full details yet. About ten acres in all. Eight are woodland. Rest fields. Cottage needs a lot of work." Gemma studied the brief handwritten notes as the agent continued, "We haven't seen it yet, so still have to agree an asking price with the seller. Was planning on going out there this afternoon to meet him and get the full information. You're welcome to come with me if you're interested?"

Gemma nodded, "Yes, please."

"Of course, I can't guarantee it'll be in your price bracket."

"That's OK. It'll give me an idea of what I can afford if nothing else."

***

The damp February air didn't diminish her mood. If she weren't such a lump, she would've skipped along the path. The place was perfect. She expected a long search, so to find her dream property so quickly was a bonus. It was a shame she would have to stick to her plan to stay in Reading until she went on maternity leave, but she needed to save as much money as possible and she doubted temping work for pregnant accountants was easy to come by in the middle of the Welsh countryside.

Leaving the woodland, she stopped to catch her breath. In front of the ramshackle cottage, her parents were in deep discussion with the seller and estate agent. *Oh, gawd.* Such a perfect property was bound to be beyond her budget. She trudged across the drive, dodging the larger weeds.

"I love it," she announced, interrupting their conversation.

"The house needs a lot of work before it's habitable," her mum pointed out.

"I don't mind. You've still got my tent, haven't you?"

Her dad rolled his eyes in despair.

"So, we just need to agree the price?" the agent directed the question at Gemma.

"I've got one hundred and fifty grand."

"I'll take it," the farmer responded, holding out his grubby hand.

She shook it.

Her parents gawped. "So much for negotiation," her father muttered. "You're supposed to start low with your bidding."

She didn't care. The property was hers.

# FORTY-FIVE

Pausing for a breather before she entered the baby shop, her left hand rested under her bump, supporting the extra weight as the baby practiced its gymnastic routine. There were four car seats in the window. Plastic and polyester. Her eyes drifted to a pram. Not much better. Maybe she could find one manufactured from recycled tyres or bottles or something? Alleviate her guilt that way. If not, she'd just have to suck it this time. Baby's safety comes first. As the activity subsided, she turned and looked down the street. A few days ago, it would've been a pretty winter scene with a fresh layer of snow. Now it was a disappointing grey slush that had ruined her boots with a salt mark across the toes. Her eyes lifted from the pavement to see a familiar face.

Matt. Out shopping, hand in hand with two infant boys; aged about three and four, maybe five? Is there no end to his deceit? She glowered as he sploshed along the wide pavement in her direction. But he acted as though she wasn't there, keeping well over to the far side. As he drew near, he did a double-take, quickly glancing at her, but didn't acknowledge. As he walked past, he totally blanked her.

She spun to follow his trajectory and, hands on hips, shouted, "YOU COULD AT LEAST SAY SORRY."

He glanced over his shoulder, his eyes quickly running over her. Turned away and quickened his pace. He picked up the smaller child to carry him on his hip. The other he held by the hand, as he strode away, the poor child skipping to keep up. If Matt had been on his own, she would've chased after him and given him a piece of her mind. There was no need to be rude and ignore her. She was the injured party after all. All she wanted was an apology. Was that so hard to give?

Outside a hairdresser's, he stopped as a blonde woman came out; easily identifiable as the bride in the wedding photo. She kissed him on the cheek and ruffled the hair of the two children. He said something to his wife, and she glanced at Gemma before speaking herself. She then started to walk towards her.

"Shit." Gemma turned and walked as fast as she could in the opposite direction—which wasn't very fast. Last thing she wanted was to have a confrontation with his wife in the middle of a busy street—well, anywhere to be honest.

She ducked into a boutique shop.

"Please can I use your loo? Bit desperate." She jiggled to stress the urgency.

"Err, yes. Through there, on the right." The shop assistant pointed to the back of the shop.

"Thank you." She dashed past the clothes carousels, sending one in a spin, and crashed through the door into a corridor. Then into the loo. She closed the door and turned. Lovely! Wet floor, dotted with damp bits of loo paper. Drips on the seat. A brown stain in the bowl. Yuck. "Don't kick, baby."

\*\*\*

She hid in the toilet for a good ten minutes before re-emerging. She peeked through the face-sized window in the shop floor door. Matt's wife was standing just outside the shop entrance, waving both arms in the air; trying to attract the attention of someone—her husband. Gemma turned round, "Must be a back exit down here somewhere." Off she waddled.

\*\*\*

Once home, she slumped onto the sofa; too exhausted to remove her coat. She struggled to kick her boots off... and lost her socks in the process. She rested her tired and swollen feet on the coffee table. Puffy and red. The skin hot to touch. What did the midwife say about pre-eclampsia? She rifled her coat pocket for her phone and searched for the causes of the condition on the NHS website. It seemed to be a medical condition with underlying causes rather than due to a temporary bit of high blood pressure. She leant back and tried to relax, willing the symptoms to dissipate.

She closed her eyes, but her mind whirled with the unexplained. Where had Matt's wife and kids been last July? On vacation? The two boys both looked very young, so no school. Maybe they went to stay with his in-laws for a holiday. Matt wouldn't have been able to go because of the farm. That made sense... and the bastard had taken the opportunity to have a bit of fun and get revenge on Tim, killing two birds with one stone.

But there had been no toys in the house. Then again, he'd been redecorating. Maybe they were packed away somewhere. One of the three bedrooms had been devoid of furniture, but newly painted in a pale blue. Blue for boys. Sexist pig! He obviously decided not to reintroduce the kids' beds after hatching his plan. He'd also hidden away any other evidence: children's crockery, cups, clothes, etc. Photos were probably just stored in the cloud or on his phone; she never printed out her own these days. Who did anymore? He made a mistake leaving out the wedding photographs. Hence his concocted explanation of the twin brother.

Was this all a bit far-fetched? The only other explanation was a temporary separation. His wife got custody and removed all their belongings, except a few items of clothing she no longer wanted. He had redecorated the bedroom for weekend visits. But that didn't absolve him. He should've told her he had a wife and kids, even if he was planning on getting divorced. And he should have told her about his relationship to Tim.

His wife was welcome to the lying, cheating bastard. More fool her for taking him back. He was a total ratbag! All men were. They could all go to hell. She wanted nothing more to do with any of them. She rammed the arch of her foot into the coffee table, "Bastards!"

# FORTY-SIX

The following Saturday, she braced before stepping out of the foyer into the freezing wind. Shivering, she pulled on her gloves, carefully tucking them up her coat sleeves to keep out the icy cold. She toed the pavement with one boot. The snowfall earlier in the week had compacted into slippery glass. *Must be careful.* She hesitated; maybe it was a bad idea to go out in this weather? But she needed to get the baby stuff she'd failed to get the previous weekend. The internet wasn't an option as she wanted to check out prams and car seats for sturdiness and ask about eco-credentials. If bought online, and they were not up to scratch, it would be a total hassle to send them back and order something else... and she was running out of time.

Her first steps did not go well. She slid clean across the path... grabbed the lamp post... held her breath. Exhaled. *Phew! Close.* Here, at the edge of the kerb, the snow was less compacted and the footsteps of a very large man—well, someone with large feet at the least—provided a safer route. She gingerly trod in the indentations, her hands gripping the pole until the last possible moment, then crunched her way along the pavement... or was it the road?

Having negotiated the crushed meringue of dirty grey without further mishap, she smiled upon reaching the bus stop. *Still in one piece.* Stamped on the spot and blew air into her hands to hold back the penetrating iciness.

A purple bus pulled into the stop, sliding straight towards her. She jumped backwards and slipped, but an elderly gentleman grabbed her elbow and prevented disaster. The bus swung out and stopped alongside the kerb.

"Thank you."

"That's OK. Glad to be of use."

She could have done with her own permanent life saver right now. A nice sturdy arm to hold on to. Warm muscle to snuggle into. Someone to carry her shopping. All daft reasons to seek a new relationship. One that would inevitably come with a good dose of lies and deceit. Where were the good men? Hiding in their bedrooms? Too afraid to ask a girl out? Or maybe they didn't exist anymore. Her dad the last of a dying breed. Responsibility and loyalty replaced by a selfish disregard for anyone but their self. The sooner she retreated to the Welsh wilderness, the better.

She grabbed the rail and hoisted herself into the vehicle. After paying with her smartphone, she waddled down the aisle, hoping the driver would wait until she was seated.

She shuffled along the seat to the window. Drew a circle in the condensation. The slate-grey clouds threatened more snow. Head for a mall this time. Fingers crossed she wouldn't bump into her ex again. She didn't want to talk to him. Didn't want to confirm to him, he was the father. To do so, meant he would have a hold over her. Would always be in her life... filling her child with lies... turning her baby against her... no, she couldn't face it. What was he doing in Reading anyway? Perhaps the in-laws live this way? Must be it. He couldn't possibly leave the farm for more than a few days, so—phew—he'll have gone back to Sussex by now.

*** 

Thankfully, the pavements in the city centre were ice-free, so she was able to make her way safely to the shopping mall. The place was crowded despite the cold weather. Plenty would be suffering from Tim syndrome: buy, buy, buy, must have more stuff. Shopping an entertainment in itself. Others, like her, would be gritting their teeth—and not because of the cold—buy necessities as quickly as possible and hurry home. A chore to be avoided unless needs must.

Her trips into the city centre, since arriving in Reading some seven months ago, had been few and far between. She'd found a good source of maternity wear in a charity shop just a short walk from her flat. And plenty of second-hand furniture retailers on the outskirts of town. She considered going for a pre-owned pram and car seat as well, but her parents put scare stories into her head about them lacking a safety guarantee or possibly being some dodgy counterfeit from China. She was not going to put her baby in harm's way, so brand new it was on this occasion.

She could've done with her mum's help right now, in making her choice, but the snow had stopped her parents travelling down from Wales. Their remote cottage was currently surrounded by four foot of the white stuff. The weather better improve before her April due date; her mum was supposed to be her birthing partner. She tried to persuade her dad to attend too, but he thought that a bit cringe-worthy. Promises that he could stay at her head end failed to change his mind. If her mum didn't make it, she would have to persuade one of her best friends.

They all lived in and around Horsham. That was about an hour and a half away and they all had busy jobs, so she wasn't hopeful of a volunteer unless it were a weekend delivery.

***

After a lengthy discussion with the shop assistant, she finally made her decision. Relief swept across the woman's face that there would be no more questions. Gemma paid for the goods, arranging for home delivery of the larger items. She staggered out of the shop carrying four bags of washable nappies, bibs, babygrows, sheets and blankets, etc. She totally lost it in there. Bought far more than she intended, but it had all been so cute... argghh... hormones. What had she turned into? She couldn't watch tv without blubbing along to the slightest tear. Had developed an intense attraction to cartoon animal motifs. The sight of them always instigating an "Awww, I want one." She couldn't pass a teddy without snuggling her face in the fur. God knows what the shop assistant thought. Still, she had a great excuse. And now she had everything, she could steer well clear of any further temptation.

The exit took her onto the first-floor walkway that circled the mall's atrium. She yawned. The baby kicked. "Ooo." She walked over to the balustrade, dropped her bags, and rubbed her belly. "Not a good time, littlun." She leant sideways against the railing. On the floor below was a collection of bistro tables and chairs, next to a counter serving coffee. She froze. Matt was there, sitting in one of the chairs, sipping from a cup. Between sips, his head flipped from person to person, scanning the passers-by. He glanced upwards. She quickly stepped back. "Shit."

Odd that he was searching for her now; after he'd blanked her the other day. Then again, it was his wife who chased after her. Maybe she told him to find out whose baby it was. It must be awful for her, finding out he'd cheated on her whilst she was away... even worse, maybe got someone pregnant.

Or perhaps, he was just waiting for his wife? She glanced around the first floor. There was no sign of Mrs Begood there. She peeked over the railing. Big mistake. Matt spotted her. Stood up, spilling his coffee, and waved, shouting something indistinguishable from the background grumble of busy shoppers. He ran towards the escalator. She scuttled to the other end of the walkway and took the stairs down.

On the ground floor, she headed for the exit. *No, he'll catch me*. She halted. What she needed was a... She scanned the shops. Three along was the perfect place. She ducked inside the sportswear outlet. Hurried past the rails of tightly packed clothes to the back corner. Crawled under the bottom rail of puffer jackets.

"Err. Are you OK?" asked a teenager, pulling aside the coats.

"Yes, I'm fine. Hiding from someone, so..." She put a finger to her lips "...shssh."

"Sure." He sauntered off. Regrouped with his pals. Pointed and chuckled. *Great. Some promise*. She slid the hangers back. Would those lads tell on her? No. Teenagers. They won't be arsed.

She yawned. How long to stay put? How thorough would he search? Would he assume she'd left the mall and concentrate on looking outside? Probably shouldn't stay here for more than an hour; if she got too stiff, she'd be stuck. She set an alarm on her phone and settled back for a snooze.

# FORTY-SEVEN

A fleeting glimpse, but he was sure it was her. He waved and shouted but she stepped back out of sight. He wasn't one hundred percent certain she'd seen him despite his energetic display of arm flapping. Rude for him, he barged past the waiter—who had arrived with a cloth to attend to his spillage—and sprinted to the escalator.

He leapt up the left side until his passage was blocked by a family of four. He jiggled on the step until the ride reached the top, then raced to where Gemma had been standing. There was no sign of her. Just four bulging shopping bags stood abandoned in the spot. He jogged along the walkway to the next exit. She couldn't move fast given her condition—must be seven months pregnant by now—so she couldn't have got far.

He stepped into the stairwell. The door swung shut with a bang as he stared down the shaft. "GEMMA." He listened. Trainers squeaked on the concrete. "GEM?"

"Sorry, mate. Just us," said the man appearing round the corner. Behind him, his teenage daughter trailed, a frown on her face.

"Pass anyone?"

"Nope. Sorry."

The pair went through the door. Matt followed. So, where was she? He wandered into the nearest shop. A phone store. The displays ran down either side of the oblong space. There were no racks or shelves to hide behind. The backdoor had a keycode lock. And the only customers were two confused-looking pensioners in the grip of a salesman's spiel. If nothing else came of today, at least he'd save them.

"Has a pregnant lady just come in here?"

"No," said the salesman. The couple shook their heads and inched away from their captor.

"Did you see her go out the exit?"

"No. Umm..." he spun round, "Let's try a bigger screen."

Poor sods. Far too slow. The lady handed her shopping bag to her husband.

*Her bags? Maybe there's a clue to her address in there?* He ran out of the shop.

Too late. The baby shop bags had gone. Heart thumping, he scanned the shoppers. He'd either just missed her or someone had swiped her purchases. Not seeing Gem or the overflowing bags, he leant over the banister to check the escalator and floor below. Maybe she's in the stairwell?

He dashed back to the stairwell and leapt down the steps. Bursting into the ground level, he wiped his sweaty brow. He could see sod all.

He pushed through the crowds and stopped at the coffee bar. Wrapped his arms over his head. It was clear, from last week's encounter, it was more than Tim's words that had sent her packing. There was a hell of a lot he needed to explain to her. But he needed to find her first if he was even going to get a chance to put things right. But just like last week, she had disappeared without a trace. Was this nightmare ever going to end?

***

At speed, he recced the streets outside and the attached multi-story. Then, searching the odd shop, he continued to circle both the upper and lower level for about an hour.

"Sir."

"Yes?"

"I have to ask you to leave."

"What? Why?"

"I've been watching you. I've a good mind to check your pockets though I've not seen you snatch anything yet—"

"I'm not a thief!"

"You're acting very suspicious-like."

"Just looking for my girlfriend."

"Phone her."

"Haven't got her num..." his voice trailed off, realising how stupid it sounded.

"See. Suspicious."

"She's my ex-girlfriend."

"Yeah, well, stalking's a crime too. Go home before I drag you off to my office and call the police."

"But—"

"Exit's that way." The burly man pointed to his right. "Move it." His left hand dropped to the radio on his belt.

He'd already had a run-in with the police in Guildford. Probably meant he was on some sort of database. One call and he'd be in the slammer for the night... maybe several days. And he was so close, he couldn't risk the interruption to his search.

"I'm going."

He wandered the streets for another couple of hours until his feet were frozen and his nose numb. Frostbite? Just what he needed. He trudged back to his jeep in the multi-story, scrutinising every vehicle passed.

Sitting in his car, he battered the steering wheel. There was no point searching anymore today. The shops had now closed, and darkness had long since descended. He'd come back tomorrow and search the streets again. Just as he'd done every day this week. Just as he would every day until he found her.

# FORTY-EIGHT

She checked her phone. "Oh, crikes!" Over three hours had passed. Such was her exhaustion from carrying the baby weight around town, the alarm had not woken her. She crawled from under the garments and hauled herself up using the clothes rail. She bent over and searched her hiding place for the four shopping bags. "Damn. Must have left them outside."

Wincing, she crept past the two assistants who were busy cashing up for the day.

"Sorry. Fell asleep."

They stared. Too puzzled to speak.

As she struggled to lift the security grill, one came to help.

"Please may I check under your coat?"

"Oh, right, yes. I'm just very pregnant."

"I need to confirm that."

"Of course."

She undid her coat and displayed her belly. The assistant gawped, unsure as to what to do next. Gemma lifted her jumper and shirt, exposing her bare flesh. A tiny appendage thrust against the skin, forming a hummock, perfectly on cue.

"It's real," she explained unnecessarily to the girl.

"Yes. Sorry, we just have to be sure. You'd be surprised what people will do," the shop assistant replied, lifting the grill to release her captive.

"That's OK. You're just doing your job."

Gemma scuttled out. There were a few stragglers like herself, but no sign of Matt. She went back upstairs to where she left her bags, but they'd gone. She wasn't that surprised but visited the Lost Property Office just in case. That turned up a blank too. She couldn't face the thought of another shopping trip; another chance to bump into Matt. At least she hadn't lost the car seat and pram, which were to be delivered next week. She would just have to rebuy the rest online. An expense she could've done without.... Look on second-hand freebie sites first. Which was what she should've done in the first place. She could kick herself. Fell for every marketing trick in the book. Seduced by cute motifs, soothing jingles, and warm-white lighting. Stayed far too long and bought far too much. And what did she have to show for it? Nothing, but stiff limbs, an aching back, and another stalker.

Great.

# FORTY-NINE

The visit to the maternity unit at the Royal Berkshire was interesting, albeit rather hurried. The midwife, showing them around, looked harassed and clearly wanted to get back to her proper job of delivering babies—or go home. Grey roots encircled a frazzled bun of chestnut hair as a finger pointed at the various wards. Names were uttered rapidly but there was no stopping to let the four expectant mothers and three fathers have more than a quick peek through the doors. Gemma's bump made it hard to keep up with the nurse as she sped down the corridor of delivery rooms.

"Right. In here, everyone."

They were herded into the empty suite and the midwife proceeded to demonstrate the gas and air.

"Anyone want a go?"

A blond woman raised her hand.

"OK." The midwife passed over the mask. "Take a deep breath."

It so wasn't fair. Here she was doing a fair impression of a hippo and that slip of a thing had nothing more than a small and perfectly round bump. No swollen ankles or flushed cheeks for her. No heartburn or sleepless nights. While the woman giggled, Gemma checked the other mums-to-be. She had the biggest bump there. Her fault for continually putting off this trip. Still, better late than never.

The blond passed the mask to her husband. Gemma was also the only bod with no partner. The others eyed her suspiciously. Minds ticking over as to the reason for her solitude. Wishing she had invited Louise, she stood tall and proud, pretending to be the confident woman she once was. Before the controlling Tim. Before the emotional battering from the father of her child.

No longer rocked by its mother's activity, her baby fidgeted. Her hand soothed as the nurse explained the workings of the birthing chair. A frightening-looking contraption that called out for some heavy woven straps and a helmet with wires spewing from the top. A peek behind the seat revealed no lever to instigate a powerful electric shock.

"Over there is the ensuite. Have a quick look, then I'll wrap up with a list of things you need to bring with you."

A queue formed to view the bathroom. A shower, toilet, and sink. That solved the mystery of the bathing arrangements after giving birth. TV programmes never went into sufficient detail and, presumably, you were a right sweaty, bloody mess afterwards.

"OK. You can download this list from the NHS website. Interrupt me if you have any questions. Your birth plan and hospital notes. Something loose and comfortable to wear during labour—don't wear your best nighty!" The midwife paused for breath. "It says three changes of clothes. Bit of an overkill. Your partner can always bring more in…"

Gemma made a mental note to buy maternity pads, an XXL t-shirt to wear, and snacks to keep her going. She'd been told this plenty of times at the ante-natal classes. They'd even given out that list. But still, there were so many things she had forgotten to get. The pregnancy had definitely ruined her previously infallible brain.

Tour over, she headed for the carpark. The snow of previous weeks had been replaced by a miserable damp drizzle. Not hard enough to warrant an umbrella, but persistent enough to frizz her hair into an unruly mess.

As she drove out, she stopped to let a white-coated doctor cross the road. Huddled in her collar, the medic jogged across. Reaching the other kerb, she turned to wave a thank you.

"Shit." Gemma slunk down in her seat and sped out onto the street.

She peered in her rear-view mirror to make sure she wasn't being chased. The woman was standing at the carpark entrance staring in her direction. The doctor disappeared from sight as she turned a corner and headed home.

So, Matt's wife was a doctor and worked in Reading. This could be awkward if she worked in obstetrics. Was it too late to swap hospitals? Oh, it was too much hassle. She'd just have to chance it.

# FIFTY

"Mum, my waters have broken."

The voice crackled at the end of the bad connection, "Oh, sweetie, that's early."

"Only two weeks. They said that's normal in the classes."

"Yes, but we're still snowed in. There's no way we can get to you anytime soon. Can you get a friend to go with you?"

"I'll call Louise, but it'll take her a while to get here. I'll have to get a taxi to the hospital."

"I'm sure you've got plenty of time. I had a seven-hour wait after my waters broke with you. Have you had any contractions?"

"Just tiny ones. Do they count?"

"How frequent?"

"Gosh... um... every few minutes."

"Since when?"

"Since yesterday afternoon."

"Gosh, Gemmie, why didn't you phone sooner?"

"I thought they were Braxtons. They're not like painful or anything."

"Well, I think you better call that taxi straight away. Let me know when you've got to the hospital. Our mobile signal's bad at the moment, so best to use the landline number.... Good luck. We'll be thinking of you. Both of you. Really really sorry we can't be there."

"Me too. But don't worry, Mum, I'll be fine."

"I'm sure you will. Love you, sweetie."

"Love you, Mum."

"PUSH HARD, GEMMIE. WE'RE CHEERING YOU ON!" her dad's voice shouted out in the background.

"THANKS, DAD."

\*\*\*

She climbed into the taxi. Sat down with a puff.

"Where to?"

"Royal Berks maternity block."

He twisted in his seat to stare. Frowned. "Keep your legs crossed. Don't want any mess."

He faced forward. She stuck out her tongue. The car pulled out into the road. She feigned an extra big sigh and embellished with a whimper of pain, just to wind him up.

"Are you OK?"

"Think it might be coming." A bit mean, but it was funny... and he deserved it. She turned her attention to the side-window view and sucked in her lips to prevent a giggle escaping. The roads were quiet. Hardly surprising, given the time: 3am. The car sped along the bypass, well above the speed limit. If they were stopped, she'd have to do a bit more acting. If they crashed...

"Please can you slow down a bit?"

"I'm not delivering your fucking baby." He pressed his foot down.

She braced. It wasn't far. There wasn't any traffic. They'd be OK.

\*\*\*

The taxi screeched to a halt in front of the unit. The driver sprang out and flung the door open. Snatched her labour bag and dumped it in a puddle. Her mouth dropped open. *I'll teach him.* She inched her way across the seat, stopping at the edge to give some heavy pants. He thrust his sweaty hand out. She lifted hers. Hesitated. He grabbed her wrist and dragged her out.

She placed one hand on the car boot and one on her stomach, "Ooooh... think it's coming. Arghhh... how much do I owe you?"

"Don't worry about it."

"Are you sure?"

He nodded, jumped in his car, and sped off.

She pressed her lips together. She hadn't intended to do him out of a fare. In fact, she was planning to give him a big tip because of her teasing; not that he was aware it was a joke. Still, he had no empathy for women in labour. How he thought he'd arrived in the world, she could only guess. Anyway, the battle of wills had kept her mind off the impending arrival.

She waddled into the building and took the lift to reception.

"Name?"

"Gemma Williams."

"Did you phone?"

"No."

"You're supposed to phone before coming in."

"Sorry."

The receptionist frowned. "I'll get a midwife to assess you. You might get sent home if you're not far enough along. We're very busy. That's why you HAVE TO PHONE."

Gemma grimaced. So much for 'joyous occasion'. She'd already pissed off a taxi driver. Now the officious gatekeeper to maternity services. If she got through this without screaming blue murder at the midwife, it'd be a miracle. One that deserved chocolate cake with chips.

# FIFTY-ONE

Gemma thumbed through the magazine as she waited for a midwife to see her. She could not concentrate anymore; the contractions had upped their game. She stroked the restless bump, "Soon, Baby, soon. Don't fret now."

"Gemma."

She looked up. *Shit.* She glanced towards the exit, but an excruciating pain shot across her back and stomach. "Yeeow." The worse one so far.

"Contraction?" She nodded, breathing deep, as Matt's wife sat down next to her. "I'd advise not trying to run away this time and listen to what I have to say. OK?"

She doubted she could even crawl right now. The woman had her trapped.

"I'm so sorry but I really didn't know. I don't want anything from him. If I'd known he was married, I wouldn't have touched him with a barge pole."

"Er..." The doctor's eyebrows scrunched together, "Matt's not married."

"But I saw him with you. I saw the wedding photos."

"That wasn't him. That was Mike, his identical twin. My husband."

"But there wasn't two of them in the group photos."

"Matt wasn't at the wedding. He had an accident on the stag night. Tripped on a kerb and smashed his knee. He was in too much pain to leave the hospital and was so drugged up, he probably wouldn't have remembered anything anyway." Gemma stared at the medic. She never considered there might be a reason as to why only one twin was in the photos. "Can I ask, Gemma, why did you leave him?"

"My ex turned up at his house. He was surprised to see me there. Said Matt was only with me for revenge. Which seemed reasonable given the circumstances." The doctor's head flinched in query, so she added, "Tim Starling."

"Ohhh, you're that Gemma?"

"Guilty as charged."

"Interesting." Her eyes wandered in thought. "Solves a mystery. Sue was very sketchy with the details when she came to stay with us. She said Matt had been in a fight over a girl. She didn't mention it was Tim's missing bride-to-be. Neither did Matt. Me and Mike had no idea Tim was involved. But that's beside the point; Matt was well and truly over that awful Bella woman by the time he met you. Glad to be rid of her by all accounts. So, no way was it revenge."

"Are you sure? There definitely seemed to be bad blood between them. Matt never said anything nice about Tim. Tim never said anything at all about Matt. Not one word."

"Oh, they fell out years ago. Long before the Bella saga."

"So how did they fall out? Matt said they used to be best friends."

"They were, umm... until Matt went to visit Tim at his uni. They were in a club and Tim had sex with a girl in the toilets, then totally blanked her afterwards. She clearly thought it was the start of something and was in tears. Matt was furious with

Tim. By all accounts, they had a right old shouting match and both got chucked out of the club. They ended up fighting in the street. Police came. Tim legged it. Matt got arrested and received a caution. He didn't give the police Tim's details, so Tim got away with it. Just as well, cos it could've ruined his chances of becoming a barrister."

"So, there's still bad blood between them?"

"Don't think so. Just not best buddies anymore. Well... that was until you stirred things up. Tim punched him, you know."

"When?"

"The day you left. You said Tim spoke to you at the house?"

"Yes. Then he went to look for Matt."

"Well, he found him. Knocked him clean out before Matt knew what was happening."

"Was he OK?"

"He needed a few stitches, but otherwise fine. Well, except for the broken heart."

"So, they might hate each other's guts now, but before—there's no reason why Matt would try to ruin Tim's life by stealing me away?"

"Absolutely not. As I said, he was well and truly over Bella. Anyway, Matt's not that sort of bloke. He wouldn't hurt a fly."

Gemma said nothing. This was sounding like she'd made a terrible mistake.

Picking up on her discomfort, the doctor continued, "Can I ask, how did you meet Tim?"

"Xmas do."

"You worked at the same place then?"

"No. It was one of those mega events with lots of different companies attending. He was really nice and polite. I had no inkling he was such a cad."

"Didn't ask you to accompany him to the toilets then?"

"No. He was a real gentleman."

"Probably because his bosses were there." The medic's face twisted. The doctor wasn't telling her something.

"What?"

"How long before Christmas was that?"

"A week or so... Fifteenth."

"And this was 2017?" Gemma nodded. "And did you start dating straight away?"

"Yes. Why?"

"He chucked Bella out on Boxing Day."

"No! That's when I agreed to move in with him. Oh god, I feel awful now. Poor girl."

"Don't feel sorry for her. Total gold-digger."

"Still, he threw her out to make way for me."

"I think that's pretty much par for the course with Tim."

"I'm so rubbish at judging characters. Every boyfriend I've ever had has turned out to be a right toe-rag. I thought I'd done it again with Matt. That's why I fled without giving him a chance to explain. He's not going to want me now, is he?"

"Course he will."

"But he once told me trust was important in a relationship. I haven't exactly—"

"You made a mistake. You're only human after all. We all make them from time to time. He'll understand. He's that sort of guy. And he definitely wants you back in his life. He's been very depressed ever since you left. Another contraction?"

Gemma nodded, grimacing, "Bloody hurts."

Dr Begood squeezed her hand, "Breathe through it. Nice and slow."

She drew in the air. Exhaled. "OK. Going now.... Thanks."

"Um, when we told Matt we'd spotted you in Reading, he rushed over to try and find you. He's divided his time between hanging around the city centre and searching street by street, ever since."

"Did you tell him I'm pregnant?"

"Yes.... It is his, isn't it?"

"Yes."

The doctor sighed, "Phew. I was a bit worried you were going to say it's Tim's. Matt was a hundred percent sure it was his. Made him more desperate to find you. Can I phone him and let him know you're here?"

She nodded in reply as a midwife approached.

"Gemma Williams?"

"Yes."

"This way, please.... Is Doctor Begood your birth partner?"

"Err..." She looked at the doctor, who now paced to and fro across the corridor, her phone to her ear. "I'm on my own at the moment. A friend should be here in about an hour or so. I just need to wait a min..." She wagged her finger at Matt's sister-in-law, and whispered, "...until she's finished."

The midwife's chest heaved. They waited in silence.

Dr Begood ended the phone call, "He's on his way," and checked the time. "Sorry, Gemma, but I've gotta go now." She marched over and hugged her, "I would love to stay, at least until Matt arrives, but I've got a plane to catch." She stood back, "Holiday. Really sorry. Hope everything goes OK. We'll come and see the new baby as soon as we get back. Good luck."

"Thank you. Have a good time."

Gemma watched the doctor leave via the lift, then followed the midwife into the delivery unit.

# FIFTY-TWO

"Still eight centimetres," the midwife reported after examining her nether regions. "I've got to check on the other lady. Any news on your friend's whereabouts?"

Gemma fumbled for her phone on the bedside table. Checked for a reply to the million sent texts. "No. She must be driving. She won't even use hands-free at the wheel."

"Good for her."

"Oooo..."

"Deep breaths, remember." The midwife stood, "Back in a min," and dashed out the door.

Poor woman. Rushed off her feet. And the absent birth partner only added to the midwife's stress. The reluctance to leave her patient on her own meant she was dashing from the room every twenty minutes to check on the 'neighbour'. Five minutes later she'd be back. Apparently, help would come once 'things got going' but for now she was stretched thin.

Her phone dinged. At last, a text from Louise, «*Broken down. Waiting for the AA. Sorry.*»

She replied, «*Don't worry. Matt's coming.*» and signed off with a smiley face.

«*Whoooa!!! Great news!*»

Unfortunately, she had no idea when he would arrive. If coming from the farm, he could still be at least an hour away even if he'd left immediately upon receiving the news. She wasn't sure she could keep her legs crossed for that long. There was some definite downward pressure going on. And she felt like having a shit. But she mustn't push until the midwife gave the go ahead. Splitting like a ripe tomato didn't appeal.

She closed her eyes to breathe through the next contraction. Someone walked into the room. Presumably the midwife. The door clunked shut. A chair scraped over the lino flooring and rattled to a halt next to the bed. She exhaled slowly as the pain tore at her belly. Eyes still closed.

"Gemma, I'm here."

She opened her eyes and turned towards the deep husky voice that was cracked with emotion.

Close to bursting into tears, she blurted, "Matt. I'm so so sorry. I've been a total idiot."

"No, I have to take the blame. I wasn't upfront with you—breathe—We'll talk about this another time. Concentrate on the task in hand." Lips together, he smiled. His eyes glistened with a coating of tears, matching her own. "Don't cry, Gem. I'm here now. I'm not going anywhere, ever. Do you want me to rub your back?"

"Yes, pleeease. It's really bad." She shifted into a more upright position with Matt's help. His strong hand stroked over her t-shirt. She pulled her clothing up, "Underneath would be better." His gentle touch travelled across her skin. The roughness of his farmer's hands didn't diminish the temporary relief from pain. She sighed.

The flustered midwife hurried back in, "Aah, great. Matt, yes?" He nodded. "I was worried you weren't going to make it.... Right, let's have another look."

She caught Matt's eye as the nurse prodded, "You get used to it very quickly."

He smiled, nodding.

"Ten centimetres. Time for some hard work. Don't force it to start with. Wait for your body to tell you when."

\*\*\*

Matt stood by the bed, gently rocking the baby. The love in his eyes for his daughter shone bright below a scar she hadn't seen before. He glanced over.

"Sorry, am I hogging her?"

"Just a little bit."

He perched on the edge of the mattress and placed the sleeping newborn in her arms.

"I love you, Gem."

"Despite what I did?"

"I'm pretty sure Tim was behind it. He saw you at the house, didn't he?"

She nodded. "He was surprisingly calm about it."

"Not my experience."

"No?"

"Flattened me. Not a word, just whoomph, down I went."

Mouth agape, she tapped her left eyebrow.

He nodded, "Yeah, that was him. But why didn't you return my calls? Let me explain?"

"I was so livid at that point. Every boyfriend I've ever had has turned out to be a right scumbag. Tim said you were only with me to get revenge. I believed him cos it fitted the facts. You kept your relationship to him quiet. You were positively encouraging me to leave him..."

"He's a nasty piece of work. I was thinking of you, not me."

"...and you knew where my engagement ring had come from but didn't say anything."

"I didn't say anything because I wasn't sure it was definitely over between you at that time. Yes, you'd had a major tiff. Obviously. But there was a chance you would sort it out and I didn't want to stick my fingers in the wound and poke it about. I thought it best to keep quiet. I was half expecting you to ask for the ring back in a couple of days."

"And there were your wedding photos all over the house."

"My wedding photos?"

"Well, I thought that at the time. There was no identical twin in any of the photos. I thought you had lied about that too."

"You thought it was me, even though I told you it was my twin?"

"Only after Tim put doubts in my head. I checked all the photos. There wasn't any twin."

"I was in hospital."

"Yeah, I know that now. Your sister-in-law told me."

"And you thought it was me when you encountered my brother in Reading?"

"Yes. You—he, I mean—blanked me. Then your wife chased me..."

He smiled, "His wife."

"Yes, his wife I mean." They both laughed. "Why didn't you say Tim was your cousin?"

"I thought I had, then it became obvious you didn't realise.... I started worrying you might not want to be with me as you'd be bumping into him at family gatherings. And I know you had an awkward encounter with his parents and wouldn't be that keen on seeing them again either. I thought you might think I wasn't worth the potential embarrassment. So, I kept quiet. Then I started regretting it after we got serious because then it was inevitable you would find out eventually.... I was racking my brains over how best to tell you. But you left before I got a chance. I think I'm just as much to blame as you. Let's just put it behind us and move on together. You're the one for me, Gem. I've missed you so much. I want you and baby to come home with me."

She smiled, "I want that too."

He leant over and kissed her softly on the lips. Gazing into her eyes, he paused, before going in for a longer smooch. The baby did a little grizzle, as though unhappy at not being the centre of attention.

She jiggled the bundle, "Hey, sweetie. What's wrong?"

"Maybe she's hungry?"

"Should I feed her?"

"I guess so. You're the mum!"

"I've no idea what I'm doing."

"That makes two of us."

***

As the baby suckled, Matt stroked her short fluffy bits of jet-black hair, "Got a name in mind?"

"Um... how about Mabel?"

He nodded, "Like it. Mabel it is." He checked his watch. "Right. I've just got to pop out and put some money in the parking meter. It's not far, just round the corner, so won't be long."

He kissed them both and left.

# FIFTY-THREE

She stared at the ward entrance. Where the hell was he? He said he wouldn't be long, but that was forty minutes ago. Is that long? Maybe his jeep got clamped? Perhaps he's gone to find some food? Or a coffee?

She forced a smile as Louise appeared with a bunch of flowers and pink balloon.

"Not sure I approve of the pink," she joked. Louise blew a raspberry. "Better not be buying pink stuff for my daughter."

"Oh! Is it a girl? Thought it was a boy," Louise teased back. "Would have bought blue if I'd known." Her best friend leant over and kissed her on the cheek, "How ya doing?"

"Fine." She bit her lip and sniffed.

"Oh, Gem. What is it? What's wrong?"

"Nothing."

"Doesn't look like nothing. Is littlun OK?" She peered into the bedside cot where Mabel was sleeping peacefully.

"Yes. She's perfect."

"Why are you upset then?" Gemma couldn't answer. She bit hard on her lower lip to stave off the tears. Louise glanced around the ward, "Where's Matt? Hasn't he arrived yet?"

"Been and gone," she blubbered.

"What?" Louise sat on the bed and put her arm around her weeping friend, "What happened?"

"He was here. For the birth. Then he said he was going to put some money in the parking meter, and he hasn't come back."

"Did he seem happy?"

"Yes, very. We had a long chat before he went and, well, it seemed all sorted. He wasn't blaming me. He insisted he was partly at fault. He asked me to move back in with him."

"How long ago was that?"

"About an hour."

"He's probably just got delayed. Have you tried to phone him or send a text?"

"No. I haven't got his number. I threw my old phone away, remember."

"Bummer. I'm sure he'll reappear at some point. Maybe he had to move his car. Parking's a bloody nightmare. Took me an age to find a space.... Cheer up. How was giving birth? Should I avoid it?"

"It was painful."

"But bearable?"

"Let's just say, she's worth it."

"You're not giving me much to go on, Gem."

"Everyone's different. It might pop out like a cork for you."

"Or it might not."

"Are you thinking of having one then?"

"I wasn't until you got pregnant. Now I'm all broody. Thanks for that, mate."

"You'll need to sort out your love life first unless you're going down the donor route?"

"It's sorted."

"You've got a new boyfriend?"

"Yeah."

"Since when?"

"End of Jan."

"And you didn't tell me?"

"Umm... I'm kinda embarrassed about it."

"Just because I haven't got anyone, doesn't mean you can't."

"That's not the reason."

"So, what is?"

"It's Tim." Louise winced.

"School Tim?"

"No. The other one."

Gemma stared at her cringing friend. She couldn't believe what she was hearing. "Tim Starling?"

"Yes," blushed Louise, grimacing.

"You're kidding me. You and Tim? Germophobic Tim? Tim who's allergic to you?"

"Yes. Do you mind?"

"No. You're welcome to him. But are you sure you really want him?"

"Well... yes. I love him."

"Gosh. I don't know what to say. How did it happen?"

"Well, he had a blocked drain so called me. Dad was on holiday, so I went on my own. Um... this was after he visited you. I would never have done anything if there was any chance of you getting back together. You seemed pretty adamant there was zero chance of that."

"Don't look so worried. It's OK. He's a free agent."

"Anyway, I took the opportunity to apologise for all my past hugs and kisses given his history with the slurry pit. But told him he needed to get over his phobia. I made him help me jet wash the drain."

"You what?"

"Therapy, like."

"And he agreed to?"

"I didn't give him a choice. Bossed him."

"Right.... So, how did you get from that to being in love?"

"I think he was kinda turned on by me ordering him about. I was definitely getting a kick out of it.

One thing led to another and we ended up having a frantic sex session against the fridge freezer."

"You didn't need to go into quite that much detail, you know."

"Anyway, we're together. It's good. I don't take any shit from him. Told him I'm not participating in anything I've not been consulted on. He got the message after I refused to go to some fancy restaurant he'd booked without asking me. Now, he lets me decide everything. I think he likes not having to make all the decisions outside of work..."

"Wish he told me that."

"...and in the bedroom."

Gemma stuck her fingers in her ears, "I don't want to hear anymore."

"I've bought a leather catsuit and a whip."

"Nooooo... Louise, stop it! I don't want to know."

"Got some handcuffs on order," she giggled.

Gemma tugged a pillow from behind her back and clasped it over her head in mock horror. She dropped the pillow onto the bed and shrugged her shoulders, "I guess, whatever floats your boat. Umm, you said you were broody? You know Tim doesn't want kids?"

"He doesn't get a say. I'm the boss."

Gemma laughed. "What about the vasectomy?"

"I'll book him in for a reversal once I've checked your little production doesn't put me off."

Her brow scrunched, "Are you pulling my leg?"

"No. Dead serious," laughed Louise.

Not one hundred percent convincing. But with Louise, it was often hard to tell. The catsuit would be a joke. Her friend was never one for fancy dress. The whip? Handcuffs? Wouldn't put it past the control freak. A baby? Surprising, but there's no accounting for hormones.

"Do you want to hold her?"

Louise nodded, "Thought you'd never ask."

\*\*\*

Louise stayed for a couple of hours before she had to leave. She had a job to do in the morning, and it was extremely unlikely the hospital would allow her to stay the night anyway. She promised to come back the following evening.

It was hard saying goodbye. Gemma appreciated her friend's presence, especially once it became obvious Matt had got cold feet and wasn't coming back. Halfway through her visit, Louise took a wander around the hospital and the parking lot, but there was no sign of him. Her pal tried to console her by pointing out she was merely back to where she was a day or two ago, only better because she now had Mabel. But all she felt like doing was crying. She wanted her mum badly. She'd received a phone call from Wales saying the weather was finally warming up so, fingers crossed, they would be able to come down in a day or two. But for now, she was on her own with just a tiny baby for company.

# FIFTY-FOUR

Gemma yawned. She hadn't slept and not because of her angel of a baby. Once she was back at the flat, away from all the memories of that man... at home with Mabel... she'd be too busy to dwell. She swung her legs out of the bed. Stood. Dressed. Sorted out Mabel. Cursed herself for not asking Louise to pick up the car seat from her flat. *Walk?* She started to pack her bag.

A nurse rushed in, "Where are you going?"

"Home."

"I don't think so."

"I thought we're only supposed to stay one night?"

"That's only if you've got someone at home to help you. Have you?"

"Err... not yet. Maybe tomorrow."

"So, put your things back in the cupboard and I'll get you a cup of tea. Someone's coming to visit you shortly for a chat."

Gemma's brow scrunched, "Who?"

"Oh, here she is now. I'll get that tea." The nurse dashed off, spoke briefly to the woman in a knitted tunic-dress, then left the ward.

The middle-aged woman approached, "Gemma, yes?"

She nodded. "And you are?"

"Hannah Jackson." The woman studied Mabel, "Isn't she gorgeous?" Then stared at Gemma.

Thrown by the statement being in question form, she stuttered, "Er... yeah."

"Let's talk." Ms Jackson drew the curtains around the bed, as though she believed this suddenly gave them absolute privacy. "I hear there's been lots of tears?"

"Err... yes.... Who are you exactly?"

"Clinical psychologist specialising in post-natal depression. Sorry, thought you'd been told."

"I'm not depressed, I'm upset."

"About what?"

"Boyfriend dumped me."

"Oh.... What after giving birth?"

Gemma nodded with a sniff.

"How long had you been together?"

She grimaced, "Well, we got back together while I was in labour."

The psychologist scratched her head. Her eyes narrowed, "So, you were only reunited for a few hours?"

"Yes."

"And how long were you separated before?"

"About nine months."

"I see. Reluctant father?"

"I don't think so.... Oh, I don't know.... He seemed overjoyed holding Mabel but then he buggered off without a word." She stared at the floor.

"Harsh. No wonder you're upset. And it's just that, that's thrown you? Everything OK baby-wise? Not finding it overwhelming or anything?"

"No. Well, the love I feel for..." She leant over the cot to tidy Mabel's hair, "...this little bundle is totally... wow! Can't describe it..."

"Overwhelming but in a good way."

"Exactly."

"Well, Gemma Williams, I don't think you have PND. Just man troubles—"

"Nothing new there. I'll get over it."

Hannah smiled, "I'll be off then." She fumbled in her pocket and handed over a business card, "Phone me if at any time you find yourself not coping. Good luck." With that, she whisked the curtains around the rail, nodded, and strode off.

Exposed to the gawping mothers, Gemma blushed. Hospitals. Nothing's secret.

She scooped up her daughter and hugged her tight, "Just you and me, Mabel. We don't need him, so best you forget ever meeting." Her hand stroked over the soft hair, just as Matt had done yesterday. Just before he left. The jet-black hair. Matt was blonde. His mum was blonde speckled with grey. Gemma had shown him an old album her own mum had given her, so he knew they were all reds and browns in her family. She never got to see any photos of his father or grandparents, but one thing was certain: Tim was dark-haired. Just like Mabel.

A pit in her stomach grew. No wonder Matt left. He realised he wasn't the father. The black hair must come from Tim's paternal side. Matt would know that. And it didn't take an accountant to work out she was still with Tim just over nine months ago. Mabel was not an early arrival after all—she was late. But Tim confirmed he'd had a vasectomy. Hadn't he? She racked her brains. Yes, she was sure of it. So, it must have failed. And the condom too. That would explain the ridiculously light period she had just after she left him. It wasn't due to stress. She was already pregnant.

"Oh, shit!" How the hell was she going to explain this to Louise? Louise who was apparently so in love with Tim, she was thinking of having kids with him. If her friend's new relationship was for the long-term, then it was inevitable Tim would accompany Lou on visits. She couldn't put Mabel in a balaclava, every time he came round—for the rest of her life.

He would know as soon as he set eyes on her. Tim. The child-hater. The father of her daughter. There was zero chance of him being overjoyed...

"Who's my father, Mum," the teenage Mabel would ask.

"Tim."

"What Louise's Tim?"

"Yes."

"Does he know?"

"Yes."

"But he never talks to me..."

Sure way to give a girl psychosis.

*Oh, gawd.* She'd better head to Wales and hide in the hills.

# FIFTY-FIVE

Gemma's parents had been busy since the purchase of her smallholding went through a couple of months ago. They got the roof fixed, windows replaced, the damp sorted, and walls re-plastered in the stone-built cottage. Mabel's nursery had been painted a cheerful primrose-yellow. An inflatable mattress was squashed in the tiny room, next to the cot, until her own bedroom was finished.

A two-up two-down affair—think Victorian terrace but twisted ninety degrees—the cottage was situated on a hillside with four small windows overlooking the valley below. Behind the cottage was a rocky cliff that loomed over the building. Atop that, grass adorned a steep slope to the summit. It hadn't even crossed her mind that this was a cause for concern; the cottage was over a hundred years old and had yet to be crushed by falling rock. But her dad, a worrier by nature, insisted on a land survey to make sure the whole mountain wasn't about to squash her and Mabel flat. The results were good news—solid rock—and the lay of the land meant any rain run-off naturally flowed to the left of the house, where it joined a stream running down the far side of her land. This stream was her sole water supply. The blue pipe snaked out of the kitchen wall, ran across the terrace and up the hill, to feed from the stream at a higher level. Serviced by gravity, no pump was required. Of course, her father had the water tested to check it was drinking quality. She hadn't been worried. It was pure rainwater from the top of a hill after all. She would've been happy to drink it straight from the tap, but Dad made her promise to boil it first.

As she rolled the paint over the wall, she was reminded of the incomplete kitchen in Matt's barn conversion. She sniffed. She had thought he'd forgiven her. He looked so happy holding Mabel. There'd been love in his eyes when he gave her that final kiss. And yet he left without saying a word.

Bastard!

She'd been taken for a ride again. Some sort of warped game. Pretend everything was hunky-dory. Get her expectations up. Then dump her without a word of explanation. She should've guessed what he was up to. He had history after all. Revenge. That's all it was. Revenge for her leaving him. Revenge for her trying to pass off Tim's offspring as his own. Though she could hardly be blamed for that, seeing as she didn't know at the time.

Mabel squawked from the beanbag in which she was cosseted, just beyond the kitchen doorway. Gemma put down the roller. Washed her white-speckled hands under the single tap—the cold water splashing into the old tin sink—then dried them on a tatty but clean t-towel.

"Just a sec, Mabel. On my way."

She picked up the baby and flopped backwards into the beanbag; the only piece of furniture in the sitting room. As Mabel fed, she flicked through the colour charts (a curious gift from Dad) that were scattered across the floor. The room was so small, white still seemed the best option and that would match the kitchen too. "Hmm." Did she have enough paint for both rooms? Possibly. If not, there was half a tin of primrose-yellow left. Mix it in and hope for the best. But it might not come to that; the room was miniscule. She snorted a laugh. Even smaller than the kitchen, courtesy of the boxed-in staircase that filled the back wall and exited via a tiny door in the kitchen. It was tempting to rip off the cupboard doors, to give a bit more floor space, but the understairs closet was the only storage in the house. And babies had a ridiculous amount of stuff.

It would be hard to find a sofa that didn't swamp the room. Maybe a couple of comfy chairs—or even just one—would do. A trip into town was called for. Check out the second-hand shops. She didn't want anything that might have mice or fleas living in the upholstery, but she could always strip the fabric off and have a go at recovering them if needs must.

The fire crackled in the grate, spitting out a shower of golden sparks. She must get a proper wood burner and a guard. The open fire would be unsafe once Mabel was crawling. Maybe one of those little stoves that you can rest a kettle or pot on top. Or a tiny Aga in the kitchen might be a better idea? She needed something for cooking. Gas was out of the question; she didn't want to be carting heavy bottles around and, anyway, it wasn't green. Electric would have to wait until she'd saved up for the solar panels. It would have to be a teeny-weeny wood-fired Aga. She pouted. She wasn't sure they came small enough and, even if they did, it might be hard to find one second-hand. A trip over to Mum and Dad's was therefore required... to research online.

God, it was hard to live without the internet. The initial rejoicing of being cut off from social media, constant news, and the means to answer every trivial question that came to mind, had turned into a nightmare of constant trips to her parents' to find out where she could buy paint from, source a second-hand greenhouse, etc etc. Only to find, the best options were buying supplies online or searching pre-used websites. And then there were her constant queries on how to do this or that. How to fix a dripping tap? Clean paint brushes? Wash nappies without a machine? Mum and Dad only knew so much... and then it was back to tapping in the browser. So much for cutting herself off from the world. Switching off would have to wait until the property was sorted... well, except for the matter of work.

Mabel's mouth released its grip from her breast. She quickly changed her on a towel spread out on the floor. Placed the sleepy infant back in the beanbag, then chucked the nappy in a bucket just outside the front door. On the other side of the doorstep was a large cooler. She lifted the lid and retrieved an apple and some cold soup in a milk pan. She munched on the apple as she heated the soup over the fire.

She chuckled. Tim would never cope with this, not even for a day. He would head for the nearest five-star hotel within minutes of arriving. Matt, on the other hand, would love it. He would be making her some sort of pot stand to go over the fire; would have sorted out the dodgy tap; maybe even built her an outdoor shower with hot water. She jiggled the saucepan to stir the soup. Another thing to research: outdoor showers. It can't be that hard, can it?

A knock on the door startled her from her daydream.

"Hi, Gemmie. Just me."

"Hi, Dad." He struggled to get an enormous box through the narrow front door that led straight into the kitchen. "What you got there?"

"Ham radio."

"You're kidding me?"

"No. I don't like you out here with no means of communication. You've got no phone signal. No internet. Radio's the only option."

"I haven't got any electricity."

"Thought we could power it off your car."

"I don't want to waste the battery. I can't recharge it here."

"I know, I know. It's just for emergencies. It's not going to use massive amounts of power. It'll just be less of a worry for me and your mum." He scanned the restrictive floor space, "Where shall I put it?"

"Err... shed?"

"Thought that was your loo?"

"It is, but it can double up. There's more room than in here."

"OK. Shed it is." He stared at the doorway and sighed, "Should have asked before I brought it in. Never mind. Here goes."

As he struggled back out, Gemma picked up Mabel, wrapped her in a blanket, then followed him onto the terrace that fronted the house. They crunched across the weed-free gravel, and into the ramshackle shed that stood to the right of the cottage, next to the start of a long stony track; the lone route in and out of the property.

"Are you sure there's no room for a bathroom indoors?"

"No. I don't want one inside. I'm going to build a proper compost loo and an outdoor shower."

"How about an extension? We'll pay. It's bloody cold up here in winter, you know."

"It's good for you."

"Not if you bloomin' well freeze to death."

"Think Skandi. Snow plunges. Saunas. Ice baths."

"Brrrr," he shivered. "Whose child are you? You're not mine, that's for sure."

She laughed, "Pixies swapped me."

He set up the radio on the workbench that ran down one side of the shed. As he tickled a now-awake Mabel on the head, he asked, "Car keys?"

"In the car."

He strode off, so she leant over the battered counter and examined the ham radio. She twiddled the knobs. This was a whole new thing to her. She didn't even realise they still made them. She didn't really want anything technological in her little haven from the modern world, and even planned to get rid of the car eventually. Dad would have to be managed carefully. He didn't understand her wish to live like a caveman. To her, the house was an excess. To him, inadequate. Her original dream had been a yurt or, even better, an actual cave house. She'd had a bit of a poke in the cliff behind the cottage, but it was solid granite, so no chance.

The previous occupant had the right idea. Though she was unsure whether this was by choice or not. The farmer, who sold her the property, said the place had been rented out on a secure tenancy, at a peppercorn rent, to a farm labourer. The man retired some twenty years ago, at the age of seventy, but couldn't be persuaded to move somewhere more comfortable. The farmer hadn't spent any money on the property as he didn't want to encourage the man to stay and, in any case, he refused to spend money on a property he was getting diddly squat for in terms of rent. He wanted to sell, but that was impossible with a sitting tenant who had the right to stay until he died. The farmer had a right old moan about it being his grandad's fault. The elderly gentleman finally moved to a care home last year, allowing the farmer to sell at last. Cheaply. A big mistake letting the place fall into disrepair. Serves him right for being a terrible landlord. But it meant no electricity, no gas, no phone line, no bathroom... heaven.

She stepped back, frowning. She didn't really want this radio at all. It was totally against her new ethos: no new, no plastic, no tech (except a laptop and smartphone, kept at her parents' for work purposes). But then again—she gazed at the baby in her arms—if Mabel got ill or had an accident, it could be a life saver.

Her father parked her car close to the shed. Jumped out. "Umm... might need a longer cable."

"Put the radio on the seat."

"Yep, good thinking. You are my daughter after all."

"Or just Mum's."

His head flicked towards her. "Bloomin' cheek."

# FIFTY-SIX

Too dusty in the house, she carried Mabel outside to enjoy the late spring sun. They both lay on the tartan car rug and Gemma tried to teach her seven-week-old daughter how to clap without success.

The builder had promised to finish today; ready for tomorrow's installation of the wood-burning range. The job was to knock out the fireplaces in the two downstairs rooms. The cooker would be installed in their place, so providing heat for both spaces. The chimney went up through the middle of the house, so it should heat upstairs as well. If more warmth was needed in the bedrooms, she could always leave the staircase door open.

It was a mistake decorating before checking out the stove possibilities. Hopefully, it was just dust that could be swept away, and she wouldn't have to repaint.

On Thursday (the day after the planned stove installation), her parents were to bring over all the bits and pieces she'd accumulated over the last few weeks. Eighty percent of the furniture acquired for free using a recycling site. Her parents had treated her to the tiny stove as a becoming-a-mum present;

it had proved impossible to find a second-hand one that size. Everything else had come from car boot sales and junk shops.

A bird of prey swooped overhead and down into the valley. As the raptor glided over the bubbling river, it pierced the quiet with a loud squawk. She looked towards the house. Listened. Yep, silence. Even the radio no longer blared. Perhaps Rhys had finally finished and was just clearing up? She picked up Mabel and headed across the field towards the house.

She owned two fields—situated one beneath the other on the slope below her cottage—each enclosed by dry stone walls. Or rather they would be, once she learnt how to rebuild them. Still, the gaps did allow the mobile grass mowers easy entry from the surrounding hills. And the sheep's efforts were most welcome.

In the top field, her predecessor had terraced the uppermost portion to grow vegetables. She wandered through the plots, vaguely outlined amongst the weeds. Another job to do. One to do before next spring. Dig or no-dig? That was the question. The no-dig method appealed but what about perennial roots? How long would she need to blanket the site to get rid of the brambles? No way was she spraying weedkiller all over the place. Perhaps, the answer was to dig this year, then swop to no-dig next? If only she had a Matt to advise.

Hitting the terrace retaining wall, she turned right and followed the grass path to the stone steps. Ahead was the woodland through which the access track ran. North of the road was largely fir trees—possibly the remnants of a plantation. South was a mixture of native species. Eight acres of forest in all, so no problem sourcing wood for the new stove. Or finding a site for a treehouse for Mabel. A picture of Matt sawing flashed through her mind. He would've built Mabel something amazing. Instead, her daughter would be lucky to get a few planks of wood jammed amongst the branches and a rope. And that was if her mummy ever had the time.

At the top of the steps, she halted. Swopped Mabel to her other arm, giving her a kiss on the head. It was a real shame she still had to work. And a pain that she had to go to her parents to do so. Without an internet or phone connection, she was stuck when it came to keeping in touch with clients. Without a power source, her laptop was predisposed to packing up for the day before she was ready to. So, she resigned herself to spending three days a week at her parents to fulfil her accountancy obligations. There were two advantages to this: the new grandparents could look after Mabel while she worked uninterrupted—except for the breastfeeding of course—and, secondly, they could field phone calls and check emails when she wasn't there, in case anything urgent arose. Her mum had also offered to work for her for free if she got too busy. So far, she'd declined the offer. Her parents had already done too much, and she was determined to make her own way in the world. She hadn't had any help from them before becoming a mother and she needed to get back to that state of self-sufficiency. If she could just find some old solar panels somewhere...

Approaching the house, a cloud of dust greeted her and Mabel.

"Nearly done. Just tidying up," said the grubby builder. He tipped the dustpan onto the terrace, then banged the brush on her recently painted door frame. "Come and have a look."

She waited for the dust to settle before venturing within. She nodded her approval at the hole in the wall. The stone brickwork had been neatly repointed to make a feature of what would be her new stove's home. "Love it. Thank you very much, Rhys. Great job."

"Normally I would do a bit of hoovering to tidy things like, but no power..."

"No worries. I was expecting to have to do a bit of cleaning."

"I know a good sparky. Do you want his number?"

"Err, no. I'm fine for now, thank you."

"Give me a ring if you change your mind."

"Will do. Thanks."

"Or if you just fancy going for a drink?"

"Err... oh... err..." Crikes! Wasn't expecting that. She cringed, "Not really looking for a date at the moment. New mum. Other things on me mind right now. Sorry."

"Thought that might be the case. Never mind.... Right, now for the nasty bit... my bill." He pulled a dog-eared envelope from his back trouser pocket.

She took the paperwork from him, "Thank you. My parents are going to pay, so can you wait a few days? I'll give them the bill when they come over on Thursday, and they'll pay either that evening or maybe Friday."

"That's fine. As long as it's by Monday." He smiled cheekily, "Otherwise I might have to come over and brick it up."

She laughed, "It'll definitely be paid by Sunday."

"I'll be off then."

"Thanks again," she called after him as he left the cottage. As she shut the front door, his truck started, then rattled away down the bumpy road.

It was nice to be on her own again with just Mabel for company. The novelty of having the builder around had worn off by lunchtime yesterday; only five hours after he started. The noise and dust meant she had to steer clear for two whole days, which was a disruption to her and littlun's routine. And she was at a loss how to fill the time as all the things she wanted to do were in the house. So, they spent the two days exploring the woods and sitting in the field admiring the view. Mabel was such a well-behaved baby, she was no problem at all as long as she was fed, changed, and had a leaf to wave in her chubby hand. Luckily, it hadn't rained, otherwise they might have found themselves sitting in the car or the rather less salubrious shed.

Unfortunately, the break from tradesmen would be short-lived. The stove installers were due tomorrow. Fingers crossed they were fast workers as she didn't want to waste another whole day when she had a list of jobs that ran to the moon and back. Good thing Mabel still spent most of the day sleeping. How she would cope once her daughter demanded more attention, she didn't know. But for now, it was a matter of getting as much done as possible while she had the chance.

Maybe a builder boyfriend wasn't such a bad idea?

She slapped her cheek. "Nooo... terrible reason to go out with someone. Single forever. Don't even think about men."

# FIFTY-SEVEN

A thick soup of fog clouded his brain. Flashes of memory appeared within the swirling mist: the birth of their child; Gemma's smile; his daughter's first cry; the dash to his car. His eyelids weighed down... no, glued. His call for help: a strangled gurgle. Muffled footsteps... the muted scrape of a chair.

Through the haze, a familiar voice, "Matty-moo? Are you awake, love?"

Forced through closed lips, no sound accompanied his mumbled reply. More distant murmurs, a clatter, then something round and narrow placed between his lips. A voice he didn't recognise addressed him, "Matthew, take a sip of water to clear your throat."

He obliged and the welcome freshness slipped down, freeing his voice box from its tortured constriction. "G-Gem-ma." Was that himself speaking? He didn't recognise the gravelly sounding stutter. He tried again, "Ge-em-ma." It was him. Why couldn't he speak? Why couldn't he open his eyes?

"Gemma's not here, Matty-moo."

"Ge-em-ma."

"I'm sorry, Matty. But she's not here. She hasn't visited once. I did warn you. She's no good. Best to forget about her and concentrate on getting better."

He tried to shake his head, but bright explosions of pain shot through his brain. He groaned, "G-em-ma... M-may-b-el."

"Who's Mabel, Matty-moo?"

"B-ba-by."

"Oh. As far as I know, she's fine. Not heard anything, mind you. You'd think that woman would've at least kept in touch to see how her own child's father's doing. But no, not a peep from her. When you're better, we'll help sort out visiting rights for you. But for now, you need to concentrate on getting back on your feet."

This couldn't be happening. This could not be right. They had sorted things out between them. Just moments ago, she said yes to moving back in with him. It didn't make any sense. He needed to speak to Gemma, "Ge-em-ma."

"I'm sorry, Matty-moo. She's not going to visit."

With focussed effort, he blinked his reluctant eyes open, rolled onto his side, and then—when his legs failed to respond to the instructions from his brain—promptly fell out the hospital bed. Thump!

# FIFTY-EIGHT

For the sixth time that day, she clicked on 'Submit Tax Return'. She'd got a lot of work done over the last three days and was making decent headway through the tax returns and accounts that had accumulated in her inbox over the last few months. She leant back and took a sip of just-warm coffee. Through the window, her dad was carrying Mabel around the garden. The five-month-old was grabbing at the late summer flowers; knocking them with her tiny hands as the attentive grandad held her facing away from him. She smiled at the joyous sight as her mobile rang.

"Hi, Gemma here."

"Gemma Williams?"

"Yes, that's right. Who's speaking, please?"

"I'm Doctor Patel of St Richard's Hospital in Chichester."

Somewhat unexpected, to say the least. She had no idea why a hospital near the Sussex coast would want to speak to her. "Err... why are you calling?"

"We have a patient here. A Mr Matthew Begood." Her mouth dropped open. All that wishing him dead had come back to haunt her. "I understand from his family you were in a relationship with him some time ago?"

"Yes, that's correct. Is he OK?"

"Yes and no. He was in a coma but regained consciousness yesterday. He's asking for you. Well... shouting is more accurate. He's very confused and distressed. Keeps trying to escape his bed, which is not good in his state. His family can't get through to him that you are no longer together. We were thinking, if you could just explain to him face to face it might help."

"Err..."

"I understand you have a daughter?"

"Yes, I do."

"His family think it might help if you let him see her?" She remained silent. She was unsure of seeing him again. He dumped her after all. Abandoned her and Mabel without a word of explanation. "Are you still there?... Miss Williams?"

"Oh... yes. Still here. Umm... yes, I suppose I could come if you think it will help."

"Thank you. His family will be grateful.... What time can we expect you?"

"Well, I live in Wales, so it's a bit of a journey. If we leave now, we'll have to stop somewhere to sleep. So, tomorrow morning sometime?"

"That would be great. I'll let his family know. Safe journey."

The doctor disconnected the call.

She sat still. Strange that Matt's family wanted her to take Mabel to see him. Surely, he must've told them. But what did he say? She'd heard nothing from Tim or Louise on the subject, so it would seem the barrister had not been implicated... unless the usual line of communication between the two families remained broken by the fallout between her two former lovers? Or maybe the Begoods were hoping for a bit of shock therapy because that was exactly what Matt was going to get once he set eyes on the infant. There was no doubt about it, she was Tim's daughter. His raven-haired, blue-eyed daughter.

"MUM!"

"Here, sweetie. What is it?"

"I've got to go to Chichester. With Mabel."

"Chichester? Why?"

"Matt's in hospital. He's asking for me."

"Is he very ill then?"

"The doctor said he'd been in a coma, but now awake. Sounds like he's in a bit of a state. Thinks we're still together or something, so they want me to talk to him. And let him see Mabel."

"I thought you decided he wasn't her father?"

She nodded, "Maybe he's forgotten. He's been in a coma."

"Why was he in a coma?"

She shrugged, "I don't know. He didn't say.... I forgot to ask."

"Did he say how long he was in the coma for?"

Gemma grimaced, "Sorreee. Didn't do very well, did I?"

"No, blooming hopeless. Anyway, we'd better come with you. It's a long trip, especially with a baby. We'll use our car, so we don't have to worry about finding charging points."

"Are you sure?"

"Yes. Come on. Let's go pack."

Gemma puffed, regretting the promised visit. She closed her laptop and stared out the window. All that way, to see a man who had treated her so badly. And who now thought they were still together! She flopped back in the chair. Christ! Well, at least it would be a chance to give him a piece of her mind. Get rid of that pent up anger that had been gnawing away for the last five months. Only problem was, he'd been in a coma. Was confused. And she couldn't very well shout at a sick man in a hospital. She growled from the throat. Well, she could, but not with Mabel present.

Her mother rapped on the door. "You coming? Or just going to sit there like a lemon?"

She sighed. "Coming."

# FIFTY-NINE

"Hello, Gemma. I'm Mike... before you get confused."

She stared at the twin, baffled by the unfriendly greeting. He hadn't said it like a joke. His tone was distinctly scathing. Cross.

His wife addressed her, "We know you don't want anything to do with Matt, so we're grateful that you agreed to come."

Slightly more conciliatory, but still an undertone of hostility. Why were they so angry with her? He was the one who walked out and left her in her hospital bed alone with her newborn. She could hardly be blamed for getting pregnant by a supposedly infertile man; especially when they'd used condoms so diligently—though, obviously, not as diligently as she'd thought.

"Did you bring your daughter?"

She nodded, "She's with my parents in the café. Where is he?"

"This way," Mike turned to walk through the open doorway into a ward for eight. She spotted Matt's mother sitting by a bed, holding the hand of a thin pasty-looking man. A shadow of his former self. His tan was gone. His hair shaved short. A long scar ran from the middle of his forehead, at the hairline, diagonally down to his right ear. It was healed, so not recent. The scar over his left brow—Tim's masterpiece—was still prominent. She glanced at his twin to remind herself of his healthier form.

"G-em! Ple-ease te-tell me it's not tr-ue," he shouted across the ward as she approached. His voice was slow and stilted, as though each word was hard to locate. He struggled to get up into a sitting position. Mike rushed to his aid and hauled him upright before arranging the pillows behind him.

"Hello, Matt." Her eyes drifted to his mum. Talk about getting the evil eye. "Hi, Sue."

Mrs Begood scowled but didn't respond, vacated her seat, then left the ward with Mike. Gemma sat down. Matt fumbled for her hand. She pulled it away and crossed her arms.

"I d-don't un-der-stand? Ev-very-one k-keeps say-ing we're n-not to-gef-fer an-ny-more. Pl-ease t-tell me it's n-not tr-ue."

"I'm sorry, Matt. It is true."

"B-b-but... w-why? I d-don't un-der-stand. I f-ought w-we s-sort-ted our pr-ob-blems. Y-you s-said you w-would m-move b-ack in wiff me."

"Don't you remember what happened?"

"No... L-l-ast f-fing I re-mem-ber is k-kiss-sing you b-boaf goo-goodbye and le-lea-ving to... go to p-parking tic-ket m-machine. Nest fing... w-wa-king up here in hos-pi-tal. Ev-very-fing be-tween is a bl-blank."

"Well, you didn't come back," she retorted.

"B-but... w-why w-would I d-do d-dat? It d-does-n't m-make any s-sense. I l-ove you. I love Ma-bel.... W-where is she?"

"She's here. I'll go get her." She left quickly, glad to escape. This was just too much to bear. The man had forgotten how he treated her, and now he wanted to pick up as though nothing had happened. Yes, she still had feelings for him. And it broke her heart to see him in such a bad way. But she didn't want him back in her and Mabel's life if he was just going to bugger off once his memory returned and he realised why he had left in the first place.

***

She placed Mabel on Matt's lap. He was silent. His brow furrowed, "Err..."

Mabel chuckled and lunged for the drip in his arm.

Gemma gently unfolded the tiny fingers from around the tube, "You need to watch her... she'll grab anything in reach."

"Sh-she's... a lot bi-big-ger than I ex-pec-ted. How l-long was I in a co-ma for?"

She shrugged, "Don't know.... Don't even know how you came to be in one, to be honest."

"M-mum s-said I g-got kno-knocked o-ver. S-seem to be... mak-ing a ha-bit of it."

"Why do you say that?"

"M-my f-fir-ty b-burf-day. Got kno-knocked o-ver den as w-well. N-not fink-ing. St-stepped out in-to ro-road."

He stroked his daughter's ebony hair, his hand trembling over the tresses. Any minute now he would remember. She braced herself for the expected rejection.

He twirled a lock around his finger, "Gra-an-dad's h-hair."

"What?"

"Gran-dad's hair. Bl-ack and w-wa-vy. Eyes tooo."

So, he WAS Mabel's father. That was something. She could stop avoiding Louise and Tim now. But that meant he had no excuse for walking out on her, so she wasn't about to let him off the hook anytime soon.

"Your curls then?"

He slowly lifted his hand to his head and clumsily rubbed his stubbly scalp, "W-what c-curls? It's all... gone... She's gor-ge-gess. Like her... mum. De-fin-nit-ly got your... your ears and m-ouf. S-so how old is sh-she n-ow?"

"She'll be five months next week."

"Th-th-th-at l-l-lo-ng? I f-fought I was on-ly out f-for a f-f-foo da-days. B-but den a-gain, look-ing at me, I gu-ess it m-ust have be-een lon-ger. D-do-es it say a-ny f-fing on my ch-charts? I n-need more de-tails. It's hor-ri-ble not re-mem-ber-ring any-anyfing. And I ca-ca-can't be-lieve I wa-walked out on you."

Gemma stood and walked to the end of the bed to retrieve the clipboard from its slot. She brought it back to her chair and rifled through the pages.

"RTA... road traffic accident?"

"D-dat's wh-what Mum sa-aid."

She stared at the date. This could not be happening. She'd done it again.

"What's wro-wrong?"

"Eighth of April, two thousand and nineteen... Mabel's birthday." She mumbled, unwilling to vocalise her blunder, "You've been in a coma since Mabel's birthday."

"So, I did-n't wa-walk out on y-you?"

Her stomach churned. She'd made the biggest mistake of her life. She'd been cursing him left right and centre for the last five months, while all the time he'd been in a coma in hospital. Unless... he got knocked over after leaving her? Serves him bloody well right then! No... that was too harsh. She wouldn't wish that on anyone.

"I... m-must have got kno-knocked d-down out-side the hos-pi-tal."

She wasn't so sure. The accident could have happened nearer his home. That would prove he had walked out on her and Mabel. After all, if it happened in Reading, how had he ended up in hospital in Chichester? She searched through the pages. "It says you were knocked down by an ambulance." But where? The pit of nausea grew. Flustered, she scanned the page. She stared at the sentence.

"W-what du-us it s-say?"

She gulped. "Transferred from Royal Berkshire to St Richard's on the fourth of June." To be closer to his mother and home. "Fractured skull, bruising on the brain, possible brain damage, broken right hip and double fracture of right leg."

"Ooouch! Gl-ad I was in a co-ma."

"Don't joke. It's awful."

"Sor-ry."

"I should have been with you, but I didn't know. No one told me. Why did no one tell me? I thought you'd left me."

"Go g-et my mum and bro-bro-fer."

She rushed out of the ward. The three members of Matt's family were sitting further down the corridor. She waved them over and went back to Matt's side. He was teasing Mabel with a banana; waving the fruit around as she tried to grab it.

"Can sh-she have... it?"

"Yes, she loves bananas. Just give her a little bit at a time, otherwise you'll regret it. She's messy."

He peeled the banana shakily and broke off a chunk to give to the outreached hands. He then turned his attention to his family.

"M-um, Mi-mike, Cl-claire. We've j-just looked at my char-arts. I had my ac-ci-dent on Ma-bel's burf-day. W-why did none of you tell Gem-ma?"

The three accused glanced amongst themselves before Mike spoke up, "Because she knew."

"But I didn't. Nobody told me."

"But you were at the hospital when it happened."

"I was in the postnatal ward. Nobody told me Matt had had an accident. I thought he'd left me. I thought he'd changed his mind about getting back together. Either that, or just being mean—raising my hopes before dashing them."

"We thought you knew. We didn't know he was in hospital until we got back from holiday. The hospital staff said you hadn't visited once. So, we thought you weren't interested in him anymore. Thought you didn't want to be saddled with an invalid."

"No, no. That's not true. I would have been by his bedside day and night if I'd known."

All five adults stared at one another. Matt pulled her close for a hug. His lips gently kissed her cheek.

Mike ran his hands through his hair, "I'm so sorry, Gemma. It seems we made a mistake. I think because you'd already left him once, it seemed the most likely explanation."

"D-dat was-n't her f-fault," Matt defended her. "D-dat was a mis-un-der-stand-ing. If any-one's to bl-blame it... Tim."

"Talking of Tim..." Mrs Begood Senior interrupted. She'd remained quiet throughout the conversation so far and her tone was far from pleasant, "...not much of a gap between him and Matt. You seem to swop boyfriends like it's a hobby. Have you ever been dumped or is it always you doing the dumping?"

Stunned, her mouth dropped open. How could she answer this without incriminating herself? It was true she'd always been the one to end a relationship. But with good reason. Not a spur-of-the-moment thing like Matt's mother was suggesting. Was she supposed to put up with being beaten, cheated on, and disrespected?

"Mmmmu..."

"Mum, that's uncalled for," Mike complained, coming to his brother's rescue.

"It wasn't like that. I left Tim because it wasn't working for me. And then I met Matt. I fell in love. I wasn't expecting it or looking for it. It just happened. And then I blew it. I know that. I made a mistake... and then another." She turned towards Matt, tears streaming from her eyes, "I'm so sorry. I should have been here for you."

"I w-was in a co-ma, Gem. I did-n't no-tice you weren't here, so d-don't up-upset your-self about it. Any-way, your time was m-much bet-ter sp-ent wiff our dau-daughter than mo-ping bout a hos-pi-tal ward day and ni-night."

"Still—"

"No, I don't w-want to hear it. It wa-wasn't your f-fault. Once I'm ou-t of this b-bed, we'll st-start a-fresh. You, me, Ma-bel.... May-maybe it's time to f-ink a-bout buying d-dat w-wilderness i-dyll w-we talked a-bout?"

"Done it."

"Wh-at?"

"In Wales. Woodland, couple of fields, a stream, tiny cottage... no services whatsoever," she laughed. "Paradise."

# SIXTY

She walked into the farmhouse for the first time in over a year. The smell of new carpets supplanted by the musty odour of a home abandoned. She placed the car seat, containing the sleeping Mabel, on the living room floor; avoiding the trail of mud that led to the sofa. Then flung open the windows. The fresh autumn air breezed in.

"That's better."

She turned. Blew a raspberry. Better get to work. Coffee table first. She stacked up the food-encrusted plates. Piled the moldy cutlery on top. Picked up the lot and headed for the kitchen.

In the hallway, Mike was still rummaging through the mail on the doormat. He'd made two piles. One for junk. One for official. 'FINAL DEMAND' was a reoccurring theme.

"Aaachoo!"

"Bless you."

"Dusty," said Mike as he stood straight, flicking his nostrils. He wiped his finger across the console. Sighed. Pouted. "I'll take those and scout the kitchen for health hazards. You check upstairs."

She passed him the plates, then ran up the treads. She stopped at the top. Dirty clothes were strewn across the landing. She dodged the worse, jumped over the whisky bottles blocking the bedroom door, then dashed for the window...

Sticking her head out, she gasped, "It's all my fault." But blubbing wouldn't help. She pressed her hands against her cheeks. Closed her eyes. Breathed deep. "Right... bin bags... kitchen." She ran back downstairs. Did a quick check on Mabel—still asleep. Then walked into the kitchen.

Mike was holding his nose, peering into the sink. Filthy plates and ready meal cartons littered the room. A pile of empty beer cans had accumulated in the corner, next to the fridge freezer, below a beer splashed wall. This was not the Matt she knew. Tidy. Organised. House proud.

Mike faced her, "Any better upstairs?"

"Not really."

"Sorry, I didn't realise. Haven't been here for ages. I guess Mum hasn't either.... Well, she hasn't had much chance too. She was with us in Australia for the second half of last year, until we moved back in January. Then she helped us move into our new house before going off on yet another cruise in March. And then she came on holiday with us in April, you know, after Claire spoke to you in the hospital. We all felt a bit shitty about going away when you were about to give birth, but the holiday was booked and the travel insurance didn't cover the circumstances. Anyway, we didn't know what would happen with you and Matt. You might have not let us visit anyway. So, we went."

"That's OK. Totally understandable."

"Anyway, bloody rubbish internet in our hotel but Matt wasn't answering emails anyway. Or phone calls. But that had been par for the course since you left, so we assumed things had gone badly and you didn't want to get back with him. We never thought for one moment he'd had an accident. It was a bit of a shock, to say the least. Since we got back from

Bulgaria, Mum has been spending most of her time at the hospital. We all have."

"How long did you live in Australia for?"

"Five years."

She nodded slightly, satisfied with the answer. It explained why there had been no sight or sound of him or his family in those few weeks she had lived at Willow Farm. Of course, she now knew Matt hadn't been lying about having an identical twin. How could she have been so stupid to ever doubt him. It all seemed so ridiculous now. If only she could go back in time...

"Let's prioritise," declared Mike. "Correspondence first." Leaving the kitchen, he chuckled, "Least messy."

Standing in the doorway, she asked, "Claire's a doctor, but what is it you do? I don't think Matt ever told me."

"Cyber security. I'm the nerdy one."

"So, you were never into the farming side of things?"

"God no. Hated it. Spent my childhood hiding in my room in front of the computer."

Another mystery solved. No wonder Matt never said much about Mike. It was Tim who roamed the farms with him in his youth—well, until the slurry incident—and it was solely Matt who had taken over the farm.

"So, you're not the kind of twins who live in each other's pockets and can't bear to be apart?"

"Definitely not. We might look the same, but that's about it. But don't get me wrong, we don't hate each other or anything. We get on just fine. Rib each other rotten. Probably more like normal brothers than twins. Do you have any siblings?"

"No. Only child."

"Did that bother you, growing up?"

"No. I had lots of friends. Ours was the 'go to' house. I think my parents felt guilty about me being an only child, so I was allowed to invite over all and sundry... and I sure did take advantage of it."

"Do you want more kids yourself?" She nodded. "That's good. Matt wants loads."

"Define loads?"

"Err... five... six?"

"Crikey! I was thinking two."

He laughed, "Don't fall out over it."

"No. We'll find a compromise... Two," she laughed, then pushed the rubbish off the kitchen table to clear a space for Mike.

He dropped his collection and started to open the envelopes marked with red warnings. "I think most of these, I've already sorted over the phone."

Gemma retrieved a roll of bin bags from under the sink and started to collect up the cans.

Mike gave up on the correspondence and joined her in the task, "I knew he was missing you, but he kind of withdrew into himself. Couldn't get much out of him over the phone whilst we were still in Sidney. Didn't want us visiting when we got back to the UK. I can see why now. I should've been more forceful." He pushed his hands through his hair. "I'm an idiot. Too wrapped up in my own family to see what was happening. I let him down, big time."

Noticing Mike's watery eyes, Gemma rested her hand on his shoulder, "No, it's my fault. I should never have left him."

She expected the doppelganger to agree with her, but he held back, letting out a drawn-out sigh instead. "It's all a bit of a nightmare.... You are going to stay this time, aren't you?"

She nodded, "Yes."

"Regardless of disabilities?"

"I love him, faults an' all. I promise you, I'm not going anywhere."

"Good." He stared at her. "Sorry for insinuating..."

"Don't worry about it. I can only really blame myself if you have a low opinion of me."

"Still, Matt's only ever sung your praises. And as we've never actually met before, I should have listened to him. Instead, I've been cursing you left right and centre. Sorry."

"Well, we all make mistakes. Not least me." Her voice broke into a tremble, "I've spent the last year cursing Matt." She blinked and a tear fell. Mike took her in her arms and hugged her tight.

He pulled away, "OK. The past is behind us. The future beckons. Do we dare go outside and look at the crops?"

"Let's do it."

"I'll get my niece."

"Thanks."

She dropped a few more cans into the bag before Mike returned with Mabel in his arms, "She was already awake. Very smiley, isn't she. Cute. A mixture of you and Grandad. I'll leave it to you to decide who's the cute one out of those." He winked. "I'll carry her if you like?" Gemma nodded.

Mike led the way through the back door, "I'm your Uncle Mike, sweetie-pie. Try and not get me confused with your daddy. Though I can't say I'll mind." Mabel gabbled back nonsense in reply. "Yeah, I know, I'm the better looking one."

Gemma laughed as she caught up to walk by his side, "I'm not sure I agree with that."

"You think he's got a better hairstyle?"

"Undoubtedly," she lied. She was hoping the hospital crop grew out quickly. "Are there any differences between you?"

"Yeah, I'm the all-round better model. No, seriously, there's a few wayward moles and freckles that differentiate us." He tapped his neck, "This one, for instance." She peered over. Just above his t-shirt collar line, the dark freckle was only about four millimetres across. But if that was what it would take to tell them apart, she'd better take note of it. "Apart from that, it's the tan. I'm ahead of him on that at the moment. Normally, it's me who's the pasty

one. Err, then there's a slightly different pattern of..."
He grimaced, "...acne pockmarks. Then, of course,
there's Matt's delightful new scars."

She halted. Why was she even bothering to
commit that freckle to memory? Her man had
whopping great scars across his face. If Matt
remained in a wheelchair, or his stutter didn't
resolve itself, then there wouldn't be a problem
identifying him even if the scars faded away. As it
was, it was early days. He'd only just come out of
his coma, so the doctors were still running tests and
monitoring his progress. So far, they'd not been able
to give any predictions of what the future might
hold. Of course, she wanted him to make a full
recovery, but if he didn't that wouldn't change how
she felt. There was something about Matt she found
intensely attractive. And it wasn't just looks because
she didn't fancy Mike in the slightest even though he
was arguably the more handsome of the two right
now. With Matt, there was a 'connection'. It had been
there all the time. She tried to suppress it. Put it out
of her mind, such was her misplaced anger. But it
persisted like an itch that couldn't be scratched.

They arrived at the field in which she helped Matt
pick beetroot last year. A sea of dead weeds. The
odd spike of green thwarted the autumn struggle
for survival. Mike handed Mabel over, then yanked
out a handful for a closer look, "Rotten. Last year's
crop?"

"Could be. I was picking them here with him, last
summer."

"So, he never finished harvesting them.... Shit!
This is worse than I thought. Do we dare look
further?"

"Potatoes were behind that hedge," she pointed to
the back of the field.

They walked to the open gate that had come loose
from its top hinge. It hung lopsidedly, neglected like
the crops. Scanning across the field, she could just
make out the furrows under the weeds. Mike kicked

at a mound between the trenches, then dug his hands in and retrieved a couple of scabby shrivelled spuds. He sighed. "Must be last year's again. Damn."

Gemma's eyes filled with tears. It was all her fault. After she left, he'd just given up. Let his business go to ruin. Stopped looking after himself, his house, his customers. He really did love her. How could she have not seen that? So blinded by her anger with Tim—and Dan, and Josh, and Yousef—she had cast Matt in the same boat.

"No wonder there was zero concern from customers over his illness... he didn't bloody well have any by then."

She wiped her eyes, "Did you contact them then?"

"Not individually. I couldn't be arsed to come all this way to look for a customer list. Probably wouldn't have been able to access his computer anyway. I did manage to get a message put on his website and I sent a comment to his Facebook page explaining what had happened. Nobody got in touch with me as a result. That should have rung alarm bells."

"You had other things on your mind."

"True.... Anyway, how is he going to run this place if he doesn't get his mobility back?"

"I was kind of hoping he'd come to Wales with me and Mabel, rather than us stay here."

"Is it suitable for a wheelchair user?"

"No less than here."

"We'll have to have a chat with Matt and Mum. Work out what's best. Whether to sell this place or not. You know he only has a third share?"

"Yes. Which has a mortgage on it, I believe."

"Just on the house. He'll still have some capital once that's paid off. So, you'll have plenty enough funds to make any necessary alterations."

"If they're needed."

Mike nodded, "Let's hope not."

# SIXTY-ONE

"So, she didn't turn down the offer?"

"Err, no... but..." stumbled Mike.

"Another money grabber. You don't half pick 'em, Matty."

"Sh-sh-shh-iz n-n-"

"It wasn't like that, Mum. Ohhh... I can't explain. I said Matt will have plenty of capital left to make alterations. She said, 'if they're needed'."

"Still, she didn't offer to pay herself."

"Perhaps she hasn't got the money. Anyway, you can't expect her to pay for things Matt needs."

"I don't trust her. Flipping from fella to fella. Gold-digger, like Bella."

"T-t—"

"I don't want her anywhere near my son."

"T-t-im."

Mike faced him, "Tim? What d'ya mean, Matt?"

"L-l-efff T-t-im."

"Left Tim?" Matt nodded. "Gemma left Tim?" Matt nodded again. If only he could get the words out.

"Lucky Tim," grumbled their mum.

"I think he means she wouldn't have left Tim if she were a gold-digger. Is that right, Matt?"

He nodded. Finally.

"Tim's not as wealthy as you seem to think. Big spender. Big mortgage. No wonder Bella came crawling back to Matty. Your brother might be cash poor, but he's land rich. You can bet all those improvements she was planning for the farmhouse were all to do with increasing its market value. She was never going to be happy as a farmer's wife. She'd be badgering him to sell up as soon as she got him down the aisle. Thank god, he saw sense and didn't take her back. And now this Gemma's got her claws in. Didn't want to know our invalid until money was mentioned. Now she's all over him."

"That's not exactly true, Mum. There was no mention of money until I took her to the farm."

"Yeah, just playing for time. Waiting to see what's what. Discovered Matt wasn't in as bad a state as she'd thought. So just needed to check out the money situation. Now she knows there's a few quid to have, she'll stick around long enough to get what she wants."

Matt wanted to scream. She never claimed child support. Surely, that was proof enough of her innocence. "Ma-a-bel."

"Yes, you can still see your baby. If she is your baby, that is. We should get a DNA test done."

*Argghhhhh!*

# SIXTY-TWO

The catering assistant cleared away his lunch while the nurse puffed up his pillows.

Visiting time. Gem and Mabel were a sure thing. His mum another. Mike was working, so it was unlikely he would make another appearance until the weekend. Without his brother to provide the voice of reason, the thought of a Mum versus Gem battle was disconcerting. His mother wasn't known for giving the other party a chance to speak. And he wasn't one hundred percent sure Gem would be up for the fight. By her own account, her relationship with Tim had been one of doormat. That didn't bode well. And he couldn't defend her. His words were stuck in his throat and the more agitated he became, the less likely they were to find freedom.

His mother bounced into the ward, smiling, "Hi, Matty-moo. How you feeling today?"

He nodded. The trapped words swirled through his brain, *A million times better now Gem's back in my life.*

She dropped a farming magazine on the bed, "Article on soil degradation might be of interest to you."

He smiled. Glanced towards the door. A visitor strolled in, silver balloon bobbing along behind. A stranger, not Gemma.

"I'll read it to you."

"I-I c-ca-ca—"

"OK. Page ten." She flicked through the magazine.

"I—"

"Here it is. The UK has one hundred harvests left warn scientists..."

What was he? Four?

She rattled on about topsoil erosion, compaction, over-ploughing, water runoff, soil fertility... All things he was well aware of and had been doing his best to mitigate on his farm. But she was on a roll. His stuttered protests not even worth consideration. She had her baby boy back and she was in control. Nightmare.

He gazed towards the door. Only Gem and Mabel could save him now.

"She's not coming."

"Wh-wh-ot?"

"She's not coming."

"W-wh?"

"Not good enough for you, Matty-moo. I won't let that slut ruin your life. So don't you worry, it's all sorted. She won't bother you again."

The room whirled. What had his mother done? He opened his mouth, but the words sunk to his stomach, churning his chicken sandwich and soup. The pillows suffocated. The walls caved in. This couldn't be happening... not again. Blackness swallowed him...

# SIXTY-THREE

The countryside whizzed by in a blur, like her mind. The ticket sweaty and crumpled in her hand. A sodden tissue in the other. Her daughter, tucked in her car seat, waving her stumpy legs up and down, pointing at random strangers, and gurgling joyfully at the adventure. Her first train ride. Ignorance is bliss, as they say.

She replayed the events in her head. Sue had turned up at the farmhouse...

"Hi, Sue."

"Mrs Begood to you." The first indication something was up. "Making yourself at home then?"

"Yes. So much better than a hotel."

"And cheaper."

"Yes, bonus," she joked trying to lighten the woman's mood—her first mistake. "To what do I owe the pleasure?" Her second.

"How dare you act as though you own the place."

"I'm sorry. Didn't mean—"

"Waltz back into his life. Move in before he's even left the hospital..."

"Mike said I—"

"...I see you've even rearranged the furniture..."

"I'm spring—"

"...well, I've got news for you, it ain't your house and it never will be. If you think I'm going to sit by and let you get your claws into my son like that Bella woman, you can think again, missy."

"Err..."

Matt's mother thrust out a piece of paper, "This is for you." Gemma took the sheet and stared at the print. A train ticket to Cardiff. "That's all you'll be getting from this family. That and a taxi ride to the station. So, pack your bags, the car's waiting outside."

"But—"

"GET OUT. NOW."

Christ! She scarpered. There was no arguing with the woman. In a haze of disbelief, she let the taxi take her and Mabel to the station. She should've asked him to drive to the hospital. See Matt. Or even Mike. But, no, she got on that train. Changed at Havant. And was now on her way to London Waterloo.

As the train pulled out of Godalming station, Mabel tugged her jacket sleeve and babbled, "Na na na na... na na na na."

"Oh! Banana?" She rummaged in her holdall for the fruit. Peeled off the skin and popped a chunk in her baby's mouth. Did that count as first words? If it did, Matt had missed it, just as he had—and would—miss every milestone in his daughter's life. A tear fell. She could go back, confront his mother... but where would that get her? The woman didn't want her around and while Matt was still struggling to vocalize, she couldn't expect him to speak up for her. If she couldn't get a word in edgeways, what chance did he have?

She handed Mabel another piece. She had to do something, for their daughter's sake if nothing else. But what?

The train trundled to a halt. "We're getting out here, Mabel." She stuffed their belongings in the bag, picked up the car seat, and raced for the exit.

# SIXTY-FOUR

She hauled Mabel out of the taxi while the driver retrieved her bag from the boot.

"Do you want me to carry it to the door?"

"No, I can manage. Thanks."

He dropped the holdall at her feet. "Thank you for the tip."

She nodded. The man jumped back in the white saloon and drove off.

She turned to face the drive. The house was exactly how she remembered it. New car. No surprise there. Parked alongside, a transit van: 'The Drain Girl' followed by 'and father' in smaller lettering. God, she had some explaining to do. Five months of avoiding her friend. Elaborate excuses as to why Lou couldn't come to her cottage: building work, no spare bed, ground too sloped and bumpy for a tent, aga not working, no electricity, no hot water.... Claims of being too busy to visit Louise, now ensconced in Tim's home. Lying that the camera on her phone had packed up and she couldn't send any photos of her baby. All because she thought Tim was Mabel's father. Yep, she could expect a frosty reception.

She rang the doorbell.

The door flung wide. Louise's mouth dropped open, startled. "Gemma! Please say you've forgiven me?"

"Err... forgiven you? What for?"

"Tim."

"What about Tim?"

Louise scratched her neck, "I thought you weren't happy about me being with him?"

"No, not at all. I told you I wasn't bothered, so why would you even think that?"

"Well, for one... you been avoiding me like the plague."

Gemma grimaced, "Yeah, we need to talk about that. Can I come in?"

"Absolutely." Louise stood aside, holding the door.

She held out the holdall, "Here, take this for me."

"Sure."

She passed over the bag, then went to retrieve Mabel from the bottom of the steps. She hurried by Lou and into the kitchen. Placed the car seat on the floor.

Louise marched in and crouched down for a close look at the baby she hadn't seen since birth. "She's grown." She tickled Mabel under the chin, "Hi, cutie. Ain't you got a fab smile just like me fella." She sat back, staring at the grinning infant. "You look just like..." her voice trailed off.

"Don't worry, she's not Tim's." She cringed, "but I did think she was for a while. That's why I've been avoiding you."

"Ohhh.... But she don't half look like him?"

Gemma nodded, "Tim and Matt have the same grandad..."

Lou stood up, "Figures. Being cousins."

"...Tim and Mabel take after him."

"You are a twit sometimes, Gem. You knew they were cousins."

"I just thought it was why he abandoned me. You know, saw Mabel's hair... realised she was Tim's... scarpered. But I was so wrong."

"So why did he scarper then?"

She bit back the tears, "He didn't." Failing to hold back the floodgates, she bawled, "He got knocked over outside the hospital. He's been in a coma."

Louise stepped over to hug her tight, her hand rubbing her shoulder, "Jeez, Gem, you've really fucked up this time. Didn't you even stop to think how unlikely it was given Tim's snipped state?"

"I assumed it failed," she sobbed. "And the condom."

Lou backed away, "OK, time to cheer you up with some juicy gossip."

"What?" she sniffed.

"Let's crack open a bottle first. Red or white?"

"Red, please."

Her friend walked over to the wine rack, "What d'ya think's most expensive?"

"Those at the bottom."

***

Sitting on Louise's lap, Mabel grabbed the spoon and splattered the yoghurt over the island. Lou took back the cutlery, delivered another mouthful into the gaping hole... Mabel snatched and flicked...

Gemma sipped her wine. "So, what's the juicy gossip you were going to tell me?"

"Oh right. Not sure it actually counts as gossip, but I've solved the vasectomy plus condom conundrum."

"Yeah?"

"Yeah." Louise gulped a mouthful of wine, then battled Mabel for the spoon.

"Well, go on. The suspense is killing me."

"Is every mealtime like this?"

Gemma nodded, "Pretty much. So?"

Her friend wrestled the teaspoon from the tiny fingers and stabbed it back in the pot. "It wasn't because he didn't want you to know he couldn't have children." Louise stared at her, "Though that doesn't absolve him from not telling you that." She shovelled in another mouthful.

"Too right, it doesn't."

"It was because of... don't take this the wrong way, he does the same with me... err..."

"What?"

"Err... germs."

Gemma sat back on the bar stool, just the tiny back rest stopping her from toppling.

"Not STDs. Just germs generally," Lou continued. Gemma shook her head, speechless. "He's having counselling."

"Slurry pit?"

"Yeah, think so."

Mabel, seeing an opportunity, did another grab and splash...

"Tim will have a fit when he gets home," pointed out Louise.

"Nah. Chucking yoghurts is allowed." Her BFF raised her eyebrows. "Sorry. Probably shouldn't say things like that."

"No, it's fine. You have history. You've shagged Tim in our bed and god knows where else. I know that and I'm OK with it. If I weren't, I shouldn't have taken up with my best friend's ex. So don't be pussyfooting around me.... So, tell me, did it end it sex?"

Gemma nodded, "Don't most things with Tim?"

"Sure do. Despite the germs!"

*** 

Gemma fell into the sofa, "She's fast asleep."

"Here, have some more wine."

She took the glass, "Tim in London?"

"Yeah. Should be home around ten. Which gives us plenty of time to discuss what you're going to do about Matt?"

"I think I'll just head back to Wales. If he wants me, he'll find me. He has my address."

"Thought you said he was still in hospital?"

"When he's better, he can find me. Or phone."

"You don't think the evil mother will stop him? He's stuck in a bed, unable to speak. She's in control and she's not going to make it easy for him. Does he even have a phone?"

"His brother will help him."

"His brother, who's also his mother's son. How far do you think he's willing to go without upsetting her?"

"So, what do you want me to do?"

"Grow a spine, Gem. Confront her."

"That's easy for you to say. I'm not like you. And she was impossible. Totally ignored anything I said. Might as well shout at a brick wall."

"Dan has a lot to answer for."

"Excuse me?"

"Well, before him you gave as good as you got. Now you buckle at the first sign of trouble."

"You can hardly blame me for that."

"I'm not saying it's your fault. Just it changed you. You don't fight back anymore."

"I was arguing with Tim all the time over politics and stuff."

"To what extent? Did you ever scream blue murder at him?"

Gemma chewed on her lip. "No." Her nose crinkled, "I always gave in, once things got heated."

"See, it's like you're frightened you're going to get the shit beaten out of you again."

"I'm not thinking that. I just don't like the confrontation."

"Might be subconscious."

"Possible, I suppose... Are you some sort of counsellor now? Sorting out Tim. Now working on me?"

Lou chuckled, "Might change career.... Anyway, I doubt Mrs Begood is going to start throwing punches, so stand your ground. Tell her she's wrong."

"But she's not going to listen. Maybe I'll write her a letter. Yes, that's a better idea. I'll go back to Wales. Write to her. Write to Matt... via Mike. To make sure he receives it."

"As I said, spineless."

Gemma stuck out her tongue at her BFF.

# SIXTY-FIVE

"Matty... Matty... wake up... Oh, thank god. Here, have some water."

His mother put the straw to his lips. He sipped once, then pushed the cup away, "H-ow lo-ong ou-t?"

"About a day. You need to stop getting yourself wound up. It's not doing you any good."

"Ge-ge—"

"Don't you worry, Matt, she's long gone. Now rest. Concentrate on getting better."

He rolled onto his side and swiped his hand towards the handle, missing by a mile.

"M-mum... m-my fo-fone."

She retrieved the new mobile from the drawer and held it just out of reach, "Who do you want to call?"

"Ge-ge—"

"You can't. I know you think badly of me, but I'm doing this for your own good. You're not capable of sensible thought at the moment, so you just have to trust me to do what's best. I am your mother after all. No one loves you more... and that's why I've deleted her details from your contacts. I'm not letting the bloodsucker near you. You're easy prey, Matty-moo, easy prey. Sorry to be so blunt, but that's the fact of the matter." She handed him the phone, "I'm sure Ash would love to hear from you."

His hand dropped to the bed, the mobile slipping from his grasp... just like Gemma. Was this his life now? To be treated like a naughty five-year-old. No say in his future. Friends vetted. Girlfriends vetoed. Diet imposed. A prisoner in a wheelchair with no voice. His only hope, his twin.

"M-m-ike?"

"Yes, he'll be visiting on Saturday."

He fumbled for the phone to check the date. Wednesday. Shit. He glared at the person he hated most in the world. Still loved... but despised. How could she do this to him?

His mother looked towards the entrance. "Tim!"

Matt turned. His cousin was striding down the middle of the ward towards them. A man on a mission. *What the!* His head couldn't take another fist right now. He couldn't run. Couldn't protest. Couldn't hide. Instead, he cowered, shrinking back into the pillows.

Tim halted at the side of the bed. He glowered at his aunt, sitting the other side. "Susan," he boomed. "Be advised, Gemma Williams is no gold-digger. How could you even think that of her? A woman who was born twenty thousand years too late. Who would rather live in a cave and bathe in a ditch..."

Well, this was a turn-up for the books. Tim to the rescue—unexpected, to say the least. But most welcome.

"...Who has never bought anything new in her life. A woman who gave me all her savings, every last penny, all twenty-six grand of it, to spend on my kitchen without a moment's thought and not long after meeting me. And never once asked for it back. That is NOT the action of a gold-digger..."

His mum was doing an impression of a goldfish. For once, silenced.

"...How dare you cast aspersions on her character. She fell out of love with me, and in love with Matt. True to her heart. What's wrong with that? Yes, she made a mistake leaving Matt. She knows that. She doesn't need you to rub it in her face. She feels guilty enough as it is. And I'm to blame. It was my words that put doubts in her head..."

Wow, Tim accepting blame. That was new.

"...Doubts compounded by the string of shitty boyfriends she had before me..."

Not admitting to being one of them, then?

"...So you can hardly blame her reaction. And as to Mabel, I had a vasectomy years ago, so she's not mine. She definitely looks like a Begood, so who else do you want to accuse? Mike?"

His mum shook her head.

"Matt loves Gemma." He faced him, "Yeah?"

Matt nodded.

"Hell, he was scouring the country for her. Kept banging on my door. Really annoying, but that's love for you. And Gemma loves Matt. Can't understand why, but the girl was distraught when she turned up on our doorstep. You need to apologise, Sue. Put things right. These two are meant to be together." He glared at his aunt, jutting his head forward.

She nodded. Tim strode out.

Biting on her lip, she faced Matt. "I'm so sorry. Too quick to judge."

A kerfuffle in the ward made them both look up. Tim had reappeared, this time dragging a teary-eyed Gem. All patients and visitors stared in anticipation of Act Two, joined by a gaggle of doctors and nurses at the door.

Tim manoeuvred Gemma to stand aside the bed. "You have something to say, Susan?"

"Err... yes. I'm sorry. I was mistaken. I take it all back."

Gem nodded. "I do love him, you know." She reached out for his hand and squeezed it. He grabbed the fingers and tugged her towards his mouth. Kissed. Oh, how he'd missed this. The soft lips. The caress of her tongue. She sidled onto the bed. He wrapped his arms around her. If only he could say those words... "I lu-lub y-ooo."

In the background, Tim whispered, "Auntie. Come on. Time to go."

There was a scrape of a chair and the rattle of a curtain being drawn. Privacy at last. Not that they were bothered...

# SIXTY-SIX

"We should have come in my jeep," Matt commented as they bounced up the rocky lane.

"Sorry. Are you OK?" She braked to a slower speed.

"I'm fine. No need to go like a snail."

"Are you sure? I don't want to hurt you."

"Remember, the consultant said I don't need to be wrapped in cotton wool. I need to exercise my back and legs as much as possible."

"I don't think she meant like this." A chipping hit the underside of the car, making her jump. "I'm going to keep at this speed. Dad's car needs it, even if you don't."

"How much further?"

"Just round the next bend."

Out of the corner of her eye, she could see him surveying the surroundings. A slight smile showed he was happy with what he'd seen so far. As they swung round the curve she braked, bringing the car to a halt at the edge of the woodland. She watched his face. He broke into a broad smile.

"It's brilliant, Gem. Just look at that view. Wow."

He turned and planted a kiss on her lips. His eyes returned to the valley. A morning mist still lingered over the river. Frost iced the grassy slopes. But the sun shone bright despite the cold. By lunchtime, the moisture would be gone, leaving the golden leaves upon the terrace crisp and crunchy. At the moment, the wet litter was a distinct hazard for her fella.

He reached for the door handle, "I'm going to look around."

"Hang on. Let me park properly first."

She drove the car forward and positioned it as close to the cottage as possible. Matt already had the door open and was struggling to lift his legs out of the footwell.

"I'll get your wheelchair."

"No, no, I want to walk. I just need my frame."

She sprang out the car. Poked her head back in and smiled at their daughter, "Be with you in a sec, Mabel." She jogged to the back of the estate and lifted the rear door. Retrieved the off-road frame—specially designed for walking and hiking on rough terrain—and hauled it round to the passenger side. She yanked the wheeled contraption open with a bit of help from Matt, who was now standing, supporting himself with the car door. He got into position and trundled off slowly across the terrace. After getting Mabel, Gemma followed.

"I love it. You've done well, Gem. Great find." He nodded to the vegetable plot below, "I see you've been digging. Grow anything this year?"

"No. Been dealing with weeds, weeds, and more weeds!"

He smiled, then turned to the left. "Are those apple trees I see over there?"

"Yep. Apples and pears."

"Perfect. We can put a polytunnel or two down there," he let go of the frame to point to the side of the top field, losing his balance in the process. She grabbed him. "Thanks. Getting too excited. I love it, just love it." He turned to her and, in a calmer more serious tone, added, "I love you."

"I love you too. Come on, Mabel's getting chilly. I'll show you indoors."

She carried Mabel inside and made sure she was comfy, sitting against the beanbag, before returning to help Matt. He had shoved the walking frame into the kitchen and was clinging onto the door surround as he heaved himself up the step. He paused to look around the kitchen.

"Tiny," was his only comment.

"Cosy," she countered as she stood next to him. "Here, put your arm over my shoulders."

"I weigh a ton." She gave him the once over. "OK, half a ton. Still a lot."

"I'll manage. Head for that chair," she nodded towards the armchair, not six feet away in the sitting room.

Sideways, they shuffled through the internal doorway. Reaching their destination, Matt dropped down suddenly. Still holding his arm, she fell against him, knocking him off the edge of the chair. They tumbled to the floor with a thump. Mabel burst into giggles.

"Ow, ow, ow," squealed Gemma.

"What's wrong?"

"My hair's caught on your button. Can you?"

"Yep. Hang on... OK. You're free."

She sat up. Patted her head, "Thanks." Matt stayed prostrate on his back. "Are you OK?"

He nodded. "That went well." He arched his neck to face the chuckling baby, "Are Mummy and Daddy silly billies?"

Mabel leant forward. *She's gonna topple*. Gemma scrambled towards their daughter. But the little mite put out her hands, got on all fours, and crawled across to Matt. She then rolled onto her back, joining her father in his horizontal state.

"Huh. That's a first!" Gemma exclaimed.

"What crawling?"

She nodded, smiling. "Who's a clever girl? Can you do it again? Here, follow me." She crawled around the room, but Mabel just stared as though she were mad. She gave up and went to lie down on the floor next to Mabel. She looked across to Matt. He was grinning through clamped lips, his body quaking. "Do you want to see upstairs?"

"Err... I'm quite happy here for now. I think best leave that adventure until bedtime."

"So, are we just going to stay here? Lying on the floor?"

"Don't see why not."

"I don't need to call an ambulance, do I?"

He laughed, "No. I'm fine. Just need a bit of a lie-down. I'll get up in a bit... or maybe just crawl?"

# Sixty-seven

An eventful year. After visiting the cottage for the first time, last November, Matt agreed with his mum and brother to sell the farm. Whilst there was some reluctance to let go of a family business that went back five generations, all three owners agreed it was the right thing to do. Mike had no interest in taking over. Their mum was too busy enjoying her retirement and grandchildren. Matt... well, he couldn't wait to get back to Wales and start their new life together.

The farm sold quickly. The Starlings wanted the land to expand their own operations, so a private arrangement was made to avoid agent fees. The house and surrounding outbuildings proved easy to sell as one lot, and the barn conversion was being finished by a builder. Once complete, Sue would move into one of the units, and the other two would provide a rental income for the twins. They also retained the orchard, some woodland, and the field the barn overlooked—for a garden. So, the family's connection to the area would not be totally lost.

Packing a couple of disassembled polytunnels and a greenhouse onto the back of a trailer, they finally moved to Wales permanently in February.

Matt used some of the sale proceeds to settle his debts, pay off her mortgage on the smallholding, buy the much-needed solar panels, and add a wood-clad one-storey extension to the cottage. The latter was currently being used as their main bedroom. The plan was to convert it to a kitchen-diner, once Matt could cope with the stairs. Oh... and yes, there was a shower room at the far end, complete with compost loo. The additions to the cottage were a compromise to her ideals, but she was happy to make them for the sake of Matt's comfort. And the cottage, whilst roomy enough for just her and Mabel, seemed to have shrunk once inhabited by her partner's bulk.

And she no longer had to work. Hooray! She sold her practice for a tidy sum and bought a wind turbine.

Matt had made good progress with his recovery. His speech returned to normal within a month or so of regaining consciousness. His mobility remained an issue but was much improved, and he could now manage with just the one walking stick.

They laughed over Mabel's resemblance to Tim. Louise and Tim thought it very funny too. Apparently, Tim was the dead spit of Grandad Sid. And Mabel was a female version. Gemma had to do some serious grovelling after cutting her best friend out of her life for five months. And Lou certainly knew how to milk things. She and Tim had been regular visitors to the smallholding over the winter months. Tim even got his hands dirty helping with the extension build. Never thought she'd see that in a million years. Somehow, a miracle had happened and he'd changed. He clearly doted on Louise and hung on her every word. Bounced Mable on his knee; getting in the practice for his own offspring now the reversal op had proved successful.

The animosity between the two men had mellowed into a back and forward exchange of banter. Tim would claim credit for getting them back together. Never mind, it was his words that send her packing, and his fist that stopped Matt from explaining. Tim liked to tease that Matt had his cast off. Matt would counter, Tim had his first. They shut up when she pointed out they were both dumped. There was also some teasing over their grandmother's ring. It turned out, Tim had taken it from Bella as a contribution towards all the debts she had run up. But he never once asked for it back, which was just as well because she had no idea where it was. The jokes kind of ground to an uneasy silence when Louise suggested it be returned to its predestined owner: Gem. Matt had shifted uncomfortably in his seat and professed ignorance as to its location. That would be her fault. She had pulled out the fridge before they left Willow Farm, but there was no sign of the heirloom.

Of course, it would now be a while before they could see Louise and Tim again. The Covid-19 pandemic had put paid to any social visits. Here, in their little haven of tranquillity, it was hard to believe anything had changed in the outside world. They'd been oblivious to all the goings-on until a trip to the supermarket in late March revealed empty shelves. They had driven away, confused and frightened, noticing for the first time the lack of traffic. "I can't see any zombies," Matt had joked. It had taken a detour to her parents' empty house to find out what was going on. Lockdown. Her parents stuck in Mexico on their once-in-a-lifetime world tour. Sue just back from a cruise-turned-quarantine nightmare. If that didn't put her off, nothing would! Doctor Claire moved out from the family home to protect Mike and the boys while she battled on the frontline. Thankfully, no one had succumbed to the virus. They rifled the cupboards for food and loo roll, dug out her old work mobile, and headed back to their refuge in the hills—only to find they had no phone or internet reception without driving halfway to the nearest village.

As she sat on the homemade bench enjoying the summer sun, Matt played football with Mabel. She smiled. They were as bad as each other. Both unsteady as they travelled across the terrace. Both wobbling as they kicked the ball. Mabel kept falling on her bum. Matt would have followed suit if it weren't for his stick.

Mabel shot the ball over the edge of the terrace.

"Goal!" the toddler shouted. "Me wind. Daddy loser."

Gemma laughed. Matt pouted.

He limped over and sat down beside her, "Our daughter's a massive cheat."

"Moveable goalposts. Ingenious."

Mabel was now crouching down, peering at the gravel.

"What you looking at, Mabel?" asked Matt.

"I looksing ants."

"Don't let them crawl up your legs, sweetie."

A discomfort caused her to look down at her stomach. With her finger, she gently pushed the protuberance that was causing a bulge on the left side of her swollen belly. The tiny foot retracted, then kicked. "Ouch."

Matt laughed and placed his hand on top of the bump, "Serves you right."

His eyes twinkled with joy as the baby swivelled within her womb. He had missed the first pregnancy. And the first five months of their daughter's life. Her voice cracked, "I'm sorry."

He faced her, brow wrinkled, "Sorry? Why?"

She stroked over her baby bulge, "You missed so much."

"If you were puking as much as this time round, I'm glad," he joked but there was a hint of sadness in his tone.

"Can you ever forgive me?"

"There's nothing to forgive. I'm just as much to blame. I made mistakes. Didn't tell you things I should have... but that's all in the past. Right now,

I couldn't be happier. There's only one thing that could make things even better."

She gave a slight shake of the head. Life was perfect. How could it possibly be improved? "What's that?"

He fumbled in his pocket and retrieved a small object which he placed on her belly.

"Mabel and Sid's ring," she said quietly. She picked up the band and slipped it on her wedding ring finger.

She smiled at him. He smiled back.

# FROM THE AUTHOR

I hope you enjoyed reading A Glass of Milk and didn't find Gemma too preachy!

My aim was to write a story that is thought-provoking in a numbers of ways. Not just the green issues, but how the past can effect present behaviour; the sometimes opaque nature of abuse; and how we judge others.

Please help this book beat the algorithms, and get noticed, by leaving a review or rating on Amazon and/or Goodreads.

Follow me on Goodreads for updates on new releases.

Thank you for reading,

Jo.

# ALSO BY JO EDDY

**The Oron Nexus: Empathy** (Book 1 of 2)

**The Oron Nexus: Discord** (Book 2 of 2)

Printed in Great Britain
by Amazon